John!
Happy Christmas.
[signature]

THE KRAMPUS CHRONICLES

THE THREE SISTERS

SONIA HALBACH

CURIOSITY QUILLS PRESS

A Division of **Whampa, LLC**

P.O. Box 2160

Reston, VA 20195

Tel/Fax: 800-998-2509

http://curiosityquills.com

ISBN 978-1-62007-962-1 (ebook)

ISBN 978-1-62007-963-8 (paperback)

ISBN 978-1-62007-964-5 (hardcover)

For Grandma Ruth and Grandpa John,
and our many Christmas Eves.

And in memory of Lily, Sarah, and Grace Badger

Learn more about the Lily Sarah Grace Fund
at: lilysarahgrace.org

TABLE OF CONTENTS

Chapter One: *Chelsea Manor*..5

Chapter Two: *A Man From Poughkeepsie*..................... 11

Chapter Three: *Night Before Christmas*....................... 23

Chapter Four: *An Unexpected Visitor*.......................... 33

Chapter Five: *Another Unexpected Visitor* 44

Chapter Six: *Ashes and Soot*.. 52

Chapter Seven: *Myra Lane*... 59

Chapter Eight: *Nicolas Poppelius*................................. 68

Chapter Nine: *Foundling Row*...................................... 78

Chapter Ten: *Visions of Sugarplums*............................ 88

Chapter Eleven: *Nestled All Snug*.............................. 100

Chapter Twelve: *The Sister Wheels* 112

Chapter Thirteen: *New Head Garrison*...................... 122

Chapter Fourteen: *Stoomboot and Boeken Kamer*...... 131

Chapter Fifteen: *Furnace Brook Men* 140

Chapter Sixteen: *Sir Pringle Taylor* 147

Chapter Seventeen: *Krampus*..................................... 157

Chapter Eighteen: *Down the Chimney*........................ 170

Chapter Nineteen: *Return to Poppel*.......................... 180

Chapter Twenty: *Horologe*... 190

Chapter Twenty-One: *The Wheels and Key*................ 199

Chapter Twenty-Two: *Seneca Village* 212

Chapter Twenty-Three: *Lustre of Midday*.................. 222

Epilogue 231

About The Author.. 233

More from Curiosity Quills Press.............................. 235

CHAPTER ONE

CHELSEA MANOR

As soon as the carriage came around the street corner, Maggie Ogden glimpsed the snow-powdered sycamore that stood beside the west porch of Chelsea Manor. Strips of its brown and gray patterned bark desperately clung to the trunk as though sensing an impending storm, for even the estate's distinguished trees knew of the disturbance brought on by the arrival of the holiday season.

"Was it last Christmas when there was too much brandy in the plum pudding?" Clemmie Ogden mumbled while the carriage bumped along the cobblestone road.

"That was two years ago, Clemmie," corrected Catharine, as she gripped the black lace shawl draped around her porcelain neck. The ends of Catharine's mouth turned up as she recalled the incident. "Aunt Lucretia had three slices and was giggling all evening."

Fourteen-year-old Maggie was seated between her older siblings in the back of the carriage. She listened to the hooves trotting up the avenue before adding, "Last Christmas, Grandfather Clement went missing at Jefferson Market. Remember? We couldn't find him for hours."

Clemmie snorted. "Grandfather was attempting to escape Aunt Emily's endless Yuletide cheer. His disappearance was quite intentional, I assure you."

Before Maggie could respond to her brother, the carriage lurched to a stop in front of their grandfather's mansion.

Chelsea Manor had been built upon farmland, but by the mid-nineteenth century the city had nearly crept to the mansion's front stoop. South of the Manor, a brownstone church and seminary campus stood where once had been an apple orchard. Row houses pressed against the borders of the estate while a railroad company laid its tracks along the west end, dividing Chelsea and the banks of the Hudson River.

But Chelsea Manor itself remained untouched, sitting on top of a hill that was supported by high stone walls where New York City's streets and avenues had been carved out. And inside the Manor was even less affected by the wafting scent of industry and change making its way across Manhattan.

Grandfather Clement had lived in Chelsea Manor all seventy-five years of his life, and he planned to die there, possibly sometime soon. But even though Grandfather Clement had deemed the past year to be his last, Christmas arrived once again to the Manor in 1854, and with it, the entire family. By late December, Grandfather Clement's five living children, two daughters-in-law, one son-in-law, and seven grandchildren were settled in his mansion for the holidays.

Maggie didn't mind staying at Chelsea Manor. The tradition was a fairly predictable one. From the moment Maggie walked into the mansion's foyer, greeted by a handful of servants and chattering relatives, her body seemed to fall into a simple state of holiday routine. Every year the same family members were seen, the same meals were eaten, and the same conversations were had.

"Why, Catharine, I dare say that you have become the most beautiful woman in all of Manhattan," Aunt Lucretia squealed, grasping Catharine in a tight embrace.

"Young Clement, have you reconsidered studying at the

seminary?" Uncle William said, poking Clemmie's chest with a stubby finger. "I still believe that you would make a fine theologian."

"And Maggie," Uncle Benjamin greeted, turning to acknowledge the least noticed person of her party. "What's it that you do to occupy your time these days?"

Maggie smiled accordingly. "I remain in a constant pursuit of betterment." Her response was received with approving nods.

Yes, it was a predictable tradition indeed.

But there was one annual occurrence only Maggie knew about. And it was the peculiar dream she had each Christmas season where the legendary St. Nicholas would fall from Chelsea Manor's rooftop. And this year proved to be no different.

After the family retired for the evening, Maggie once again dreamed that St. Nicholas stepped too close to the rooftop's edge and his polished boots slipped from the shingles. As the bearded man's plump body tumbled through the misty air, the tattered sack clutched in his hand burst like a Christmas cracker, and a colorful explosion of red, green, and gold tinsel decorated the glittering lawn below while hundreds of baby dolls, snare drums, and wooden guns rained down from the sky.

Although Maggie had dreamed the same thing many times before, after awakening in the early morning of Christmas Eve Day, she still anxiously ran over to the window. The family would never tolerate some jolly old elf sprawled on Grandfather Clement's prominent estate—and on Christmas Eve Day, no less. Such a scandal would cause quite the outrage within the household, undoubtedly spoiling the entire holiday.

"How rude!" Maggie pictured Aunt Maria squawking at the sight of the motionless Christmas saint.

Then Uncle Clement Francis would surely prod the bulbous body with the tip of his cane, shaking his head in disgust while muttering, "I do not know what is more tragic—his fall or his fall's lack of propriety."

So Maggie felt a silly sense of relief when there was no trace of St. Nicholas as she looked out Chelsea Manor's third-story window where swirling flakes greeted her like an early present. It appeared the night had only brought a gentle, agreeable snow.

But then a chilling thought froze Maggie at the window. There was something about her dream that had been different this year.

Was another figure on the rooftop with St. Nicholas?

Had the old man been pushed?

Maggie shook her head. No, that couldn't be right. The dream was always the same. St. Nicholas simply slipped from the rooftop. And she brushed aside the nonsensical idea of him falling any other way.

Maggie ordinarily wouldn't leave her bedroom until the pink sun drifted over the cusp of the estate, but the dream had left her feeling uncomfortably wide awake. Also, the portrait of late Aunt Margaret that hung over Maggie's bed wouldn't stop staring. The painted eyes of her beautiful—yet deceased—aunt usually followed Maggie around the room, but today they were even more penetrating.

Maggie glanced across the bedroom and watched as twelve-year-old Gertrude continued to sleep soundly. Maggie's younger cousin appeared free of nightmares as she muttered, "But, Mother, it was Gardiner who took a second bowl of lemon sherbet..."

As the stale predawn light leaked into the bedroom, Maggie slipped out to the hallway with a coat in hand, mindful of her sleeping relatives.

Maggie's other cousins Gardiner and Louis resided in the bedroom just down the hallway. Before even opening the door, Maggie heard snores coming from Gertrude's twin brother, Gardiner. On the far end of the room, Louis was slumped on a separate bed, back arched with his arm draped to the floor. The curly-haired boy's hand was still mindlessly clutching the blankets that had been tossed to the ground during a lively slumber.

Maggie got along with fifteen-year-old Louis. He was a good-humored boy who often mocked the family's obsession with the city's high society and their efforts toward being above reproach. And whether the target was Uncle William's ability to weave misquoted scripture into most daily conversations, or Aunt Emily's well-intended pleasantries that were spoken even when things were not all that pleasant—Louis was provided with much fodder for his ridicule.

Also, Louis' gangling body was similar to Maggie's own boyish frame, so upon spying a stack of clothes casually folded on a nearby chair, Maggie snatched a pair of trousers and snuck away.

Two mirror image staircases wrapped downward through Chelsea Manor. Having stayed in the mansion many times, Maggie knew that the east staircase creaked, so she carefully drifted down the west one. In need of a shirt, Maggie stopped on the second floor landing. One large lonely door led to Grandfather Clement's master chamber, while the other bedrooms housed Catharine, Clemmie, Maggie's parents, and all the remaining relatives. And just as she had done earlier, Maggie crept into one of the rooms and came out gripping a beige shirt.

When Maggie reached the main floor, she momentarily paused and listened. Normally, the servants wouldn't be there for another hour, but being Christmas Eve Day, Maggie thought they might arrive earlier to prepare for the evening's meal. But she heard nothing.

Maggie crossed the circular stair hall to the music room. Her brown hair was held in a tightly pinned bun, and she hurriedly put the borrowed clothes over her nightgown. And then a dense coat on top of that. Tucking her hands into her sleeves, she opened the door that led to the west porch.

Maggie's exposed face tingled in the cold air. The roads were quiet as she stared out at the untouched snowy ground of the estate. There were no carriages to be seen and even the regular locomotives weren't running this early. But beyond the railroad tracks, the Hudson River flowed freely.

Maggie hopped off the porch and found her sled tucked beneath the steps. The paint on the pinewood was beginning to peel, but its vibrant royal blue color still looked brand-new. Two mustard-colored stripes ran across the top and bottom of the sled, framing a red-painted badger wrapped in a cluster of ivy. The sled didn't feel as big as it once did, but Maggie planned to ride it until its metal runners fell off.

Gripping the ends of the sled, Maggie pranced to the back of Chelsea Manor, which was the clearest of trees. She dropped the sled where the hill dipped and jumped on top, sinking the runners into the immaculate snow.

Maggie glided the sled forward until the earth's natural pull took hold. And then down she went.

Maybe it was Maggie's excitement, or possibly the freshness of the snow that morning.

Or maybe it was an aging sled wanting an extraordinary final run.

Or perhaps, just maybe, the planet had momentarily shifted on its axis, making hills steeper, snow slicker, and sleds faster.

As the sled continued to gain speed, causing brittle ice crystals to dot her face and blur her sight, Maggie was struck with panic. The sled wasn't going to stop before reaching the stone wall overlooking the street, she realized.

But before the sled was airborne, visions from last night's dream flashed through her mind.

There *was* another figure. And St. Nicholas *had* been pushed.

Then into the air Maggie flew, over the wall and above the city's gravel road.

But only for a moment.

The ground quickly moved up and met her sled with a violent *thud*. And then all went dark.

CHAPTER TWO

A MAN FROM POUGHKEEPSIE

Maggie tasted wet salt as a cold blend of snow and blood soaked her lips.

"Are you all right, Miss?"

The voice sounded distant, but a warm breath grazed her cheeks. "Miss?"

Squinting, Maggie opened her eyes—first the right and then the left.

"Are you all right?"

An unfamiliar face bent over her supine body. The young man looked around Clemmie's age of seventeen. A felt cap sat upon his puffy bronze hair, and there was a dimple in his chin that Maggie focused on until the gray sky stopped spinning.

"Are you hurt?" The stranger kneeled next to her, one arm casually propped on his leg while the other hand carefully touched the side of her head. "That was quite a fall."

Maggie slowly steadied herself upon her elbows as pebbles from the road roughly dug into her skin. She spotted the sled partially buried in snow a few feet away. But it didn't look broken.

"Perhaps this will be of use." The man took a long handkerchief out of his coat pocket. Grabbing a fistful of snow, he swiftly packed a snowball into the handkerchief then tied it tightly. He placed the cold, round cloth into Maggie's palm. When she didn't move, he smiled and guided her hand up to her bleeding bottom lip.

"You also have a small bruise on your forehead." The man pushed his cap back on his head as his radiant blue eyes examined the top of Maggie's face. "But I think you'll survive."

Maggie looked at the wall surrounding Chelsea estate where she had just dropped. Her back ached and her head throbbed, but she was glad it hadn't been much worse.

The stranger continued to watch her closely.

"Who are you?" Maggie asked.

The man's face relaxed and his eyes widened.

"Henry."

Maggie stared blankly at Henry who returned her gaze with a look of concern.

"And do you know your name?" he gently asked.

Flustered more by Henry's presence than from the sledding accident, Maggie struggled to find words. Each time his eyes scanned her face, her mind dizzied and her mouth went dry.

"Maggie," she finally murmured. "My name is Maggie."

Henry gave her a fleeting smile. "What are you doing outside at this hour?"

She thought the answer to the question seemed somewhat obvious and she weakly pointed to her sled lying nearby.

Henry cocked his head to look.

"I went sledding before the others woke up," she explained.

"Others?"

"My family," Maggie said, nodding toward Chelsea Manor.

Henry looked up the hill to the Manor then stared back at Maggie.

"You are related to Clement Clarke Moore?"

She couldn't pinpoint Henry's exact tone. It seemed like feigned admiration and, unless she had imagined it, a bit of disdain.

Maggie nodded. "Are you a student?"

Most young men in the neighborhood attended the General Theological Seminary down the road. Besides being built on his Chelsea property, Grandfather Clement had also taught at the seminary before his retirement. Although the name Clement Clarke Moore was recognized throughout New York, Henry's response was similar to the other students who knew the professor as somewhat of a legendary figure.

"A student?" Henry repeated, seeming confused.

Maggie began to wonder if Henry had actually been the one to smack his head in a sledding collision.

"At the seminary," Maggie said, looking down the avenue where the large brick campus could be easily spotted.

"Oh, no, I'm not a student," Henry said, following her gaze. "I'm from Poughkeepsie."

"Poughkeepsie? What are you doing here?"

Henry seemed uncomfortable with the attention and he leaned back on his knees, shifting his blue eyes away from Maggie's face for the first time. She instantly missed the intensity of his stare.

"I was just picking up a few things for Christmas Eve," he stammered.

"Down in New York?"

"The shops in Poughkeepsie are closed today, and I thought I'd have better luck in the city." Henry nodded to a carriage with a brown-spotted horse standing in the street.

Now it was Maggie's turn to be baffled. She shook her head, convinced the fall had knocked something loose. "You took a carriage from Poughkeepsie to pick up a few things? And then you're going all the way back today?"

Even if weather and road conditions were ideal, the trip from Poughkeepsie to New York would be a day of travel each way. Although Maggie rarely ventured outside of the city, she still recognized there was no logic in that.

"How do you make such a trip in one day?" Maggie blinked

several times. "Is that a flying carriage you have there?"

"Uh, actually," Henry stuttered as his face became flushed. "I was visiting an acquaintance here in New York the last couple of days. I am now returning home to Poughkeepsie, but I'm picking up some items before I leave."

Henry couldn't hide the dishonesty in his tone. But Maggie wasn't too concerned with the young man's whereabouts. So she attempted to diffuse the unease created by his puzzling explanation.

"Can you help me up?" Maggie sweetly reached out her arms.

Henry seemed taken aback again. "Why, of course." He shot up from the ground, brushed the snow off his knees and then helped Maggie to her feet. His gloves were warm against her exposed pink hands.

Maggie stared up at his glowing face. "How old are you?"

She didn't mean to ask the question. It just slipped out.

Henry raised an eyebrow and smiled. "Nineteen."

Silently, Maggie concluded that their five-year age difference would someday not seem so significant.

"Would you..." Maggie started to say, but stopped. She wanted to invite Henry to Chelsea Manor for breakfast. But then Maggie pictured her older sister drifting down the stairs and arriving in the dining room, looking as beautiful and refreshed as always, and Henry falling for Catharine's charms as most people did.

"Would you... show me your horse?" Maggie finally said. But she didn't wait for a response before heading over to the carriage.

"Hello, girl," Maggie said, rubbing circles along the animal's coat.

"Boy," Henry playfully corrected, coming up beside Maggie. "His name's Dunder." Henry caressed the horse's long muzzle, and Dunder responded with an affectionate nudge.

Maggie scrunched her nose. "Dunder? Sounds like the noise my brother makes when clearing his throat."

Henry chuckled and gave Maggie a wink, causing her stomach to uncomfortably whirl. "Dunder is the Dutch word for thunder."

"Well then, Mr. Dunder," Maggie said, patting the horse's side and trying not to think about Henry's striking eyes. "Since you're a Dutch horse, does that mean you wear wooden clogs on your hooves?"

Maggie hoped Henry would appreciate her rather witty quip, but the Poughkeepsie man appeared lost in thought as he stroked Dunder's mane.

"Tell me, Maggie," Henry finally said and Maggie's ears perked up. "How are you related to Clement Clarke Moore?"

Disappointed that the conversation had turned back to her family, Maggie indifferently replied, "He's my grandfather."

There was a pause before Henry asked, "Well, what do you think of him?"

Maggie slid closer to Henry as she rubbed the horse's neck. "He's beautiful."

Henry appeared perplexed at her response, but then he gave an amused smile. "No, not the horse. What do you think of your grandfather?"

Maggie furrowed her brow. "What do you mean?"

"Well, is Clement Clarke Moore the man his writing makes him out to be?" Henry uneasily stared out toward the river. "Would you say he's, uh, full of the Christmas spirit?"

Maggie eyed Henry inquisitively. "You mean to ask about his poem?"

It was no secret that even though Grandfather Clement had led a successful life as a professor and scholar, most people associated him with his famous poem.

Something Grandfather Clement severely resented.

"He is the writer of *Twas the Night Before Christmas*," Henry remarked dryly. "Is he not?"

"What about it?"

"Does he talk about the poem often?"

Maggie shrugged. "He never really mentions it."

"Not at all?"

Maggie shook her head.

"Don't you find that curious?" Henry arched an eyebrow.

Maggie shrugged again, still petting Dunder's mane. "Grandfather Clement is like other old men. He mostly sleeps and reads, occasionally mumbling to himself from time to time."

Maggie had spoken seriously, so she was surprised when Henry laughed. His broad lips drew into a childlike grin, curving his cheeks that were rosy in the cool morning air.

Realizing that she was staring, Maggie looked off toward Chelsea Manor. They were standing in the avenue on the west side of the estate, but the rising sun was beginning to peek through the trees on the opposite end.

"Thank you for your assistance, Henry," Maggie said, reluctantly offering back the handkerchief, which was now just a soggy cloth. "I should return to the Manor."

Henry nodded. "It was a pleasure to meet you, Maggie. And do be careful sledding."

She touched her forehead lightly. "I don't believe that I'll be sledding again for a while."

Maggie walked back to the stone wall. After retrieving her sled, she turned around to wave goodbye to Henry, but he had already left with Dunder and the carriage. Her heart dropped low in her chest at the sight of his abrupt departure.

Maggie's warm tongue traced her mouth, grazing the bruise on the bottom lip. Her thick hair had come undone and Maggie tried to pull it back with the remaining pins that hadn't been tossed from her head during the crash. But since there weren't many left, long strands of brown hair freely hung over her face.

As she stared down at Louis' soaked trousers, Maggie imagined what her appearance looked like to Henry, and she was embarrassed that the Poughkeepsie man had witnessed her in such a state of disarray. But she concluded that it didn't much matter since she would likely never see the handsome stranger again. And her insides burned at the thought.

"I really must need breakfast," Maggie mumbled to herself, rationalizing the unusual sensation in her stomach.

Maggie walked to the back of Chelsea Manor. It took only a second after entering the kitchen before she heard, "Good Lord, Miss Margaret. What happened to you?" With her dark plump arms braced on her hips, the older house servant, Ann, scanned Maggie from head to toe.

"Miss Margaret!" Hester had been cutting a loaf of bread, but stopped mid-slice when she saw Maggie. "What in the world?"

Maggie realized that her haggard appearance was shocking to the servants since no one knew of the sledding accident, and she hurriedly explained.

"An accident?" Thomas stood up from the kitchen table where he had been eating a buttered roll. His back was partially hunched and white stubble peppered his face. "Why, you look like you've been through battle, Miss Margaret."

"I am quite all right," Maggie insisted. "I promise." Maggie said goodbye to Ann, Hester, and Thomas, claiming she just needed to get cleaned up.

While leaving the kitchen, Maggie snatched a cinnamon stick from the table. Catharine taught her years ago that chewing cinnamon was like being able to taste Christmas Day before it even arrived. But it just reminded Maggie of Chelsea Manor and all the times she had hidden from Grandfather Clement behind the curtains in the music room.

Maggie had barely walked into the round hall to go upstairs when she heard her brother's voice.

"Margaret Van Cortlandt Ogden!"

Clemmie leaned over the second floor banister, and after getting Maggie's attention he straightened up and whipped down the steps.

"Did you pilfer my shirt?"

A long, red robe hid Clemmie's form-fitting long johns while his wavy, black hair was tousled like he had just woken up. His solemn face was handsome like their father's, except Clemmie was quite vain about it—always stealing prolonged glances in passing mirrors, dark windows, recently polished soup spoons, and all other reflective surfaces.

"I went to get dressed and it had mysteriously vanished."

Clemmie paused in front of Maggie with arms folded across his chest. He stared at his younger sister expectantly, and she blankly stared back, casually munching on the cinnamon stick. Their sibling relationship often teetered between marked indifference and casual annoyance.

"Well," Clemmie pressed. His pointy nose and searching eyes tensed as he waited for an answer.

Maggie sighed and unbuttoned her coat, revealing the oversized shirt underneath.

Clemmie threw up his hands in a halfhearted celebration.

"Maggie, I've repeatedly instructed you to stop taking my belongings."

Rolling her eyes, Maggie quickly pulled off the shirt and tossed it to Clemmie. "Are you pleased now?"

Clemmie looked at his sister who was now just wearing wet trousers with a wispy nightgown tucked into the waist. Her hair was coming undone while the bruises on her forehead and lip glistened in the hall's light. Leaning forward, Clemmie examined the injuries. He often pretended to have a passion for medicine, but the actual sincerity was sometimes hard to find. But Clemmie certainly was sincere about people thinking he was interested in the medical field, especially their father, Dr. John Ogden.

Feeling content with the inspection, Clemmie relaxed his shoulders, stared at the shirt in hand and then back at Maggie.

"You look dreadful," he said dully before walking back up the stairs. "Kindly refrain from touching my property again."

18

Maggie remained standing in the middle of the hall, a puddle pooling under her dripping trousers. But when she heard the Chelsea Manor front door open, Maggie quickly covered her nightgown with the coat she had been absentmindedly holding.

A servant, Charles, walked out of the foyer, carrying a pile of wood. "Miss Margaret," he said, startled by her presence. Even on his dark skin, Maggie saw a red tint begin to burn his cheeks. "You surprised me."

Charles didn't ask about Maggie's battered face or point out that her coat was on backward. Instead he just nervously stood between the two staircases.

"I didn't think anyone in the household would be awake yet," he stammered.

"I was sledding," Maggie replied simply.

"Ah, I see," Charles said and then hurriedly added, "Oh, please, Miss Margaret, don't say anything to your grandfather."

Maggie raised her eyebrows. "What about?"

Charles nodded to the stack in his arms. "I ain't supposed to be bringing wood through the front door, Miss Margaret. Mr. Moore wants Thomas and me to bring it through the kitchen. I get yelled at if I don't. But when I got the wood this morning, the front door was mighty easier. Please don't say anything to Mr. Moore." Charles' wide eyes pleaded to her.

"I won't tell anyone, Charles."

Charles gave a relaxed smile. "Ah, thank you, Miss Margaret." Then finally noticing Maggie's appearance, his mouth shifted into a frown and he added, "You all right, Miss Margaret?"

Maggie sighed. "Yes, Charles, I'm fine. Thank you."

She pulled some pins out of her knotted hair and attempted to run fingers through the clumpy strands. But they got lodged within the dense tangles and she struggled to free her hand.

Charles looked at the girl and shook his head doubtfully, but continued toward the kitchen. However, catching sight of the hall's grandfather clock, he stopped in his tracks. The three weights were resting against the bottom of the clock.

"Ah ha!" Charles exclaimed, setting down the wood next to the grandfather clock.

"What is it, Charles?"

"Oh, nothing to worry about, Miss Margaret," Charles replied, reaching between the split pediment on top of the clock. "It just needs some winding."

Charles pulled down a brass crank. Maggie watched with interest as he opened the panel, placed the crank inside one of the clock's tiny holes and began turning. One by one, he wound all three weights until they were swaying together at the top.

"Do you have to do that often?"

"About once a week, Miss Margaret."

"That seems rather tedious."

"Oh, it's quite fine," Charles smiled. "You know, my father used to work at the home of your great-grandmother, Elizabeth Van Cortlandt Taylor."

Maggie nodded in acknowledgment. Grandfather Clement's late wife, Catharine, had been a direct descendant of the Van Cortlandt family, one of the most prominent names in all of New York. When Chelsea Manor was in need of another house servant long ago, Grandmother Catharine had looked toward her mother's childhood home. There she discovered a young Charles and offered him a position at Chelsea estate.

"Well, there was a key for winding them old clocks that never worked. My father would stick it in the holes, and it'd fit just fine, but when he turned it, it'd never wind them weights. Peculiar thing." Charles then looked at Maggie with growing eyes. "But my father never got rid of the bad key. You see, he believed that everything's got a rightful place. And he planned on finding where the key belonged. Don't think he ever did though. As far as I know, it's still on top of one of them clocks in that old house, not being used." Charles chuckled and picked up the wood again. "Yes, sir. Just lying around. A worthless tool."

The kitchen door swung behind Charles as he left the hall.

Maggie headed up to the third floor, but as she was about to open the door to her room, Louis exclaimed, "Maggie, what happened to you?"

Louis leaned out his bedroom doorway. A green nightshirt came down over his knees, making his arms and legs even lankier. His droopy eyes observed Maggie closely.

"Are you wearing my trousers?" Louis asked with a suppressed chuckle.

"I went sledding."

"Oh, is that why you look so beaten?" Louis scratched his curly chestnut hair, which matched the faint freckles on his nose and cheeks. "For a moment, I worried my mother was making her ghastly fruitcake again, and that you had been assaulted by precarious walnuts and currants." Louis studied Maggie again. "Are you badly hurt?"

Maggie shook her head. "Just a small accident."

"Does sledding require much ability?" Louis smirked. "I was under the notion that the sled and hill did most of the work."

"If you must know, some of us more gifted individuals are capable of sledding beyond the hill," Maggie responded, placing a hand on her hip and blowing a strand of hair away from her face. "Unfortunately, it just happens that there's a bit of a drop after the hill ends."

Louis nodded, still grinning. "Well, you should change before Grandfather Clement sees you." And then raising his eyebrows dramatically, he added, "Or we'll have to lie and say you were involved in some great knitting catastrophe in the music room."

Maggie rolled her eyes as Louis disappeared back into the bedroom, but she knew her cousin was right. Grandfather Clement believed that trousers and sledding were strictly meant for boys along with most other things.

Although Maggie enjoyed challenging antiquated ideals, during the holiday season, she surrendered to hiding books within the folds of her dresses and staying mum while Grandfather Clement and Uncle William discussed the nuisance of the suffrage movement.

As far as the Moore family was concerned, Christmas at Chelsea Manor was a sacred event best left undisturbed. And even Maggie had no intention of changing that.

CHAPTER THREE

NIGHT BEFORE CHRISTMAS

Christmas Eve dinner that evening was the finest one ever observed at Chelsea Manor. The turkey had never been bigger. The wine had never been redder. The flame on the brandy-drenched plum pudding had never glowed so long. And the Christmas crackers had never popped so loudly.

Bright paper crowns adorned the heads around the dining room as tiny trinkets were whistled and twirled. Even Grandfather Clement at the head of the table sat rosy-cheeked in a green crown. Maggie could have sworn she caught the ends of his mouth twitching into a smile.

But it was merely for a moment.

The merriment continued as the family gathered in the Great Room of Chelsea Manor. Maggie took a seat near the Christmas tree while presents were passed out. Soon piles of wrapping paper were scattered around the sparkling evergreen. But Maggie quickly became distracted from the happenings of the room.

Henry.

Maggie thought she saw the face of the Poughkeepsie man peering through the window near the fireplace. But when she looked again, nothing but a few feathery snowflakes floated in the night.

Maggie shook her head. It wasn't the first time that had happened. While attending Christmas service earlier that evening just down the road at Saint Peter's Church, Maggie swore she had spotted Henry.

During the final stanza of *Hark! The Herald Angels Sing*, Aunt Maria had been belting to the heavens. Louis–Aunt Maria's own son–once compared his mother's voice to a dying crow with a cold. And if Catharine or Clemmie weren't nearby to deliver elbow jabs to Maggie's ribcage, she would be sent into a fit of giggles.

Trying especially hard to hide her laughter on Christmas Eve, Maggie spun around in the pew, and that's when she saw the familiar bronze-haired man standing in the mezzanine, looking down at her with his bright blue eyes. Her knees had nearly buckled at the sight. But then the mezzanine crowd shifted and Maggie lost him.

Before Maggie could continue to ponder these visions of Henry, something unexpected pushed her thoughts away.

"Dear family," Grandfather Clement declared, standing next to the fireplace with one hand gripping the mantel and the other holding a small book. "If you would be such a willing audience, I would like to share with you a Christmas poem."

The entire Moore family looked at Grandfather Clement with surprise. They could not believe that after all these years Grandfather Clement would finally read his most beloved poem.

"*Old Santeclaus*," Grandfather Clement announced.

Maggie sensed the disappointment sweep across the room. The poem *Old Santeclaus* was written years before *'Twas the Night Before Christmas*, but came nowhere close to the latter's popularity—and for good reason.

Although the poem started on a light-hearted note...

Old Santeclaus with much delight
His reindeer drives this frosty night,
O'er chimney-tops, and tracks of snow,
To bring his yearly gifts to you.

It eventually took a grim turn.
But where I found the children naughty,
In manners rude, in temper haughty,
Thankless to parents, liars, swearers,
Boxers, or cheats, or base tale-bearers,
I left a long, black, birchen rod,
Such as the dread command of God
Directs a Parent's hand to use
When virtue's path his sons refuse.

The Great Room was silent as Grandfather Clement came to the end of the poem. But after a few long seconds ticked by, Aunt Emily finally spoke, "Oh, Father, that was lovely!" She clapped her hands together with feigned enthusiasm. "How I do enjoy that poem. Perhaps you could continue the reading by giving us a bit of *'Twas the Night Before Christmas.*"

The request was made by varying family members every Christmas Eve. And each year, Grandfather Clement gave the same pithy response.

The poem was a trifle.

That's what Grandfather Clement would say. "No, it's nothing but a trifle."

"Then why did you write it?" Francis' deep voice grumbled.

Francis was sitting in front of the Christmas tree, one knee perched up for his chin to rest on while his middle finger and thumb flicked a round, red ornament hanging on a low bough. His white sleeves were rolled up to the elbows as his shiny vest stood unbuttoned. A general look of boredom washed over his face and he let out a wobbly yawn.

Francis was sixteen—just two years older than Maggie. But she liked him the least of all the cousins. And Maggie had quite a few—Louis, Francis, and the twins, Gardiner and Gertrude. Catharine and Clemmie were also not to be forgotten, since in addition to being her siblings, they were Maggie's cousins as well.

But that was a different matter.

Maggie did not care for Francis. He always walked around with his chest puffed out, resembling an angry rooster. Even his wavy auburn hair sat upon his head like a bird's comb. And when smiling, his thin-lipped mouth drew pointy like a beak. Maggie was just waiting for the day Francis would start sprouting feathers.

But, nevertheless, Maggie had found his question to Grandfather Clement quite bold. The seven grandchildren did not usually speak to Clement Clarke Moore. So Maggie was glad Francis had said something about the poem. She had also wanted to know why Grandfather Clement would write a trifle.

And more importantly, Maggie wanted to know what exactly was a trifle. It sounded like a mushroom. But Maggie could not fathom why Grandfather Clement would call his poem a mushroom. Mushrooms were ugly and tasted grimy. Not to mention, some were said to be poisonous.

So perhaps, Maggie thought, Grandfather Clement hated his poem as much as she hated mushrooms.

"Never you mind," responded Grandfather Clement before whipping off his paper crown and tossing it to the floor.

The Christmas tradition of asking Grandfather Clement to read his most famous poem had once again ended, and with the same unhappy results as the prior years.

Clemmie and Louis returned to their chess game being played in front of the fire while Gardiner and Gertrude unsuccessfully spun new tops on the rug in the middle of the room. Catharine eventually took the twins over to a corner where they could attempt the toys on the hardwood.

Being the eldest grandchild, Catharine was the best with the younger ones. She was also the prettiest, having long brown hair that always glistened like a burnished banister. Her plump lips would expand into a wide yet knowing smile. And her deep green eyes were shinier than the holiday garland draped over the fireplace mantel.

Maggie had similarly dark hair, but with a thinner mouth, longer limbs and dirt brown eyes. And even though Catharine was eighteen, Maggie still found it unfair that her sister was already so much smarter, kinder, and more endearing in every way. It seemed impossible to catch up. And as Maggie stared across the room at Catharine, she became convinced that Henry would have fallen in love with her older sister if given the opportunity.

Christmas Eve dinner had long ago been eaten, but the lingering smells of turkey, roasted vegetables, and plum pudding occasionally wafted through the cracks of the doors as the fire noisily danced in the fireplace on the south end of the room. Although Chelsea Manor stood alone on the hill, a few scattered lights from the General Theological Seminary across the road dotted the darkness.

"Father, could you please read *'Twas the Night Before Christmas* this once?" Aunt Emily asked from where she sat in a chair behind Francis. Her voice was cheery, but Maggie noted how tensely her aunt stirred her tea. "It would be such a wonderful treat."

Grandfather Clement and Grandmother Catharine had brought into the world six glorious children: Margaret, Benjamin, Mary, Clement Francis, William, and Emily.

Margaret and Clement Francis had been the most physically blessed of the Moore children, while Benjamin and Maggie's mother, Mary, were the cleverest. William, on the other hand, got the short end of the stick with everything from looks to intellect.

But Emily was the most unfortunate of them all. For she was right in the middle, not too attractive but not too ugly to pity, not too smart but bright enough to realize she wasn't particularly clever. She fell terribly halfway in every category. It also didn't help that Emily was unmarried and childless. And therefore, in the eyes of her father, she served no real purpose.

Furthermore, Grandfather Clement only ever cared for three women: his mother, his wife, and his eldest daughter, Margaret. And all three were now dead.

"It is beneath my dignity to regale you all with such a silly little bit of writing."

Grandfather Clement's pale, bony hands were folded over his chest as he leaned back in the armchair next to the fireplace. The professor often looked like he was posing to have a portrait painted—unexpressive with a smidge of stodginess. Even in his younger days he had appeared somber with eyes always a tad beadier and a mouth bent a bit more downward than those around him. Against the hopes of everyone else, Grandfather Clement had refused to soften with age, and now at seventy-five years old, he was as hard as ever.

Uncle Clement Francis, or Uncle CF as he was commonly called, disrupted the silence with a tap from his brass-handled cane. "But Father, it's Christmas Eve. What better time to read *Twas the Night Before Christmas!*"

Like Aunt Emily, Uncle CF was unmarried. But this was not met with the same kind of disapproval. Uncle CF was the most handsome of the Moore sons—smooth skin, high and defined cheekbones covered in long sideburns that matched his wavy golden hair tinted with red hues. It was said that Uncle CF was biding his time and savoring life before marriage. But Maggie believed her rather self-involved uncle just didn't want to get rid of any cherished belongings to make room in his cramped home for a family.

"What do you say?" Uncle CF asked, tapping his cane once more out of habit. "Would you give us a reading, Father?"

The eyes in the room returned to Grandfather Clement. His hands had moved to the armrests and were now gripping them tightly, causing the knuckles to grow whiter and whiter. The orange light from the fire reflected off his square forehead, and as Maggie watched transfixed, her grandfather's ghostly strands of hair appeared to be drowning in a sea of flames.

Grandfather Clement's brooding was not unusual. Maggie could never actually recall seeing her grandfather fully smile. His wrinkled mouth probably couldn't hold such an expression anymore. And as Maggie stared at Grandfather Clement from across the room, the ornate patterns in the rosewood of the armchair seemed less rigid than the scholar's face.

The family anxiously awaited Grandfather Clement's response, but before the request could be repeated, he finally stood up. His legs shook unsteadily at first, but after regaining his footing, he stated strongly, "So now, my good family, I have been long awake."

Grandfather Clement hobbled over to the far end of the room. Without another word uttered, he exited through the gentlemen's parlor door.

Now this caused quite a stir within the Great Room. Not only had Grandfather Clement suddenly left the company of his beloved family, but on Christmas Eve of all nights. A cadence of murmurs trickled through the room, and after the initial shock settled down, the family instantly turned on each other.

Someone had to be blamed for chasing away Grandfather Clement.

"You just couldn't leave him alone, Emily," snapped Uncle William, pointing a finger at his younger sister and then shakily reciting, "Let the woman learn silence... no suffering nor usurping man... but to be silent in transgression."

Maggie caught Louis' eye as they both sucked in their lips to conceal their smirks.

Uncle William was a squat man with a small mouth and twitchy nose as well as other mousy features. Tawny hair curled around his ears while his face was patterned in pockmarks. Uncle William had a tendency to use extravagant hand gestures in order to make his short stature appear a bit larger.

"Why did you have to continually pester him about that—that *poem*?" Uncle William continued, extending his arm toward the parlor door while the other reached up to the ceiling, as though beckoning to the heavens for answers.

Aunt Emily may have been the youngest and plainest of Grandfather Clement's children, but she certainly wasn't the weakling. Stiffening her back, she pursed her lips together until they nearly disappeared into her mouth. Her gray eyes narrowed on her older brother.

"My dear, William, you must not speak to me that way," Aunt Emily replied in an overly sweet tone. "It was sadly CF who had angered him."

Now it was Uncle CF's turn to get huffy. He straightened up from where he had been leaning against the wall.

"How was I to know it would upset him? It's just a poem." He tapped his cane on the floor and gripped the collar of his polished red jacket in a dignified manner.

"A poem he hates," pointed out Aunt Lucretia.

Uncle William's wife was a short, pudgy woman with ears that stuck out. These ears were passed down to the twins who had also received their father's mousiness. The odd combination on a pair of children was actually quite adorable, but Maggie wondered how peculiar Gardiner and Gertrude might look when older.

"Someone should go to him," Maggie's mother said. She looked over to her husband who was standing behind the sofa a few feet away, deliberately avoiding the conversation. "John, could you go check on Father?"

Dr. John Ogden appeared uneasy at his wife's request. His fair skin flushed while his eyes darted back and forth. The doctor's black hair was streaked in gray, making him the most dashing man in the room if he didn't look so uncomfortable being there.

Maggie's father was a strange case within the Moore household, since he had twice married into the family. His first wife was Margaret, the eldest and favorite child of Grandfather Clement. Dr. Ogden and Margaret had had Catharine and Clemmie. But tragically, Margaret died shortly after Clemmie's birth some seventeen years ago.

Dr. Ogden waited a year before getting married to Margaret's sister, Mary, and eventually having their daughter, Margaret Van Cortland Ogden.

Or known as Maggie.

So that was why Catharine and Clemmie were in fact Maggie's cousins as well as her siblings. But even though Dr. Ogden had twice married into the Moore family and gave Grandfather Clement three lovely grandchildren, the good doctor always seemed to feel that his situation made him more of an outsider than a true family member.

"I think it would be better if someone else goes to him," Dr. Ogden suggested quietly with a subtle cough.

"I'll go," Uncle Benjamin volunteered, rising from his chair near the gentlemen's parlor door.

As the eldest child since the death of Aunt Margaret, Uncle Benjamin usually went out of his way for the family. This caused Uncle Benjamin to often appear worn down—his dark eyes were saggy, and even his graying hair, carelessly tossed about on his head, looked tired with life. But Maggie liked him the most of her uncles. Uncle CF could be entertaining and Uncle William was unintentionally amusing, but Uncle Benjamin had a gentle way about him—much like his son, Louis, and unlike his other son, Francis.

As Uncle Benjamin disappeared through the parlor door, a restless Francis jumped up from where he had been sitting next to the Christmas tree.

"Well, if he's not going to read it, I will!" Francis snatched Grandfather Clement's poetry book from the mantel. Grandfather Clement had reluctantly included 'Twas the Night Before Christmas in his poetry collection when it had been published a decade earlier.

Francis began flipping through the pages as the rest of the family advised against it.

"We should obey Father's wishes," Uncle William insisted. "Be obedient to your earthly masters… with trembling flesh… and fear in your heart."

"It's also bedtime for Gardiner and Gertrude," Aunt Lucretia added.

"Oh, Francis, you do have such a lovely speaking voice," Aunt Maria cooed. "But perhaps this isn't the best time."

"You'd better not read it, Francis," Dr. Ogden bleakly warned. "Grandfather Clement might return with a birchen rod."

It was often told that when the Moore children were growing up, they were threatened, or possibly struck with a birchen rod when disobedient. None of the parents used such disciplinary methods on the grandchildren. But if any of them ever deserved it, it was Francis. And he knew it.

Grandfather Clement suggested the punishment to Aunt Maria years ago when Francis had been throwing one of his theatrical tantrums. Of course, Aunt Maria would have sooner traded away her revered singing voice before ever laying a finger on Francis' dear head. But it seemed that now even the mere notion of a rod caused Francis to squirm a bit.

Still, Francis ignored the others, and when finally coming upon the correct page, he gleefully cleared his throat and began reading, "'Twas the night before Christmas, when all through the house, not a creature was stirring—"

A knock suddenly sounded on the front door of the mansion. Francis stopped reading and anxiously looked up from the book.

In all the years at Chelsea Manor, no one had ever come to call on Christmas Eve.

CHAPTER FOUR

AN UNEXPECTED VISITOR

Who on earth could that be?" asked Aunt Maria.
"Could something be wrong at the seminary?"
Uncle William squeaked.

"Maybe one of the servants got locked out," suggested Uncle CF just as Thomas popped his head out of the kitchen.

"No, sir. We're all here."

Grandfather Clement and Uncle Benjamin stormed out from the parlor.

"Who is that?" Grandfather Clement bellowed.

Charles and Hester appeared beside Thomas in the kitchen doorway.

"I'll answer it," Charles said, wiping his hands on a rag and tossing it back into the kitchen.

The Moore family remained quiet as Charles and Hester walked across the hall and into the foyer. After the heavy front door was hurled open, the servants could be heard speaking with the visitor.

"A gentleman is here to see you, Mr. Moore," Hester announced, reentering the Great Room. Her expression was uncertain. "His name is Henry Livingston and says you know his family."

"Actually, just my father," Henry said, slipping in from behind Hester. "You may recall the name Sidney Livingston, Mr. Moore."

Maggie stared in shock. Perhaps her eyes hadn't deceived her earlier. But Henry was supposed to be returning to Poughkeepsie. She couldn't think of a logical reason that would bring him to Chelsea Manor, especially on Christmas Eve.

Maggie was not the only one unnerved by Henry's appearance. Grandfather Clement studied the young man with obvious contempt.

"What business do you have here?" Grandfather Clement grumbled.

With his cap in hand, Henry stood before the Moore family looking uneasy. He ran shaky fingers through his bronze hair while the room watched him curiously.

"I am most sorry to come unannounced like this, especially with everyone celebrating Christmas Eve together." Henry gripped his cap tighter. "But I wasn't certain of the next opportunity where the family would all be here. You see, Sidney Livingston died last month, and I was not aware of my father's connection to the Moores until after his passing."

Grandfather Clement held up a long, bent hand. "Do not waste your words, young man. I remember that many years ago a student by the name of Sidney Livingston was kicked out of the seminary for plagiarism, something I consider to be the worst sin in academia. And such a man would not have any association with this family. I am sorry for your loss, but you are clearly here under false pretenses."

Henry looked slapped in the face. His blue eyes widened and cheeks reddened.

"Sir, with all due respect, I know that not to be true. I have countless journals and letters that indicate my father did in fact have a close relationship with your late wife, Catharine, and daughter, Margaret. As well as some of your living children." Henry patted his left breast pocket. "I have a few papers with me if you wish to see."

Uncle William jumped up. "There is no need to see anything. You come here claiming a family connection to two of our loved ones who are no longer around to verify your claim. How very convenient. Except I do not remember your father. And I'm certain neither of my siblings do as well."

Uncle William looked around the room for affirmation. Aunt Emily shook her head and Uncle CF rubbed his chin in puzzlement. However, Uncle Benjamin and Maggie's mother exchanged knowing looks, which did not escape Uncle William's searching eyes.

"Benjamin, do you know what Mr. Livingston is talking about?"

Uncle Benjamin cleared his throat. "How could I when we haven't even heard what has brought him here? Surely, there must be something to all of this." Uncle Benjamin stepped toward Henry. "What is it that you want?"

Henry smiled for the first time since entering Chelsea Manor. "I just thought the great Clement Clarke Moore might be interested in the current whereabouts of the Livingstons. Both his professional and personal reputation depends upon it."

"Well, come on. Out with it," Uncle William snapped. "Say what you want to say."

"I just wish to acknowledge that something was plagiarized over thirty years. But it was not my father's seminary work."

"Enough," Grandfather Clement said. "I have no time for the son of a disgruntled former student to bombard my home on Christmas Eve, making false accusations because he has an old bone to pick with the seminary." And then in a moment that may not have been intended, Grandfather Clement added, "Now go back to Poughkeepsie."

Henry was silent before smiling tensely. "You remember my father better than you let on, Mr. Moore."

And with that Charles and Hester showed the visitor back outside. But Maggie and Henry locked eyes before he disappeared from the Great Room. His look was apologetic as though he was ashamed he hadn't mentioned anything that morning. And Maggie couldn't help but feel similarly sorry.

Maggie walked over to the hall just in time to see Henry adjust the cap on his head before the front door shut behind him. They shared one last glance as Maggie tried to convey her sadness for how poorly Grandfather Clement and Uncle William treated him.

The Moore family, still stunned by Henry's sudden arrival and even quicker departure, didn't notice Maggie in the doorway.

"What balderdash!" Uncle William finally spat. "On Christmas Eve! To come here like that? The man must surely be insane."

"Are you all right, Father?" Aunt Emily asked.

No longer paying attention to his family, Grandfather Clement was facing the window, looking out at the seminary.

"What? Of course, I'm all right," Grandfather Clement grunted. "I have dealt with my share of unhappy students and their family members. It's just unfortunate that the young man decided to call at this hour while everyone is here for Christmas. He's no doubt overcome by his father's passing. Only amplified by the holiday season. In my lifetime, I have witnessed what such grief can do to men." Grandfather Clement spoke rather manically.

"What did he mean when he said something was plagiarized thirty years ago?" Dr. Ogden mumbled to himself, but the rest of the room easily heard.

"What do you mean, what did he mean?" Uncle William asked sharply. "The man was clearly crazy. Spouting strange things. All of it." Uncle William then added another bit of flimsy scripture while waving his arms. "Like a madman who throws deadly flaming arrows at his neighbors and then he comes around and says, oh! I'm sorry. It was just in sport!"

Although Maggie was standing in the doorway with her back toward the Great Room, she sensed Louis mouthing *problem verb* her direction. They had made up the term for when Uncle William inaccurately recited a biblical proverb, which happened more often than not.

"It was all quite odd. No doubt about that," Uncle CF commented. "But there has to be something behind what he was saying."

Unable to contain the question nagging her the most, Maggie spun around and spoke before Uncle William could burst into another confusing tirade.

"How did you know Henry was from Poughkeepsie, Grandfather?"

The entire room focused its attention on the girl in the doorway.

If the question had surprised Grandfather Clement, he didn't let it show. Instead he replied harshly, "Most Livingstons live up in the Hudson Valley, particularly around Poughkeepsie. A ridiculous lot."

The family continued to speculate about the true intention of Henry Livingston's visit. But Maggie couldn't help notice that Uncle Benjamin and her mother didn't contribute to the discussion.

The Christmas festivities did not return to the same level of excitement they had reached right after dinner, and soon everyone began retiring for the evening as the clock chimed ten.

Maggie headed upstairs with Gertrude who whispered giddily, "The rest of the family can say what they wish, but that Henry Livingston is one of the most handsome young men I've ever seen."

Maggie couldn't decide whether or not to be amused at Gertrude's overt adoration. Since Maggie had met Henry first, she felt a strange claim to him.

"Surely, you must agree!" Gertrude looked up at Maggie with glassy, gray eyes. She playfully tugged on the braid that curved around her pronounced ear.

"I found him to be very adequate looking," Maggie mumbled. "But wasn't the whole episode peculiar? Do you think it could be true? That his father knew Grandmother Catharine and Aunt Margaret."

Gertrude shrugged. "What difference does it make if Henry's father knew our family?"

"Grandfather Clement seemed to think it made one. Otherwise, why would he so adamantly insist that there was no connection between us and the Livingstons?"

"It just seems like a lot of nonsense. A waste of a perfectly good evening," Gertrude said, sounding like her father, Uncle William.

After getting undressed, Gertrude sat on the bed and pulled the covers over her tiny legs.

"Maggie?"

"Yes?"

"Why does Grandfather Clement call his poem a trifle?"

Maggie shook her head, not knowing the answer. But then she remembered the mushrooms and whispered, "I believe he finds it to be poisonous."

Gertrude squinted her eyes in a questioning manner, but she eventually just shrugged before turning over on her side.

Maggie couldn't imagine going to sleep; her head was buzzing with too many questions. She didn't understand why Henry hadn't mentioned anything that morning. He had been inquisitive, but nothing that alluded to his intention of paying Chelsea Manor and Grandfather Clement a visit.

Feeling restless, Maggie pulled on the trousers that had yet to be returned to Louis and quietly left the bedroom. The adults were still downstairs, no doubt discussing what had transpired earlier. And Maggie wanted to listen.

Maggie snuck down to the main floor, but paused at the bottom of the staircase so those in the Great Room wouldn't see her through the open doors. With her back pressed to the wall, Maggie slipped through the foyer and then ducked into the dining room where everyone had enjoyed the Christmas Eve dinner. In the corner there was a doorway that led to a narrow passage near the kitchen pantry. Beyond the kitchen was the small dining area and a backroom with a cot.

Grandfather Clement occasionally would request a servant to spend the night, watching over the Manor. But even with the night's unusual visitor, all the servants had been allowed to return to their nearby housing for the remainder of Christmas Eve.

Maggie peeked through the crack of the door separating the dining area and the Great Room. Only Grandfather Clement's children had stayed behind after the others had gone to bed, and they were now gathered around the fireplace having a rather serious discussion.

"This is a complete and utter waste of time," Uncle William huffed, pacing in front of the mantel. "If that Sidney Livingston had visited Mother, I surely would remember it."

Mary sighed. "How many times must we tell you, William? You had yet to be born."

"I believe Sidney stopped coming around sometime after William's birth," Uncle Benjamin recalled.

"Even as a baby William had the ability to chase people away," Uncle CF joked.

Nobody else found the comment amusing and Uncle William looked downright enraged.

"Then why didn't either of you say anything when Henry was here?" Uncle William snapped.

"Because I wasn't sure to trust my own memory," Uncle Benjamin defended. "I was five years old at the time. Mary was just four." He nodded toward his sister.

"CF was just a toddler," Mary added. "Margaret was..." She trailed off.

"Margaret was about eight," Uncle Benjamin continued. "I believe Sidney was closest to her. And to Mother, of course."

"What do you say, Clement Francis?" Aunt Emily asked. "Do you know what they're talking about?"

Uncle CF scrunched his brow as though there was a memory just waiting to be discovered. But he just shook his head, doubtfully. "I don't know," he admitted. "When I think I have a memory, I'm not sure if it's real or just sprung from the conversation we're having now."

"Well, what does all of this show?" Uncle William asked. "What if there was a man named Sidney Livingston? And what if Mother and Margaret knew him? What does that prove?"

Uncle Benjamin muttered, "I dare not say."

"Why?" Uncle William said, his eyes growing large. "What are you afraid of saying?"

Uncle Benjamin sighed. "I do remember a man—a man named Sidney. To think I had nearly forgotten. He was just a mysterious shadow sitting in my memory for all of these years. But I do recall him. He was a handsome man. And he was kind to us children. Is that what you remember, Mary?"

Mary looked taken aback. "I do remember such a man. And though his face isn't completely clear to me, I recollect his character. And the feelings attached to him."

"What feelings?" Uncle William scoffed.

Uncle Benjamin and Mary caught each other's eye.

"You sense it, too." Uncle Benjamin observed. "Don't you, Mary?"

She nodded.

"What are you talking about?" Uncle William was growing even angrier. "What feelings?"

"Love," Uncle CF said. The word was blurted so suddenly that his voice barely seemed to believe it had spoken it. "Sidney and Mother—they loved each other. And I believe... I believe he loved us, too." Uncle CF looked around at his siblings. "Am I wrong?"

"Of course, you're wrong!" Uncle William spat. "You were a baby. Just a minute ago you said you don't remember this man, and now you're insinuating that he and Mother were romantically involved. Have you gone mad as well?"

Uncle CF glanced over at Uncle Benjamin who gave a weak smile.

"No, CF is not mad," Uncle Benjamin said. "I do not know the extent of Sidney and Mother's relationship. But it was a loving one. No specific moment leads me to this conclusion. But when I search my mind and return to that time, I know it to be true. There was a young man named Sidney Livingston. He was close to Mother. For however long, I do not know. But he came to Chelsea Manor to see her and to play with the children. And when he did, even briefly, the house was full of happiness. And, yes, I dare say, there was love."

"This whole conversation is very inappropriate," Uncle William said.

"Perhaps," Mary said. "But not any less true."

"But," Aunt Emily interjected. "Why would this Henry fellow come to see us? Even if all of this is true—that Sidney and Mother loved one another all those years ago. What business does he have coming here?"

"Yes," Uncle William shook a supportive finger at his younger sister. "What's the point to all of this? You have yet to answer that."

Uncle Benjamin began to speak, but Uncle CF cut in. "Sidney was kicked out of the seminary. If there had been a relationship between Mother and him, surely Father would have disapproved. The plagiarism accusation could have been a lie. Maybe Henry wants to clear his father's name."

It seemed like an acceptable explanation to Mary, Uncle Benjamin, and Aunt Emily. But Uncle William was still not satisfied.

"You've lost your minds—all of you! This is our mother and father you are speculating about. And you're going to take the word of some stranger?"

"I remember Sidney," Uncle Benjamin insisted, rubbing his hand along his forehead. "I remember him visiting Mother here at the Manor. And there is this feeling of love and happiness attached to these memories that I cannot shake."

"Very well," Uncle William sulked. "Destroy the family and the good name of Clement Clarke Moore. As stated in Psalms: He that troubleth his house shall inherit fools!"

Uncle William then stormed out of the Great Room.

"It's actually *inherit the wind*. And it's from Proverbs," Aunt Emily mumbled as Uncle William could be heard stomping up the creaky east staircase.

Mary shook her head. "Maybe we are remembering it all wrong. It is strange that for the past thirty years we hadn't thought about Sidney Livingston. Perhaps we've just created all of this in our heads tonight."

"All three of us?" Uncle Benjamin pointed out. "I do not think that is any more likely."

"But maybe William's right," Aunt Emily said. "What does it matter now? Mother is gone. Sidney is deceased as well."

"It does seem like a useless thing to worry about," Uncle CF agreed. He flipped the jacket he was holding over his shoulder. "Let the dead rest peacefully. And let Father be. The last thing we need is to upset him—more so than usual, that is."

Uncle CF and Aunt Emily left the room more quietly than Uncle William.

"What do you think, Benjamin?" Mary asked when it became just the two of them; unaware that a third set of ears was listening in the kitchen.

"I don't know." Uncle Benjamin shook his head and ran a hand through his unkempt hair. "What's troubling is not what I remember of Sidney. It's what I feel like I'm forgetting. Like there was something specific he had said or done. Something that would make sense of it all—Sidney's sudden departure from our lives, Henry's coming here tonight, and Father's defensiveness. There's a detail missing. And I just do not know what it is."

"I feel similarly," Mary agreed. "But I do not believe the answer will appear tonight. Maybe with some rest, we'll remember."

Uncle Benjamin and Mary slowly filed out of the Great Room, leaving Maggie alone on the other side of the kitchen door, trying to process what she had heard.

Maggie's sleep that Christmas Eve was short lived.
Swish. Whack. Thud.

Maggie shot straight up in bed. The room was dark except for the moonlight trickling through the window. Gertrude appeared undisturbed by whatever had awoken Maggie. But as Maggie was about to lie back down there came a rattling from outside. It sounded like the wind was knocking about branches of the giant sycamore that stood near the window. But there was something more deliberate in the noise. It was as though someone was actually climbing the tree.

The sycamore outside the window grew higher than Chelsea Manor with its branches starting at the west porch's rooftop. If someone was able to get on top of the porch, they could potentially climb the length of the tree. Maggie had plotted it as a possible escape route in the event of a fire. But never once did she consider climbing up the sycamore.

She was too afraid of heights.

Maggie hurried over to the window and peered outside. It was impossible to see anything.

But then she heard it.

Footsteps.

And they were coming from the rooftop.

CHAPTER FIVE

ANOTHER UNEXPECTED VISITOR

Maggie listened until the stomping on the rooftop ceased.

All was quiet. And then...

Thump. Thump. Thump.

A low clatter sounded from inside the walls, as though someone was struggling to climb down the chimney.

Someone *was* climbing down the chimney, Maggie realized. She gripped the bed sheet to her chest, suddenly feeling exposed.

Although Maggie was aware that St. Nicholas didn't exist, she couldn't shake the eeriness that tonight happened to be Christmas Eve. She wondered if perhaps there was some truth to Grandfather Clement's poem after all. Or perhaps even truth to her annual dream. Maggie thought of the unknown shadow that had pushed St. Nicholas off the rooftop. Could this intruder be the mysterious figure from her dream?

Maggie soon realized the absurdity of her thoughts, and her initial concern was replaced with a need to investigate further. Maggie tiptoed into the hallway just as a door closed on the second floor. Impulsively, she rushed to the banister and leaned over. She guessed that the intruder had come from the master bedroom, since nothing could stir Grandfather Clement awake—not even someone crawling out of the fireplace a few yards from his bed.

Chelsea Manor was too dark to see anything below, but the east staircase moaned as a shadowy figure scurried down to the main floor. Maggie desperately tried to spy the person's face, but when the intruder quietly paused near the bottom of the stairs, Maggie nervously ducked behind the banister. It felt like the New Year had already come and gone before the intruder continued down the steps with Maggie following close behind.

The grandfather clock chimed midnight as she reached the circular hall on the main floor. There had been no additional noise, so Maggie suspected that her mysterious friend had gone through the kitchen door that quietly swung open and closed. Maggie cautiously made her way into the kitchen. But just as its door swung behind her, another door clicked shut on the west end of the mansion.

The intruder was now either in the parlor, music room, or library.

Maggie didn't go back out the kitchen door. With so many different entrances in the stair hall, she would be completely vulnerable. Instead she turned toward the doorway connecting the kitchen and Great Room where hours earlier she had listened to the discussion about Sidney Livingston.

During the day, the Great Room was the brightest and warmest room in all of Chelsea Manor. But alone at night, the room was cold and frightening. Jagged shadows curled around the furniture and along the walls, and even the enormous Christmas tree in the corner looked menacing with its dark twisted branches. As Maggie crossed the icy floors, she couldn't remember a room ever feeling so foreboding.

Maggie slipped into the gentlemen's parlor only to find it empty. She then crept into the music room. It also appeared vacant, but she knew only too well the room's hiding places. A bulge in the curtains immediately caught Maggie's eye, and she carefully pulled them apart, revealing the porch door and west facing windows. The moonlight blinded Maggie temporarily. But when her eyes adjusted, she saw an unusual blemish gleaming up from the floor. Kneeling down to inspect, she wiped a finger along the ground and then brought it up to her face.

Her heart stopped.

Ash.

Then someone rushed up behind her. Maggie was too surprised to scream, and even if she had garnered enough composure, a hand came across her mouth, muffling any noise.

"Remain quiet," someone whispered in her ear.

She immediately recognized the voice.

"Henry," Maggie tried to say into his hand, but it came out like a cough.

The realization that Henry was the intruder was strangely comforting, so Maggie didn't struggle as he led her into the library. Sensing her cooperation, Henry removed his hand from her mouth as the library door shut behind them.

"What are you doing here?" Maggie gasped, still locked in his arm.

Henry released his grip, stepping to the side so she could see him.

Maggie was glad she had already heard Henry speak, for he'd be impossible to identify on appearance alone. His hair, cap, and clothes were now dusted in ash, and his face was smeared in black soot.

But Maggie recognized Henry's blue eyes.

"And why did you come down the chimney?" Maggie hissed. "You could have awoken the entire household."

"I was not trying to," he muttered, wiping his mouth with an arm sleeve. Tasting the soot, Henry smacked his lips in disgust. "Is anyone else awake?"

Maggie shook her head. "And after ruining Christmas Eve, I don't believe anybody would be particularly pleased to see you again." Maggie looked up and down Henry's ash-covered body before adding, "Even with such a festive entrance."

"I mean no harm," Henry said, reaching into his jacket's inner pocket and taking out a handkerchief similar to the one given to Maggie that morning. Henry dabbed his dark face, creating pale streaks along his forehead, nose, and mouth.

Maggie folded her arms and stared at the floor. "So our meeting this morning wasn't a coincidence."

Henry stared at Maggie's disappointed expression and his face softened.

"My presence outside Chelsea Manor this morning was no accident. But meeting you was unexpected. There was no way to anticipate such a charming girl would come flying through the air," Henry said with a smile, but seeing that Maggie still looked betrayed, he continued solemnly, "But I am sorry if you feel like I lied to you. Coming here earlier tonight was a mistake. I had hoped my mere appearance might provoke Clement Clarke Moore to confess. But since it didn't, I am taking it upon myself to get the evidence I need to prove him wrong."

"But I have no idea what you want," Maggie insisted. "Some of the family remembers your father, but they have no idea why you came here."

Henry sighed. "Only your grandfather knows the true reason."

"Which is what? That your father didn't cheat at seminary? Or that Sidney and Grandmother Catharine were in love?"

Henry's mouth slightly opened in surprise at Maggie's last suggestion. "What makes you mention *love?*"

"Is it true?"

Henry still seemed stunned, but responded, "I don't know. Possibly. But that's not why I am here. At least not really."

"Then why?"

"Maggie, your grandfather..." Henry paused thoughtfully, his face lit by the colorless moonlight drifting through the library. "Your grandfather stole the poem."

"What poem?"

Henry threw up his arms in exasperation. "What poem do you think?"

Maggie didn't respond.

"*'Twas the Night Before Christmas... A Visit from St. Nicholas... Clement Clarke Moore's Famous Plagiarized Poem*—whatever you want to call it," Henry said, sounding rather frustrated. "The poem was my grandfather's. Major Henry wrote it long ago. And Clement Clarke Moore stole it."

"How can that be true?" Maggie asked. "My grandfather is many things, but he's not a thief."

"Perhaps declaring it stolen is harsh," Henry admitted. "But the poem originally appeared in a newspaper in 1823. Anonymously."

"Because Grandfather Clement never thought much about that poem. He wrote it for his children. But a friend came across it and had it published without his knowing," Maggie said, reciting the well-known family tale.

Henry crossed his arms. "It's possible that someone could have taken it without Moore's knowledge. But my grandfather, Major Henry, was the true author. It had been told at Christmastime in the Livingston household long before it was ever seen in print. My family only recently discovered that Clement Clarke Moore falsely claimed authorship to Major Henry's poem, since it took Moore twenty years after it was first published to do so. My father became obsessed with the matter right up until his death. Although the poem initially coming in contact with your family was not Moore's fault, he still lied about being the writer due to its popularity and the pressure for someone to take credit. He would rather lay claim to a poem he hates than risk exposing the real author and the story of how it came to the Chelsea Manor in the first place."

"From your father?" Maggie whispered.

Henry nodded. He wiped his face one last time and then stuffed the handkerchief back into his pocket. "After my father died, I found all his journals and letters, revealing more of the story than I knew. Sidney was a seminary student. He and Catharine became close acquaintances. She was a young mother of four with a fifth on the way. Again, I do not know the extent of their relationship. There was some kind of love, but I cannot confirm whether it became romantic. Sidney was also strongly attached to the children—the eldest one, Margaret, especially. He often visited both Catharine and the children. Many stories he had shared with them had been learned from his own father Major Henry, including *Twas the Night Before Christmas.*"

"So what happened?"

"Clement Clarke Moore found out, of course. So not only did he forbid Catharine from seeing Sidney, Moore set out to destroy my father's name. He accused him of plagiarism, shattering his academic reputation and kicking him out of seminary. Sidney had no choice but to return home to Poughkeepsie. But he had left behind many things—letters to Catharine, stories for the children, and one Christmas poem. Someone must have discovered it, and thinking Clement Clarke Moore had written it, they had the poem published. My father heard about your grandmother's death. But he didn't learn of the poem's publication until much later and was understandably upset."

"So why are you here tonight?" Maggie asked.

"I was hoping to find some evidence; maybe something in writing where your grandfather admits to all of this. Not about Sidney and Catharine's relationship. Not about framing Sidney for plagiarism. But confessing that he is not the true author of the most famous Christmas poem in the world."

Maggie wanted to ask Henry more, but something clattered in another room. The sound wasn't particularly loud, but it still got the attention of Maggie and Henry in the library.

Henry's eyes grew large. He looked toward the door and back at Maggie, silently inquiring about the noise. Maggie shook her head;

not knowing anything other than the rustling was coming from the Great Room.

Maggie and Henry walked out into the foyer and crossed the hall carefully. They each grabbed a knob on the Great Room's doors, and after Henry gave a slight nod, they swung them open.

For a moment, nothing moved—neither Henry, Maggie nor the petite intruder by the Christmas tree.

The stranger was certainly no St. Nicholas. The boy looked Gardiner's age of twelve, but was dressed much older. He wore a burgundy coat, sharply cut to expose his emerald green vest and matching trousers. His tall burgundy top hat sat loosely on his tiny head while long blond hair was swept across his brow.

After Maggie and Henry came bounding into the room, the boy seemed the most startled of the three. And now all of them stood frozen, watching to see who would move first. But then the burgundy-coated boy tightened the gray sack he was holding, slung it over his shoulder, and bolted toward the fireplace.

Maggie expected the boy to attempt the nearly impossible task of climbing back up the chimney, figuring that must have been how he had entered. But instead of watching him struggle with the chimney, the boy disappeared down an unusual opening in the back of the fireplace.

Maggie and Henry dived toward the hole, but it closed by the time they reached the fireplace. Maggie pounded on the bricks while Henry tried to pull open the ash pit cover on the ground just as footsteps sounded from the second floor. They locked eyes, both suddenly aware of the trouble that would arise if Henry were to be caught.

The footsteps drew nearer to the second floor landing and then began to slowly make their way down the steps. The Great Room doors were wide open and Maggie knew they would be discovered in a moment's time.

But just as Maggie was about to grab Henry and hide him in the parlor, Henry's scuffle with the ash pit cover exposed a round golden emblem in one of the blackened bricks. The emblem was no bigger than a half dollar with a tiny hole in its middle. Maggie spotted an engraved cursive *G* intertwined with smaller letters: *L* and *S*.

Without thinking, Maggie pressed the emblem with her thumb. The ash pit cover and its surrounding bricks disappeared, forming back into a hole.

Maggie couldn't see how far down the opening went. But as the footsteps reached the bottom of the stairs, Maggie and Henry jumped into utter darkness.

CHAPTER SIX

ASHES AND SOOT

As Maggie and Henry landed upon a giant ash pile, the hole above their heads closed, cutting them off from Chelsea Manor. Unlike when her sled dropped from the hill that morning, Maggie managed to land crouched on her feet with her hands bracing the ground while Henry ended up sprawled uncomfortably on his back. He let out a painful groan and Maggie hurried to his side.

"Are you hurt?"

Henry shook his head and attempted to sit up, positioning himself on his elbows. Through the darkness, Maggie could see his blue eyes shining up at her. And without thought, she affectionately laid her hand upon his shoulder. But the moment was broken when Maggie began to take in the shadowy sights around her. The mysterious cellar reminded Maggie of a crypt, and such a comparison caused chills to stream down her back.

"Where are we?" Maggie shakily stood on the loose residue under her feet.

Henry cupped a handful of gray powder and let it slip through his discolored fingers.

"The ash pit of the fireplace," he suggested, not sounding too confident.

Maggie pointed toward the sealed hole that hovered yards above her extended finger. "Did you see? There was a golden button on the trapdoor that caused it to open."

Still reclined on his back, Henry stared up at the ceiling they had fallen through and then around at the ash. Head to toe, Henry was marbled in gray and black filth. Maggie glanced down at her similarly stained clothes and felt relieved to be wearing Louis' trousers.

"What happened to that boy?" Henry stood up and wiped his hands together as a dust storm rained down from his body. "And *who* was that boy?"

"I don't know," Maggie said, attempting to brush soot off her nightshirt. But the soot was too layered to make any significant change. "I'm more concerned with how I'm going to find my way back into Chelsea Manor."

Henry looked across the cellar where a weak glow was coming from a passageway.

"Follow me," he said, taking Maggie by the hand. A jolt ran up Maggie's arm as Henry led her into the dim tunnel.

It was impossible to tell what lay beyond the narrow passage, but the burgundy-coated boy had left dirty footprints along the ground. Maggie and Henry followed the footprints to the passage's end where a spacious cavern appeared before their eyes. Oil lamps dangling from the walls illuminated its curved ceiling.

Maggie looked up at the doorway they were under and saw *48C* carved in its keystone. She didn't understand what it meant. But the footprints stopped there.

Maggie grudgingly let go of Henry's hand and took a few steps into the space. The cavern was empty except for heavy chains moving horizontally along the ground as far as the eye could see. Two rusty chains ran one direction and two chains ran the other, clicking along old gears that groaned loudly as they turned.

"Look!" Henry pointed toward a tunnel opening.

A wooden contraption attached to the chains appeared out of the darkness. As it neared, Maggie saw a sleigh with tattered red seats. Although the sleigh was vacant, the chains and gears slowly moved it along as though there was an old horse pulling it. When it reached Maggie and Henry, the sleigh didn't stop and instead continued to mechanically lumber along the chains, heading into the dark tunnel where it threatened to disappear completely.

Henry grabbed Maggie's hand again and tugged her toward the sleigh. It was traveling slow enough that they were able to stumble inside. Maggie took a seat across from Henry just as the sleigh passed into the musty, black tunnel.

"We're below New York," Maggie observed.

Maggie couldn't see Henry in the darkness, but she heard him clear his throat and say, "It appears that way."

"Did the city build this?" Maggie asked, trying to keep her companion talking. Henry's voice helped calm her nerves.

"I've never heard of anything being built below Manhattan. I've actually never heard of such an underground system like this being built anywhere."

The sleigh continued to glide through the tunnel. Occasionally, it would open to similar caverns that contained doorways to other passages.

"Do all of these lead to ash pits?" Maggie asked. She was pleased to be able to see Henry's face once again even though his anxious expression was a bit unsettling.

"Maybe," Henry replied. "It could be a fireplace cleaning system where workers come down here and haul away ash in these sleighs."

"But what was that boy doing in Chelsea Manor?"

Henry shrugged. "He probably was just using these tunnels to break into homes."

"Who would do that?"

Henry gave Maggie an uneasy look.

"I wasn't referring to you," Maggie said quickly. "At least you had a reason to be searching around Chelsea Manor."

Henry thought for a moment. "What if this boy also had a reason?"

"But what about that golden object?" The mysterious emblem was still troubling Maggie. "Did you see? It had a large *G* and a smaller *L* and *S* on it. What does it mean? And where did it come from?"

"I don't know." Henry's voice rose in irritation. "I don't understand any of this."

Since Henry's arrival, Maggie had learned more about her grandparents and *Twas the Night Before Christmas* than she ever imagined knowing. And now she connected their unusual circumstances to his sudden appearance. So she had expected Henry to have all the answers like he did earlier in the library.

But it turned out Henry was just as confused as Maggie.

"Perhaps *GLS* is the name of the company that helped build these tunnels and sleighs for the city," Henry suggested in a gentler tone. "And they needed a way to gain access to the ash pits from the fireplaces in case something happened to any underground entrances."

Maggie knew Henry was just inventing a story for her sake, but she appreciated the effort.

Henry sat across from Maggie in the front of the sleigh. She watched as he twisted in his seat as though he had heard something. A moment later, they both spotted another sleigh coming from the opposite direction.

It was empty.

And a few more sleighs heading toward them were also unoccupied. But just as they entered another lit cavern, voices could be heard coming from an arriving sleigh. Maggie and Henry swiftly flattened their bodies against the bottom of the sleigh.

Peeking out from the side, Maggie spotted a boy and girl dressed similarly to Chelsea Manor's burgundy-coated visitor. But they appeared around Francis' age of sixteen. The boy wore a plum coat and top hat with a red vest and matching boots. He had shaggy brown hair and a thin moustache. The girl was tall with sinister black hair pulled back into a low bun, paper white skin and almond-shaped eyes. Her skirt was blue with a cream-colored vest.

"Are you sure this is the right one, Harriet?" The plum-coated boy jumped out of the sleigh, holding a familiar gray sack. "We're supposed to visit 65G. This is 53F."

"You need to get your hearing examined, Milton," Harriet snapped. "We were assigned 53F as well."

That was all Maggie heard before her sleigh entered another tunnel. As other sleighs passed with similar passengers, Maggie and Henry remained pressed to the bottom of their sleigh.

Eventually, the caverns with the oil lamps became less and less, and soon their sleigh was coasting through darkness. Maggie's leg muscles were starting to ache, so after a few more empty sleighs went by, she crawled back up onto the seat.

"What if we never find our way out?" Maggie was unable to hide the panic in her voice.

Henry got up and took the seat beside her. He put an arm around Maggie's shoulder and rubbed it lightly. "We're going to be all right. I promise."

But soon Henry stopped rubbing her shoulder, and instead laid a firm grip on Maggie's forearm.

"What?" Maggie asked, but was instantly shushed by Henry.

A cavern appeared in the distance that was unlike the previous ones. The underground walls framed the upcoming chamber like a portrait and Maggie saw rows of motionless sleighs in the background.

It was clearly the end of their ride.

As the chamber approached, half a dozen men in tall helmets could be seen monitoring the incoming and outgoing sleighs. They weren't like the workers Maggie and Henry saw earlier. The men were older, dressed all in black with the exception of their brass belts.

And they didn't seem too friendly.

"Get off," Henry whispered anxiously.

Maggie followed Henry from the sleigh before it rolled into the guarded chamber. Hiding in the shadows, she saw an endless wall of tunnels containing similar gears and chains. Sleighs were constantly arriving and departing like a well-orchestrated station.

"Tonight always feels longer than the rest," yawned one hefty guard.

"Don't start falling asleep on me, Crofoot," another guard said. The smaller man reached into his jacket and pulled out a silver flask. "Here," he said, handing the flask over to his friend.

"Thanks, Calhoun." Crofoot took a sip and wiped his mouth. "I hate getting pit duty. Everyone is up in the Krog, drinking and playing cards, while we're stuck having to watch all the Foundlings. It ain't fair, I tell you."

"Ah, it's not so bad, Crofoot," Calhoun said, reaching for his flask. "It's fun giving the Foundlings a hard time."

After taking a long swig, Calhoun glanced about for a target. He spotted a pair of young boys arriving from another tunnel.

"What took you so long, Foundlings?" Calhoun snarled.

The surprised Foundlings looked worried, unaware of doing anything wrong.

With Crofoot and Calhoun's backs toward them, Maggie and Henry saw the opportunity to escape behind a row of unused sleighs that were stacked like kindling against the wall. Maggie and Henry crouched down and watched the guards through gaps between the sleighs. The gears and chains were noisy enough that no one could hear them whispering.

"So the young workers are Foundlings," Henry said.

"Whatever they are," Maggie replied. "I prefer them to these men in black coats."

"Well, we should leave before they become less distracted."

"But to where?"

Henry glanced around. Behind the row of sleighs in the corner of the room was a doorway. Getting Maggie's attention, he nodded in its direction.

Maggie and Henry both looked back at Crofoot and Calhoun. The guards had lost interest in the Foundlings and were back to their post, passing the silver flask between eager hands. Staying low to the ground, Henry made his way to the exit with Maggie directly behind him. Crofoot and Calhoun mumbled in the distance, but the guards didn't notice them slipping away.

The doorway led to a short flight of stairs, which Maggie and Henry climbed carefully. The farther they got from the sleigh tunnels, the quieter it became. Soon they were creeping along a constricted hallway lined with closed doors. Maggie feared that men like Crofoot and Calhoun were lurking behind them. But when they turned a corner, she didn't see any of these black-coated men.

Instead Maggie and Henry spotted a steel sign suspended above their heads.

"Myra Lane," Henry read softly.

Maggie was about to ask what it meant, but glancing under the sign quickly gave her the answer. Myra Lane stood right before their eyes.

CHAPTER SEVEN

MYRA LANE

Myra Lane was an underground village of one-story shops plastered along a cobblestone road that stretched as far as Maggie could see. The rooftops connected to a dark overhead abyss, and only the colorful building facades were visible before the rest of their exteriors disappeared into the surrounding walls.

Over the murky windows swayed battered signs that read: *Apotheker, Snop, Markt, Kleren,* and *Speelgoed* and many more strange words that Maggie didn't understand. But besides the oddly worded signs appearing deep beneath Manhattan, Maggie found the most unsettling thing about Myra Lane to be its emptiness.

According to a post clock in the middle of the road, the time was a quarter after twelve in the morning. But when Maggie drew closer, she saw it wasn't a normal timepiece. The clock was twice as tall as Maggie and didn't contain numbers. And instead of having one pair of rotating hands, there was an additional pair. These tiny hands were only a couple inches tall and clicked swiftly around the center.

Maggie tried to show Henry the peculiar clock, but he was busy studying the intricate details of a dusty shop window. He was so mesmerized by the village's seemingly quaint aesthetic that he didn't notice Maggie heading toward the pink candy shop called *Snop*.

Pressing her face against the front door's round blue-tinted window, Maggie saw rows of stout jars packed tightly on shelves inside the shop. Reaching down, she turned the knob and the door surprisingly opened.

Maggie's nostrils began to tingle as she inhaled the shop's sugary air. There were dozens of candy jars stuffed with dark, hard morsels and colorful, gooey sweets. There were fat yellow balls, pale brown cubes, angular red sticks, and a few squishy pink hearts with white speckles.

By the time Henry entered the candy shop, Maggie was behind the counter with one hand in an overflowing jar of jellybeans and the other holding a purple and white swirled lollipop.

"Maggie!" Henry said as the pink door slammed behind him. "Be careful."

"It's only candy," Maggie replied, chewing a mouthful of red jellybeans.

"But why is it here? We don't know anything about this place. It could all be unsafe."

Maggie reluctantly took her hand out of the jar and placed its glass cover on top. She was just wedging the sticky lollipop back into its wooden stand when voices came down the cobblestone road.

As they had become accustomed to doing that evening, Maggie and Henry quickly ducked. Maggie dropped to the floor behind the counter before crawling around to Henry who was crouching under the front bay window.

Three top hats drifted past the shop, but Maggie was too low to see any faces.

"We're going to be late for our shift." The voice of the passing Foundling was bleak.

"Ah, let the Garrisons wait. Most of them are up at the Krog. A bunch of drunken fools."

"Shh. They could be hiding, wanting us to think they're not around."

A third voice agreed and murmured, "Castriot's been harsher. I think there's pressure coming from the outside. I hear the Garrisons whispering about..."

The voices became muffled as the Foundlings left Myra Lane.

Maggie and Henry slowly crept up the shop's window and looked out to confirm that everyone was gone.

"This is getting strange," Maggie whispered. When Henry arched an eyebrow, she added, "*Stranger*, I mean."

Henry shook his head. "But what purpose does any of this serve?"

Maggie stood up. "We'll never find out if we keep hiding. They're the ones who came into Chelsea Manor. We didn't do anything wrong. Now let's just find out how to leave."

Henry chewed his bottom lip before responding. "Maggie, we don't know anything about these people. How can we be confident they'll even let us leave?"

"Why wouldn't they?"

Henry was silent for a moment. "I'm not sure. But none of this seems right."

Maggie opened the shop's door. "There's only one way we'll know for certain."

Maggie and Henry started down Myra Lane again, hoping now to spot a Foundling. The odd children seemed more approachable than the Garrisons.

But Myra Lane remained deserted.

Maggie and Henry reached the end of the cobblestone road where two wooden doors stood under a tall archway. Henry grabbed the handle of one door just as the other shot open and a Garrison bounded through the doorway.

This Garrison was a strapping young man who wore a small black cap, exposing his shortly trimmed red hair. His face was lightly freckled and an oval brass nameplate sat on his left breast.

McNutt.

As witnessed with the burgundy-coated Foundling in the Great Room, the McNutt fellow was more surprised to see Maggie and Henry than they were to see him. The book he held crinkled within his clenching hand.

"So sorry to startle you, sir," Henry quickly began. "We came this way by accident. I do not know what this place is or how to leave. If you could offer some assistance, it would be greatly appreciated."

McNutt looked from Henry and then down to Maggie, his green eyes dancing wildly. Apparently, people there were not accustomed to receiving visitors. It also appeared they were rusty when it came to displaying proper etiquette toward guests, because just when Maggie thought McNutt was finally about to speak... *smack!*

Dropping the book to the ground, McNutt cocked his fist and placed a punch right on Henry's jaw. Henry stumbled backward as his lip began spattering blood. He had no time to react before McNutt jumped on top of him.

Maggie watched as Henry and McNutt scuffled on the ground. Being broader than Henry, McNutt had a physical advantage. But even dazed, Henry was quick and put up a solid fight. Unable to stand helplessly on the side, Maggie stomped on the back of McNutt's leg, allowing Henry a moment to slip away from the Garrison's grasp.

Maggie and Henry ran under the arch of the double doors, which led to a curved stairwell. Maggie's bare feet throbbed as she raced up the steps. She heard Henry running close behind, but couldn't tell how far they were from McNutt. The stairwell twisted up a couple times before it opened into a banquet hall.

A grand, cobweb-adorned chandelier was suspended in the center of the hall, looming over rows of long tables. Columns were situated underneath a mezzanine that encircled the space, and Maggie dived behind the closest one. She pulled Henry into the shadows just as McNutt bounded through the entrance, running right past their column.

McNutt stopped in the middle of the hall, looking frantically around for the two outsiders. One wall was covered in a massive maroon curtain, and McNutt began prodding its fabric with his fists, swinging at any crease or bump that looked like it could be a hidden person. Then squatting on his knees, he searched under the tables.

Maggie worried that McNutt would soon start checking behind the columns, but instead he sprinted to the other end of the room where a scrawny staircase connected the space's two levels. Maggie peeked around the column as McNutt charged up the stairs and then disappeared through a bright doorway on the mezzanine. Maggie and Henry cautiously stepped out, eyes fixated on the doorway, waiting for McNutt to reappear.

Maggie started to say something, but Henry brought a finger up to his swollen lip. They silently crossed the hall, but just as they paused underneath the chandelier, loud footsteps sounded from the mezzanine.

McNutt was returning.

Maggie and Henry quickly slipped between the tables and lunged behind the musty maroon curtain. Maggie could barely breathe as she gazed through a slit in the fabric.

McNutt came back down the stairs and stood in the center of the hall, pacing between the rows of tables. At one point he came within a few feet of the veiled intruders, but he didn't bother poking around the curtain again. After a few moments, McNutt headed to the stairs that led back to Myra Lane.

Maggie and Henry remained frozen behind the curtain, but eventually, the stuffy smell was too much to handle and Maggie slid out. Henry reluctantly followed, keeping his eyes intently on the Myra Lane doorway.

"Are you terribly hurt?" Maggie stared at Henry's bruised mouth and jaw.

"It's not too bad," Henry muttered, lightly touching the side of his face. He cringed. "I guess we have matching bruises now." With a smile, Henry brushed Maggie's bottom lip with his thumb. She pretended to disregard the small gesture, but her heart rate swelled.

"We need to leave," Maggie said as a rush of anxiety pulsed through her. "Preferably without another Garrison seeing us." She searched around the banquet hall before pointing to the doorway on the mezzanine. "McNutt has already been up that way. He probably won't come looking there again. And we're clearly underground. So the higher up we go, the more likely we will find a way out of here."

Henry didn't argue and followed Maggie up the stairs. When reaching the mezzanine, they saw an additional flight of steps within the doorway. Rough voices and an accordion playing a light-hearted jig could be heard coming from whatever lay at the top.

"I guess we've found the rest of the Garrisons," observed Henry just as shouting filled the air. A cadence of drunken laughter followed shortly after.

"It must be the Krog," Maggie said.

She started up the steps, but Henry grabbed her arm.

"What are you doing?" he hissed.

"I want to see."

"Maggie, I'd be willing to bet they're not too friendly." Henry rubbed his jaw sorely.

"At least let me hear what they're saying. McNutt probably told them about us."

"That's exactly what I'm concerned about."

But Maggie was already halfway up the stairs before Henry could stop her again.

Upon reaching the top, Maggie stooped low on the steps and gazed out into what looked to be a tavern, complete with a stool-lined bar, shelves overflowing with bottles, and a table surrounded by card-playing men. Like the previous Garrisons, everyone at the bar and around the table was dressed in identical black coats and brass belts—even the half-conscious accordion player, slouched on a pile of cushions in the corner with a hat pulled down over his eyes. He sloppily performed a slow melody.

"Did you see how upset McNutt looked?" one man said with a stiffened jaw. He laid a card on the table and then bit down on the pipe wedged between his teeth.

"Mick's face was as red as his hair," another player commented.

The men laughed harshly.

"Like he saw a ghost. Blabbering about people from the outside."

"Probably just a couple Foundlings having a good joke on him. Rightly so."

"Always working," the man with a pipe scoffed. "Never even comes up for a drink. Quite unheard of for an Irishman."

The man behind the bar filled a short glass with dark liquor and shot it back into his mouth. "We don't want a stupid mick up here. What do you say?" he slurred. "Should we teach McNutt a lesson? Give him the ol' one, two, three." He pulled out a revolver and jovially spun its cylinder.

"I would worry about yourself, Comstock."

The room turned to stare at a man with a finely trimmed black beard who was leaning against the end of the bar, an empty tumbler loosely gripped in his hand.

"What did I do, Castriot?" asked the man behind the bar who had a short, stodgy build and thick moustache. He haughtily stuck the revolver back in his belt.

"All of you are just sitting around like it's a normal night," Castriot snarled. "No one taking extra shifts to watch the Foundlings."

"Why do we need to watch them? Most are working the Sleigh Pit," Comstock said, blithely. "Relax, Castriot."

Seconds later, a tumbler whizzed overhead and shattered against a nearby wall. Maggie and Henry covered their heads to protect themselves against the raining pieces of glass.

"I should just send the lot of you back to the outside. The country can never have too many mindless men." Castriot then stormed out through a door behind the bar, leaving a silent room behind him.

"Why did you have to get him upset, Comstock?" the pipe-smoking man asked through his taut lips.

"Oh, Curzon, it's Christmas Eve," Comstock defended. "Castriot is always stressed this time of year. There's nothing anyone can say that won't get him upset. He's always worried about ol' Nicky coming back."

"Nicky can come back anytime he wants," remarked another man.

"Yes, Cabell," Comstock said. "But it's only on Christmas Day that the sisters can be reunited. The old saint has no power here unless that happens."

"But how would it?" Curzon asked.

"That's what troubles Castriot the most. He doesn't know. He only knows it can happen on December twenty-fifth. And if it ever would, all of this, all of us—*pffp!*" Comstock made a slicing motion across his neck with a hand.

Henry tugged on Maggie's arm, trying to get her to come back down the stairs. Silently, Maggie scooted down the steps to the mezzanine. Henry grabbed her hand when she reached the bottom. She wanted to talk about what they'd heard, but they weren't safely out of earshot.

Maggie and Henry headed down to the banquet hall, but the moment their feet reached the bottom of the steps two men jumped out from the shadows and grabbed the pair.

One of the attackers was a red-faced McNutt, fuming as he struggled to keep Henry from slipping away. Maggie couldn't see the Garrison who had her hands pinned behind her back, but out of the corner of her eye, she read the name *Cromer* on his polished nameplate.

"We've got them," Cromer grunted.

Out of the darkness, another figure emerged. But it wasn't a Garrison or even a Foundling. Instead an elderly woman walked forward, hands folded together. Her face wore a firm expression.

"These are the intruders, Madame Welles," said McNutt. His voice held a faint Irish accent. "Shall I get Castriot?"

Madame Welles looked at Henry and then Maggie. The woman's short gray hair was feathery and her face only slightly wrinkled. She was tall with broad shoulders, appearing to be around Grandfather Clement's age. And she looked just as domineering, if not more so.

"No," she replied sharply. "Bring them to the workshop first."

CHAPTER EIGHT

NICOLAS POPPELIUS

Maggie and Henry were led down another stairwell in what felt like an endless maze. Eventually, they entered an industrial-styled space the size of the banquet hall. There were long tables covered in all sorts of curious tools and materials, including metal springs, buckets of paint, wooden shapes, and glass figurines.

But neither Maggie nor Henry had the chance to study all the clutter before being tossed through a crooked doorframe. McNutt and Cromer tried to follow, but Madame Welles cut them off.

"I'll take it from here, gentlemen," she said, sliding between the Garrisons and slamming the door closed before they could argue.

A desk took up most of the room's cramped quarters. The only window was located on the door where Maggie could see McNutt staring intensely from the workshop. Although she wanted to hate McNutt for punching Henry, after listening to how the other Garrisons made fun of him, Maggie felt somewhat sorry for the redheaded young man.

Madame Welles nodded to a pair of chairs stuffed between the desk and wall. "Take a seat," she directed, closing the blinds on the door and vanishing McNutt's face.

"Excuse me, but I have been assaulted by one of your men," Henry said, crossing his arms. "My friend and I arrived here after following a boy who had broken into her home. We never intended any trouble, and quite frankly, are not even aware of where we are. So if you could just show us how to leave, we will be on our way."

Madame Welles stared at Henry, blinked a few times and then firmly said, "Sit."

Something about her tone caused Maggie and Henry to stumble around the desk and slip into the chairs without further questions.

"Now explain who you are and what you are doing here," Madame Welles said, wringing her hands. "And do so as quickly and concisely as you can."

Maggie and Henry disclosed their night, from spotting the burgundy-coated boy in the Great Room to following him down the ash pit and through the sleigh tunnel.

"And where exactly are you two coming from?" Madame Welles asked.

"Chelsea Manor."

Madame Welles gasped. "Are you related to Clement Clarke Moore?"

Maggie hesitantly nodded. "He's my grandfather."

Madame Welles promptly turned her attention to Henry. "Henry, is it? Henry what? What is your last name?"

"Livingston."

For a brief moment, Madame Welles appeared like her legs might buckle underneath her. She stared at Maggie and Henry as though they were ghosts.

"What happened after you got to the Sleigh Pit? Who did you see? Or more importantly, who saw you?"

They talked about McNutt punching Henry in Myra Lane and then spying on the Garrisons in the tavern. But they didn't share what they had heard the men discussing.

"And you saw Castriot?" Madame Welles asked. "But he didn't see you?"

"Yes. At least I believe it was him," Maggie replied. "The man they called Castriot had a black beard. And he was quite angry. He threw a glass against a wall."

Madame Welles sighed. "That was indeed Castriot."

"Could you just tell us where we are?" Henry pressed.

Madame Welles folded her hands together. "You two have discovered Poppel, Mr. Livingston."

Maggie and Henry stared blankly at the old woman.

"Nikolaos of Myra founded the original settlement in Belgium. But Poppel eventually relocated to Manhattan in the seventeenth century when Annette Loockerman came to America and married a Dutchman named Oloff. And this underground settlement thrived independently until about thirty years ago."

"And how exactly are these names and dates relevant to us right now?" Henry asked with annoyance.

But Maggie was intrigued and wanted to hear more. "Who are Annette Loockerman and Nikolaos of Myra? And what happened thirty years ago?"

"Clement Clarke Moore's poem happened," Madame Welles stated.

"It wasn't his poem," Henry snapped, but Madame Welles and Maggie ignored him.

"How do you know about my grandfather?"

"I have never met Clement Clarke Moore. But I knew your grandmother, Catharine," Madame Welles said and then turned to Henry. "And I presume Sidney Livingston was your father."

Madame Welles finally had Henry's full attention. Maggie watched his jaw tighten. "How did you know that?"

"Catharine and Sidney used to visit Poppel with Catharine's daughter, Margaret. That was before Clement Clarke Moore published the poem. And yes, Henry, I know—Major Henry's poem," Madame Welles added, anticipating his retort. "But it really doesn't matter who wrote it at this point. What matters is that it entered into the public eye, and confirmed already established suspicions. We had struggled to stay hidden, but once the poem came to light, it didn't take long for us to be found. The city officials knew we were able to get in and out of houses, but it wasn't until the poem that they made the connection to fireplaces and Christmas Eve."

"Madame Welles," Maggie interjected. "I truly do not understand any of this."

Madame Welles sighed. "Oh, I suppose I'll have to start at the beginning. But I must make this quick."

Maggie and Henry exchanged uncertain glances.

"Very long ago there was a good man named Nikolaos of Myra who lived east of the Mediterranean Sea. He was a kind and generous bishop, known for his particular concern for the wellbeing of children and women. There were three young sisters named Grace, Sarah, and Lily whose father was very poor and unable to provide them with a dowry to be wed. He was going to sell Grace, Sarah, and Lily into slavery, but before he could, each daughter mysteriously received a bag of gold."

"From the bishop?" Henry asked.

Madame Welles nodded. "The gold was meant to liberate the sisters. But the sisters soon realized that the cruel men they were set to marry were no better than enslavement. And this is where Nikolaos of Myra gave the sisters true freedom."

Captivated by the story, Maggie leaned forward and rested her elbows on the desk, cupping her face in her hands.

"Nikolaos was a skilled seaman. He helped the sisters escape by sailing them across the Mediterranean and then up the Atlantic Ocean before finally settling in Belgium where they founded the village of Poppel. Nikolaos of Myra became known as Nicolas Poppelius, and he and the sisters focused on assisting the poor and helpless. However, Nicolas' whereabouts were nervously monitored by men of great power who did not trust individual charity, believing it undermined the need for people to rely solely on their church, monarch, or government. Nicolas was seen by many as a vigilante with an extraordinary amount of influence, offering things other institutions weren't providing."

"So what became of him?" Henry interrupted.

"At the time, there was enormous tension in Belgium and the Netherlands between the Catholics and the Protestants. And Nicolas Poppelius tried diffusing the religious hatred and violence. In 1572, after an attempt to save eighteen Catholic clerics—later known as the Martyrs of Gorkum—from torture and certain death, Nicolas Poppelius was never seen again. Grace, Sarah, and Lily continued to run Poppel until Grace fell in love with a man in the nearby village of Turnhout named Jan Loockerman."

"Was he related to Annette Loockerman?" Maggie asked eagerly. "The woman who moved Poppel to America."

Madame Welles nodded. "Jan and Grace had a daughter named Annette who married Oloff Van Cortlandt and reestablished Poppel here in Manhattan."

"Van Cortlandt," Maggie repeated. "My grandmother descended from the Van Cortlandts."

Madame Welles ignored the comment. Maggie didn't know if it was intentional, or if the old woman just didn't think it was worth the time to respond. Van Cortlandt was a prominent name in New York but not that uncommon.

"About thirty years ago we were finally discovered and taken over by the Garrisons," Madame Welles continued, "The Garrisons worked under a special department of the city."

"But what really happened to Nikolaos of Myra?" Henry asked.

"What do you mean?"

"The Garrisons seemed to think that a man named Nicky—I'm assuming Nikolaos of Myra—could return on December twenty-fifth," Henry said. "But according to your story, it sounds like he died hundreds of years ago. So which is it?"

"The man who was Nikolaos of Myra has long ago deceased, but the spirit—known by many as St. Nicholas—lives on."

"St. Nicholas?" Maggie blurted. "St. Nicholas of Christmas? But that's impossible!"

"Over the years since Annette Loockerman brought Poppel to America, most of the story had turned into myth, but Nikolaos of Myra was never quite forgotten, especially in a new country worried for its own survival," Madame Welles explained. "Officials had become less concerned about Poppel's possible existence until a certain Christmas poem immortalized St. Nicholas all over again. Although the traditional lore that has been associated with St. Nicholas is mostly inaccurate, he was still a real man who inspired the stories and whose spirit continues to embody December twenty-fifth."

Maggie and Henry looked at each other again in disbelief.

"Just so I understand all of this," Henry said slowly. "Nikolaos of Myra escaped with three sisters to Belgium, established Poppel, and eventually, the daughter of one of the sisters came to America and set up a new underground village. And now the Garrisons have taken over because of Major Henry's poem. But who exactly are you and the Foundlings?"

Madame Welles raised her eyebrows and placed her hands on her hips, seeming a bit surprised at the amount of terms Henry had already picked up that evening.

"The Foundlings are children brought to live in Poppel, because they had nowhere else to go. In the beginning, they made supplies that were delivered to the impoverished. However, it was difficult to stay undetected. If people were suddenly receiving anonymous gifts throughout the year, our whereabouts could be easily tracked. So it was decided that the year would be spent making these gifts, but they would only been given on one day known for presents and celebration—Christmas."

"But why are the Garrisons running the place now?" Maggie asked. "Just because of a poem?"

"When *'Twas the Night Before Christmas* became such a sensation, there was a panic to find whatever was left behind of the great Nikolaos of Myra. It didn't take long for those in power to discover us. The poem gave them all the needed information—Christmas and the fireplaces. Except Foundlings travel up fireplaces, not down."

"But," Henry interjected. "Why do the Garrisons continue to run Poppel? If they didn't like the place, why didn't they just destroy it?"

"Why would they?" Madame Welles scoffed. "Here was a functioning system already in place. They now have control of a world underneath the city streets full of workers and endless opportunities."

"So they weren't planning to carry on Nikolaos' vision of helping others," Maggie said dryly.

Madame Welles cackled bitterly. "Hardly."

"But why would they want Poppel?" Henry asked. "What good would come from having the Garrisons here?"

"Not good for us. But Poppel is certainly useful for them. So the city took over Poppel in 1824, assigning Garrisons to lifelong service."

"Why would they want to work here their entire lives?" Maggie asked, but Madame Welles again ignored the question.

"The first goal of this newly controlled post was not to provide services to others, but rather take them. The city had a fear of the foreigners. The sleigh tunnel offered a way to sneak around to all the fireplaces in the city. From about 1824 to 1840, the fireplace and tunnel system was mainly used to spy and steal. Foundlings were trained in this art. But then around 1840, the city's concern shifted to the boom in outspoken women for suffrage and equality."

"What would this have to do with Poppel?" Maggie asked with raised eyebrows.

"Well, if you were worried about women breaking from traditional roles, striving to gain equal footing with men in society, what would you do?"

Maggie shrugged. "Make it illegal for girls to steal their cousin's trousers?"

Madame Welles shook her head. "You give them toys. But not just any kind of toys. You give the young girls dolls and needlework and other things of that nature. Not education. Not a voting voice. Not the opportunity to join the workforce among men. Just items that help reinforce the idea that they are only to become mothers and wives. But now a new fear has overshadowed the threat of both the foreigners and women's suffrage."

"And what is that?" Henry asked.

"War, Mr. Livingston. We are now focused on war. In a country who fears for its safety from the outside and stability from the inside, the government wants a generation of fighters. The country is expanding, and with that comes a need for pliable young men. Boys are the focus now. So during the year, Poppel's workshop turns out thousands of toy soldiers and toy guns—anything to help build up a future army."

"So let me understand this," Henry said, holding up a hand. "In the past thirty years, Poppel has spied on our city's foreigners, kept women from achieving equality, and has tried to foster a new generation of soldiers?"

Madame Welles nodded. "It has become everything it once sought to prevent."

Henry let out a low whistle while Maggie asked, "But if the Garrisons have such a strong grip on Poppel, why is Castriot so nervous about Christmas? Why do they fear Nikolaos coming back and the sisters reuniting?"

Madame Welles wasn't quick to answer.

"How is it possible for Nikolaos of Myra to return?"

Before Madame Welles could respond, a pounding on the door caused a wreath to fall off the wall, clunking Henry in the back of the head.

"Do not tell them who you are or where you're from. And never

75

mention the names Moore or Livingston. And especially not Van Cortlandt," Madame Welles whispered urgently. "Everything depends upon it."

The door then swung open revealing a barricade of black coats. Two unknown Garrisons smashed their massive bodies into the tiny space. Their bulky hands reached over the desk and grabbed Maggie and Henry. Before Maggie knew what was happening, they were pulled out of the room and back into the workshop.

The Garrisons formed a tight circle around Maggie and Henry before parting just enough to allow three men to step through. Maggie recognized Castriot and Comstock, but the third Garrison was new. His face was bumpy and discolored, and his teeth were crooked. Stringy sideburns ran down his cheeks and his gray eyes were bloodshot.

"What have we here?" he said in a squeaky voice.

"They're new Foundlings," Madame Welles called from the other side of the Garrison wall.

Castriot, Comstock, and the bumpy-faced man, whose nameplate said *Cyrus*, continued to stare at Maggie and Henry.

"Who are you?" Comstock asked. "And why are you in Poppel?"

"I'm Alfred," Henry lied. "And this is Lizzie. We're brother and sister. Our parents are dead. We survive on the reluctant generosity of distant relatives. A funny boy broke into the house where we were staying tonight. We followed him down a hole in the fireplace and that is how we ended up here."

Maggie was impressed by Henry's quick thinking. But she couldn't tell if the Garrisons believed the story.

"And we would like to leave now," Henry continued.

Cyrus let out a squeal of laughter. "I'm afraid that's quite impossible."

"What do you mean?" Maggie stammered.

Castriot stepped forward. The Garrison leader had a slender frame, but his height and broad shoulders made him an imposing figure. He narrowed his beady eyes on Maggie and his lips curled within his menacing beard.

"No one ever leaves Poppel."

Above the ground and across the city at Chelsea Manor, Louis was on hands and knees in the Great Room's fireplace. Moments ago, Louis had witnessed both Maggie and Henry Livingston disappear through the ash pit. By the time he ran from the bottom of the stairs to the fireplace, the opening had vanished, and Maggie and Henry were nowhere to be seen.

Louis' hands were stained black as he pawed the ground, thumping on the bricks behind the burnt logs. He jumped to his feet and pulled aside the curtain of the ceiling-high window. Everything outside was dark, including the seminary down the hill, so if there had been any trace of Maggie and Henry escaping into the night, Louis wouldn't be able to see it.

Wind rattled the windowpane and pushed Louis back into the shadows of the Great Room, pondering whether he had simply imagined his cousin's disappearance.

Louis sat down on the sofa across from the fireplace.

"Maggie?" he whispered into the eerily quiet room. "Mr. Livingston? Are you there?"

There was no response.

"Uncle William's not going to be pleased. He'll probably misquote the entire Book of Daniel over this."

But there was still nothing except silence.

"You have to come out sometime," Louis continued with a yawn. "And I'll just wait right here until you do."

CHAPTER NINE

FOUNDLING ROW

Shortly after being told that their visit to Poppel was permanent, Maggie and Henry were forced down a long corridor near the Sleigh Pit. No explanations were given, but Maggie gathered that they were being taken to where the Foundlings were housed.

Henry was thrown into a chamber right away. He called out, but the Garrisons promptly slammed the door, muffling his cries. The Garrisons then continued to guide Maggie along the corridor, but she kept looking back, hoping to see Henry.

Although Madame Welles was leading the group, she hadn't so much as glanced Maggie's way since Castriot had showed up.

"We call this Foundling Row," Madame Welles explained, still not looking at Maggie. "It's where the Foundlings sleep. And this will be your room." Madame Welles stopped in front of another nondescript door. "You should rest a while. First days for Foundlings are long. Longer because you are busy. And longer because," Madame Welles paused. "Well, they just happen to seem longer."

Before Madame Welles even finished speaking, the Garrisons tossed Maggie into the room and shut the door. The dim room contained only wrought iron beds. Its emptiness instantly put

Maggie into a panic. She turned back around and twisted the doorknob. The door surprisingly creaked opened, but a second later Maggie closed it.

The Garrisons were guarding the door.

Or rather, making sure she couldn't leave.

Maggie slowly sat down on a bed that held a pile of folded blankets on its bare mattress. But she didn't feel sleepy. She felt scared and alone.

Suddenly, a sigh sounded from another bed, and Maggie realized that she wasn't as alone as she thought.

Maggie watched as a mound of blankets shifted on the bed diagonal from hers. Then a small body flipped over and Maggie saw the face of a young girl. Still in a somewhat sleepy state, the girl pulled a faded blanket up to her chin, which framed her caramel-toned face and curly brown hair. Eventually, the girl's eyes fluttered open and a yawn escaped her mouth. When the girl saw Maggie, she didn't seem startled. Instead she slipped out of bed with the rest of her tired body and stumbled over to Maggie.

"I'm Violet," she said, sitting down beside Maggie while letting out another yawn.

"Mag..." Maggie started to say, but then quickly remembered. "Lizzie. I'm Lizzie."

"I had an early shift so I've been sleeping," Violet said, stretching her arms above her head. "Running up and down those fireplaces got me tired. But you'll get used to it." Violet gave Maggie's shoulder a friendly pat.

The door opened and two more girls entered. Maggie recognized the black-haired girl as Harriet from the sleigh tunnel. The other girl had long, wavy blonde hair and big blue eyes. Her glowing skin was rosy, matching her red skirt that was accented with a silver vest.

"This is Lizzie," Violet introduced cheerfully. "She was here when I woke up."

Harriet and the blonde girl stared at the new Foundling. Maggie couldn't tell what they were thinking, but they didn't appear as welcoming as Violet. Violet glanced at the girls with one little eyebrow arched, clearly not understanding their hesitation toward Maggie.

"This is Harriet and Nellie," Violet explained loudly as though the girls' lack of enthusiasm was because they had trouble hearing. "They—sleep—here—too."

"You're the outsider," Nellie whispered.

"The Garrisons have been talking about you," Harriet added, gazing at Maggie with suspicion. "Castriot is furious that you and your friend got out of the Sleigh Pit unspotted. He could be heard yelling all the way from the Krog."

"What happened?" Violet asked eagerly, situating herself upon her knees.

Maggie told the girls about following the burgundy-coated boy and then being caught by the Garrisons and Madame Welles. But she left out everything that was discussed in the workshop, and also never mentioned the names Margaret Van Cortlandt Ogden and Henry Livingston.

"What will your relatives think about you disappearing?" Nellie asked.

"I am sure they'll be quite worried. What did your family think when you left?"

The girls exchanged looks and Maggie wondered if she'd said the wrong thing.

"We don't have families," Harriet said coolly.

"No family at all," Violet added.

"How did you come to be at Poppel?" Maggie asked.

"Madame Welles took me from an orphanage as a baby," Harriet said. "I don't know anywhere else."

"What about you?" Maggie asked Nellie.

Nellie's blue eyes narrowed. "I am not from around here."

She didn't seem to want to say anything else, so Maggie turned to Violet.

"I lived up there," Violet said, pointing to the ceiling.

"Outside?"

"Yes, outside. But up there!" Violet continued to point fiercely. "Right above Poppel." Violet leaned forward with a smirk. "They didn't find me. I found them."

"What do you mean?"

"I lived in the village up there. I was all by myself after my parents went away. I didn't know where they'd gone to, so I stayed on the streets. At night I hid from the scary people. That's when I saw a door—a hidden door. People were always secretly going in and coming out. One night a lady about to go through the door saw me. And I made her sad. The Garrison who greeted her also felt sorry for me, so they both welcomed me inside. I got fed lots of food and was given clothes and got all cleaned up. The lady eventually left. But I stayed."

"You came here through an outside entrance? So you know where the door is that leads above ground?" Maggie asked, unable to hide her excitement.

"Yes, I know where it is," Violet said, still smirking. "But you have to go through the Krog. And there are always Garrisons there. So there's no way to get out without being caught."

Maggie frowned at the short-lived hope.

"Don't be sad," Violet said, hugging Maggie's arm. "It's wonderful here. And there's no more living outside or worrying about scary strangers."

Harriet laughed dryly. "Oh, Violet, you don't even know the difference. I lived here before the Garrisons took over, back when Madame Welles was in charge. And it was glorious. Myra Lane wasn't gloomy and the Foundlings weren't depressed. Parties were thrown in the banquet hall as though it were always Christmas in Poppel."

Maggie studied Harriet closely. "But the Garrisons took over Poppel thirty years ago." Maggie thought Harriet looked around seventeen or eighteen—certainly, not a day over twenty.

Harriet started to reply but the door abruptly flew open and Madame Welles marched into the room.

"Come with me," she ordered to Maggie.

Maggie quickly got up and followed Madame Welles out the door, relieved to get away from the other girls. The looks on their faces were starting to become disconcerting.

Madame Welles didn't talk as they walked back down the corridor. Maggie had questions she wanted to ask, but she worried the Garrisons could be lurking anywhere.

Soon Myra Lane appeared; a couple of shops were now open and a handful of Foundlings meandered around while a few Garrisons patrolled the road. But everyone stopped and stared at Maggie as she passed.

The post clock came into view. The tiny hands were still steadily rotating about, but the two main hands showed that it had been only twenty minutes since she and Henry were last there. But that didn't seem right to Maggie. It had to have been at least an hour ago.

"Madame Welles—"

But the old woman cut her off.

"In here," she said, holding open the white door of a brightly colored shop. Over the entrance hung a yellow sign with the word *Kleren* printed in blue.

Stepping inside the shop, Maggie saw endless rows of colorful vests, shirts, and hats. Long strands of measuring tape and ribbon hung from every inch of the ceiling and walls. A clock in the corner ticked happily away. It also read thirty-five minutes after twelve.

As Madame Welles shuffled through the shop's colorful clutter, a pointy-faced man in a yellow top hat popped out from behind a rack of dresses.

"Hello!" the old man greeted. His silver hair was plastered across his forehead while his sparkling mauve eyes shined up at Maggie.

"There you are, Hostrupp," Madame Welles said, apparently unmoved by his sudden appearance. "I have brought you another one."

Hostrupp placed a hand gently on his wrinkled cheek where a deep dimple had sunk over the years. He looked Maggie up and down with an appalled expression. The ash from earlier had bled into her skin, creating a gray hue across her body.

After a thoughtful pause, he said, "Come with Hostrupp!" And with a wiggle of a finger, Hostrupp directed her toward the back of the shop.

Maggie followed him through the fabric stacks until they came to a clearing. A man stood on a wooden platform with his back toward them while he adjusted a green jacket and black top hat in front of a tall, dusty mirror. When he finally twisted around, Maggie saw it was Henry.

"Hen—" Maggie bit her tongue. Her face started to flush. "Alfred! Alfred, you're here."

Although they hadn't been separated for long, Maggie was so happy to see Henry that she nearly ran up and hugged him.

Henry also seemed quite pleased to be reunited. His blue eyes lit up. "Lizzie! Yes, Hostrupp gave me a new outfit."

He looked down at his black vest while adjusting the jacket's sleeves.

"Yes, yes!" Hostrupp went up to Henry and smoothed out the green fabric on the shoulders. "A great match for the young man. Hostrupp knows his stuff."

Hostrupp did a final review of Henry. Feeling satisfied, he pushed Henry aside and turned back to Maggie. "And now for you."

Hostrupp pulled off the tape hanging around his neck and began measuring Maggie's arms, shoulders, and waist. He went about his work so diligently that in no time Maggie was shoved through a curtain with a bundle of clothes in her arms.

"What am I supposed to do with all of this?" Maggie called from the tiny room.

Hostrupp replied on the other side of the curtain. "Put those on, of course. A Foundling's clothes are of the utmost importance. They display unity yet individuality, elegance yet comfort, safety yet strength—a way to recognize Foundlings from outsiders like… you once were… very most recently."

Maggie dropped the clothes to the floor and began sorting through the jumble. She was hoping to see some clean trousers, but not even a dirty pair could be found.

"And don't forget to wash up," Hostrupp added. "You appear a bit… unkempt."

In the corner sat a bucket of water with a white rag draped over its dented rim. Although Maggie usually didn't mind a little dirt, she had never desired to scrub her body more than at that moment.

When Maggie emerged from behind the curtain minutes later, her skin was no longer gray. Instead it glistened with a pinkish glow. But this glow couldn't mask Maggie's unhappy expression as she glared down at her new floor-length yellow skirt.

Hostrupp clapped his hands three times. "Wonderful. Wonderful, wonderful. You look wonderful."

Hostrupp approached Maggie, adjusting pieces of fabric and brushing her long, messy brown hair behind her shoulders to showcase her cobalt blue vest.

"I have to wear a skirt?" Maggie asked. She already found herself missing Louis' filthy trousers.

"Yes, yes. Of course. All young ladies of Poppel are to wear skirts. The Garrisons insist upon it. They say, Hostrupp, you must make sure all young ladies are dressed like ladies and all young gentlemen are dressed like gentlemen. They must know their place, Hostrupp."

Hostrupp reached into his pocket and pulled out a silky yellow ribbon.

"One last touch."

He motioned for Maggie to turn around. She reluctantly twisted just enough for Hostrupp to gently pull back her hair into a low ponytail, held in place by the ribbon.

Hostrupp didn't seem to register Maggie's scowl when she turned back. "Wonderful, wonderful. You shall be the talk of Poppel for years to come."

Henry smirked at Maggie's annoyed face. But his amused expression quickly disappeared. His brow creased and mouth frowned. The bruise on his jaw was now a radiant shade of purple. Caught up in the excitement of the new clothes, Maggie realized they both had temporarily forgotten the seriousness of their situation—they were forbidden from leaving Poppel.

Madame Welles reappeared next to Henry. "Very nice, Hostrupp. Now I must take the new Foundlings to the workshop."

Hostrupp waved goodbye to Maggie and Henry as they exited the shop. They didn't get very far into Myra Lane before Madame Welles stopped and looked around. Seeing that the Garrisons down the road were distracted, she shoved Maggie and Henry into a gap between the shops.

For an older woman, Madame Welles was surprisingly strong.

"I know you want to leave. And I do not doubt that you will try. Castriot and the others do not doubt it as well. So you must be careful. Since the Garrisons took over, many of the older Foundlings have tried to flee. All were caught. And all were severely punished. You two will certainly receive no second chances if you're seen escaping."

"So you're saying we shouldn't even bother trying to leave?" Henry grumbled.

"What I'm suggesting is to be careful right now. You are being closely watched."

"What about our families?" Maggie's voice cracked in frustration. "We aren't Foundlings. We have homes. We have people who will notice that we're gone. Very soon they will notice. And then what?"

"We have some time. Not much, but a little," Madame Welles explained. Maggie thought she was referring to the time before the Moore household noticed the missing granddaughter at the breakfast table. But then Madame Welles added, "This may be the only opportunity we have to reunite the sisters. But it must be done right. There is no room for error."

Madame Welles looked behind her, clearly worried about being spotted by the Garrisons. "I will explain more later. For now just stay put, be obedient, and do not give your real names."

Then Maggie and Henry were shooed back onto the cobblestone road. But the Garrisons saw the three emerge from the shadows and quickly stormed their way.

"Madame Welles, we are supposed to see that the new Foundlings report to the workshop," said a Garrison with a large forehead and hooked nose.

"Yes, Crowther," Madame Welles replied sternly. "I was just about to escort them there."

She started to walk forward, but the Garrisons blocked her path.

"We'll take it from here, Madame Welles, if you don't mind." Crowther's tone wasn't polite.

"It is my responsibility to make sure new Foundlings get acclimated to Poppel," Madame Welles defended.

"Castriot has made a special exception with these two," the other Garrison, Cabell, hissed. His slanted mouth held a thick scar above the lip. "It's a security issue now. And that's *our* job."

Cabell yanked Maggie's arm while Crowther grabbed Henry.

Maggie was getting a little tired of being tugged around.

"You are to have no further contact with these two until they have been fully evaluated, which could take days—maybe even weeks. Castriot's orders."

"I was not given that order," Madame Welles argued.

"I'm giving it to you now, old woman," Crowther snapped.

"And that should be enough for you." And with that Maggie and Henry were roughly escorted down Myra Lane, leaving a distraught Madame Welles behind.

Maggie knew Madame Welles hadn't gotten the chance to tell them everything they needed to know. And now that opportunity had passed. Perhaps for good.

CHAPTER TEN

VISIONS OF SUGARPLUMS

Laszlo wasn't a Garrison.

But he certainly wasn't a Foundling. And he was far from resembling either Madame Welles or Hostrupp. The man in charge of the workshop was a peculiar mix of young and old. Slicked down past his ears, Laszlo's hair was as white as Grandfather Clement's, but his face was as young as Henry's.

Laszlo's ghostly eyes observed Maggie and Henry with apathy when they were hauled into the workshop, pinned between the Garrisons.

"New Foundlings. Alfred and Lizzie" Cabell barked, shoving Maggie and Henry forward. "Show them to their place."

Without breaking his indifferent stare, Laszlo waved the Garrisons away with a pale, limp hand. Crowther and Cabell moved to a shadowy corner where they continued to watch Maggie closely. Other Garrisons were also stationed on the platform encircling the factory floor, monitoring the Foundlings that were tinkering and hammering away in the rows of tables below.

"Come," Laszlo finally spoke with a vacant voice.

Laszlo led Maggie and Henry down to the floor. The Foundlings were spread throughout the workshop, barely filling up a quarter of the tables.

"Most Foundlings are still out delivering. Everyone has to work the Sleigh Pit on this night, you understand," Laszlo droned. "Some Foundlings also tend to Myra Lane. But new ones are not granted such desired positions in Poppel. The Sleigh Pit and Myra Lane are for the older Foundlings. The ones who have been here longer and have proven themselves, you understand. The Garrisons certainly do not want new Foundlings toiling around the sleigh tunnels, climbing up ash pits around the city. The Garrisons do not believe new Foundlings are to be trusted. You understand."

Laszlo stopped and spun around, his oversized gray coat twirled about his slender waist like a cape. The buttoned shirt and trousers beneath the coat were also various shades of gray. Laszlo didn't wear a hat and his white hair glistened even in the faintly lit workshop.

"But I'm sure you two will have no trouble. Since you're older, I am confident you will not do anything rash. Poppel offers great benefits," Laszlo continued. "And you understand what could happen to you if you do not behave. The workshop may not seem ideal compared to getting assigned to the Sleigh Pit or Myra Lane, but it's not like being sent to Furnace Brook."

"Furnace Brook?" Henry spoke for the first time. "What is that?"

Laszlo ignored him and gestured to a table near the middle.

"Lloyd," he called.

A lanky, curly-haired boy with a button nose glanced up through his round eyeglasses. He wore a brown jacket with a green vest. Spotting Laszlo and the two Foundlings, Lloyd got up from the table and stumbled over.

"Lloyd, this is Alfred and Lizzie. Please train these new Foundlings as best you can," Laszlo instructed before swiftly returning to his station on the platform above.

Lloyd nervously eyed Maggie and Henry. "You both are old for Foundlings."

"You don't look much older than me," Maggie replied.

89

"Yes, but I've been here a while," Lloyd said, straightening his shoulders.

"How long?"

"Since I was eleven." Lloyd looked up and counted softly to himself. "So nine Christmases, I suppose."

"You're twenty?" Henry said with surprise. The boy looked much younger than Henry.

Lloyd made a puzzled face. "Fourteen."

Instead of explaining further, the Foundling sat back down at the table and motioned for Maggie and Henry to join.

"I'm working on soldiers," Lloyd murmured, picking up a knife and the wood piece he had been holding earlier. Its sides had already been nicked. "I'm the best carver here. Even Laszlo thinks so. I've got the best hands and make the most-detailed faces."

The knife between Lloyd's fingers steadily sliced into the wood. As Maggie and Henry watched, wood shavings fell to the table as Lloyd's hands worked on the block. After a few minutes a tiny, meticulous soldier appeared in Lloyd's palm. He set it on the table, proudly.

Henry picked up the toy soldier and turned it around in his hands. "That's quite impressive," he admired. "The details are so precise."

Maggie nodded in agreement. It actually looked like a little soldier.

"Do you paint him?" Maggie asked.

Lloyd shifted in his seat and frowned, scrunching his small nose. "My hands are no good when it comes to paint." Lloyd took the solider back and slid it down the table toward a blond boy at the end. "Wendell paints. He's probably one of the best."

Maggie and Henry looked over at Wendell. It didn't take long for them to recognize his burgundy coat.

"You!"

Maggie and Henry both leapt to their feet.

Wendell looked frightened and quickly peeked about to see if the Garrisons were watching. Maggie realized that the commotion could put them all in trouble, and she slowly lowered herself to the bench while tugging Henry's arm, pulling him back down as well.

"You know Wendell?" Lloyd asked, alarmed at the sudden outburst.

"Um, a little," Maggie mumbled.

"Somewhat acquainted, you could say," Henry added.

Wendell's eyes finally stopped darting around the room as he took the soldier in his hand and picked up a warped brush. Dipping the brush in the paint-filled bowls laid out before him, he gracefully applied color to the wooden toy. Wendell then slipped out of his seat and walked over with the newly painted soldier resting in his open palm. He gently set it down in front of Lloyd, but didn't seem concerned when the fresh paint smeared on the table.

"You're the one who broke into Chelsea Manor," Maggie whispered.

Wendell shifted between feet.

"Do you know the trouble you've caused us?" Henry said.

Wendell's back stiffened. Without saying a word, he turned around and picked up his paint supplies. A moment later, he was seated on the other end of the workshop, far from Maggie and Henry's table.

"Why is he upset?" Maggie asked. "It's his fault we're down here."

"Wendell didn't make you follow him to Poppel,"

A boy in an orange jacket at the next table turned around. His black oily hair hung over his forehead, partially covering his glaring eyes.

"Because of you nuisances, Wendell won't be allowed in the Sleigh Pit again. He'll be kept here in the workshop day in and day out. And he was finally being considered for a position at Kleren. He knows colors better than anybody. Even more than Hostrupp, I reckon. But not anymore. All thanks to you two."

"Excuse me, young man..." Henry started to say.

"Ward. My name's Ward."

"Wendell was trespassing," Maggie explained. "How were we to know he would lead us here?"

"Well, you're down here now," Ward sneered. "Guess that's unfortunate for you."

He twisted back around and started flattening a metal scrap with a hammer.

"What's he doing?" Maggie asked.

Lloyd glanced back at Ward.

"Oh, Ward doesn't usually work down here. So when he does, he just plays around. Hitting this, twisting that."

Maggie and Henry continued to watch Ward beating away on the table. The noise finally got Laszlo's attention and the white-haired man swooped down from the platform to inspect.

"What is that you're making so loudly, Ward?"

Ward proudly held up the dented metal square.

"It's symbolic, Laszlo," Ward explained. "It's a reminder of the brutality we face if we're not obedient to Castriot."

Laszlo shook his head and walked away.

Ward stood up and tossed the metal on Maggie and Henry's table. It rocked back and forth on top of the wooden soldier.

"Here you are, folks," Ward said, patting Lloyd on the shoulder. "Now I'm off to Snop." He pulled a cinnamon stick out of his pocket and stuck it in his mouth.

"You chew cinnamon sticks?" Maggie asked, suddenly feeling a strange connection to the unfriendly boy.

"It keeps my mouth clean," Ward said, flashing his teeth. "And I need that for all the sweets I eat." He spun about and jogged out of the workshop.

"Ward works at Snop—Myra Lane's candy shop," Lloyd explained.

Lloyd lifted up the metal square and pulled the soldier out from underneath.

"Now the paint will have to be redone. But let me show you

what I did here..."

Lloyd started to pick up his knife and another wooden block, but Henry stopped him.

"Don't waste your time showing us this." Henry placed his hand on top of Lloyd's. "We aren't Foundlings. And it won't be long until our families start looking for us."

Lloyd eyed Henry strangely and then looked back down at the block. He pretended to be examining the wood for imperfections.

"What is it, Lloyd?" Maggie could see there was something they weren't being told, but Lloyd didn't respond. "Do you think they won't search for us?"

Lloyd's eyes peeked up. "I'm sure they will. It just might take longer than you anticipate."

"What do you mean?"

Lloyd jerked his head side to side, nervously checking on the Garrisons.

"Didn't they tell you? Time moves slower here."

Maggie shook her head while Henry asked, "What do you mean time moves slower?"

Lloyd leaned forward. "Time... moves... slower."

Maggie and Henry looked at each other and then back at Lloyd.

"How long would you say you've been here?" Lloyd asked.

Henry shrugged. "I don't know, two... maybe three hours."

Lloyd nodded. "Then to your family you've only been gone about an hour."

"How is that possible?" Henry snapped as though Lloyd was trying to play a trick on them.

Lloyd blinked. "You've wandered down into an underground village that has the ability to enter any building in the entire city through a system of sleighs and fireplaces. And you ask how that is possible?"

"That's all very different than claiming one can slow time," Henry defended. "What you're talking about is... is... magical."

"Well, I suppose it is a bit," Lloyd said. "How much do you know about Nikolaos of Myra?"

"We heard about how he brought the three sisters to Belgium and founded Poppel," Maggie recounted. "And then later died helping the Martyrs of Gorkum."

Lloyd looked back down at the table and bit his lip, clearly wanting to say something.

"What?" Maggie pressed.

Lloyd's eyes began to dance with excitement as he whispered, "As the story goes, while sailing across the sea, Nikolaos of Myra received a great gift for saving the three sisters."

"Gift?" Henry scoffed. "A gift from whom?"

Lloyd shrugged. "No one knows who gave it to him. Perhaps the sea. Or the wind. Maybe a fish. But the gift was unlimited time."

"If that were so, then how could he be dead?" Maggie asked.

Lloyd scrunched his small nose once again. "Who said he was dead?"

"Well, he died, didn't he? With the Martyrs of Gorkum?"

"That's the legend. But there is no evidence of an actual death. He did, however, leave his unlimited time to the three sisters and Poppel. But the eldest sister Grace fell in love with a young man."

"Yes, Jan Loockerman. And Jan and Grace had Annette who brought Poppel to America," Maggie supplied hastily.

"So you have heard much of the story," Lloyd said. "Yes, the sisters eventually gave up their unlimited time so Grace could marry Jan and live a mortal life. But while it may not be unlimited down here in Poppel, there is more time allotted to the day."

"Is that why the Garrisons chose to work here?" Henry asked.

Lloyd nodded. "You will find when the benefits of a job include an abundance of time for drinking and playing cards; it does not attract the best kind of characters."

"But why did the Garrisons mention that Nikolaos of Myra could come back?"

"Because he can. At least it's said that his spirit can return."

"Like a ghost?" Maggie asked.

"Ghosts aren't real," Lloyd said with a slight chuckle. "Nikolaos of Myra is very real."

Out of the corner of her eye, Maggie spotted a tiny ball floating low to the ground, veering around the tables toward Lloyd's feet.

"Ghosts aren't real, huh?" Maggie remarked.

Lloyd didn't know what Maggie meant at first, but then he saw the ball gliding under the table. He dipped down and scooped it up. The ball stayed hidden in his clenched fist while he looked at the Garrisons. None of them seemed to be paying close attention. Most had been in the Krog earlier and were now too drunk and sleepy to care about the Foundlings.

"What is that?" Henry asked.

Seeing that no one was watching, Lloyd slowly opened his hand. In the middle of his palm sat a purple sphere speckled in some kind of white coating.

"Sugarplum," Lloyd whispered.

Maggie immediately thought of Grandfather Clement's poem: *The children were nestled all snug in their beds, while visions of sugarplums danced in their heads.*

With one last look to make sure the coast was clear, Lloyd popped the sugarplum in his mouth. His forehead creased in concentration as he chewed the gummy candy. After the sugarplum had been completely devoured, Lloyd's eyes lit up and he looked worried.

"Castriot now wants you both locked away until Christmas is over. Maybe even longer."

"What? Why?" Maggie asked.

"The Sister Wheel has vanished. And he thinks your arrival has something to do with it."

"I don't even know what that is," Henry said. "And how do you know?"

"Sugarplum." Lloyd pointed to his now empty mouth.

"What?" Henry stared at Lloyd's mouth in disbelief.

"No time to explain. Unless you want to be locked up indefinitely on the lowest level of Poppel, you need to get out of here."

Maggie looked at the Garrisons on the surrounding platform. "But how? There is no way to escape without being seen."

And just as Maggie finished speaking, it sounded like a hailstorm had hit the workshop as sacks full of marbles were tossed into the room. Hundreds of little balls bounced loudly down the steps, clunking over the hard ground.

As the noise filled the air, the alarmed Garrisons sprang into action. But as they stormed down the steps to the workshop floor, a shelf crammed with paint cans fell over onto the arriving men, drenching their black coats in bright reds, blues, greens, and yellows.

Garrisons coming from the opposite direction tried to assist, but the paint had created a slick ground, making standing nearly impossible. As the Garrisons slid and stumbled around, Maggie, Henry, and Lloyd slipped away unnoticed.

Henry grabbed Maggie's hand as they chased after Lloyd. Footsteps sounded behind her and she worried it was a Garrison. But when she glanced back, Wendell was running after them—his burgundy jacket was splashed in white paint. He had clearly helped knock the paint cans over.

Upon entering Myra Lane, the four Foundlings ducked into an alleyway. The cobblestone road was crowded with other Foundlings, but there were no black coats in sight. It seemed the racket had momentarily pulled the Garrisons away.

As the group snuck into Snop, Ward was waiting at the counter, spinning a red and white-striped peppermint wafer next to the lollipop stand. Seeing the group enter, he flipped the wafer into his mouth and nodded toward a decorative door behind him.

"Through here."

The door led to the kitchen. There was a wide fireplace and hearth while dozens of hanging pots and pans filled the walls. Ward directed them through another door and into a storage room where crates were stacked to the ceiling.

"I didn't think you two would fancy being hauled off to the Kelder," Ward said, sitting on a barrel and popping jellybeans into his mouth. "It's the lowest level of Poppel—a dark nightmare. I've been kept down there as a punishment. It's the waiting that gets you. Nothing to do except sit alone in the emptiness with your hopeless thoughts. I don't like that you two got Wendell in trouble, but no one—except perhaps a Garrison—deserves to be stuck in the Kelder."

"How did you know we were going to be put down there?" Henry asked.

Ward grinned, still chewing a wad of gummy jellybeans. "I have the best ears in Poppel. When I was walking from the workshop to Snop, some Garrisons were talking about how the Sister Wheel was missing and that Castriot had ordered for you two to be taken down to the Kelder."

"I don't even know what the Sister Wheel is," Maggie said with a frustrated sigh.

Ward shrugged. "Of course, you don't. Very few in Poppel even know where the Sister Wheel is hidden. The missing wheel story is probably a lie—just a reason to lock you two up. I'm actually surprised Castriot didn't put you in the Kelder right away. Madame Welles probably had something to do with it. She looks out for the Foundlings. It's just unfortunate you arrived at the time of year when Castriot is at his worst."

Ward took a handful of peanut brittle out of his vest.

"I heard them talking about shutting you away in the Kelder until Christmas is over. But it'll probably be even longer than that. So I sent sugarplums to Lloyd and Wendell. You can hide here until we figure out what to do next. The shop always slows down after the holiday. Houten's a grump, but he won't be around the next couple of days."

"Houten is the old man who runs Snop," Lloyd explained.

"He knows his sweets and has taught me loads," Ward continued, loudly crunching on the jagged brittle bits. "But he sure wouldn't approve of having stowaways in the backroom with all the ingredients."

"I still don't understand these sugarplums. What do you mean you sent them to Lloyd and Wendell?" Maggie asked. "How did they know to bring us here?"

"Oh, the sugarplums. Of course, you don't know!" Lloyd slapped his forehead with his palm. "Since the Garrisons took over, the Foundlings use sugarplums to secretly communicate."

"How?" Henry asked doubtfully. He crossed his arms over his chest.

Ward jumped down from the barrel and shuffled to the other side of the room. After sliding aside a crate, Ward removed a floorboard and pulled out a jar full of purple sugarplums.

"A special recipe," Ward said with a sly grin as he unscrewed the lid and plucked one out.

Maggie watched Ward closely, waiting for something spectacular to happen. But Ward just pinched the sugarplum between a finger and thumb. He then released the candy and it astonishingly hovered above the ground before slowly drifting over to Maggie. But when it bumped into her knee, she was unsure what to do.

"Eat it," Ward instructed.

Maggie arched an eyebrow and stared down at the floating confection.

"It's quite safe," Ward reassured with a chuckle.

Maggie reached down and hesitantly snatched the sugarplum. After turning it back and forth in her hand, Maggie slipped the candy into her mouth and began to chew carefully. It tasted surprisingly floral. But still nothing happened for a few moments until finally a warm sensation filled her mouth and the air became hazy. Suddenly, she heard Ward's voice, but it wasn't coming from where he sat on the other side of the room.

It was coming from inside her head.

"You are the only one who can hear this, Lizzie."

Maggie could see a vision of Ward cooking sugarplums in the shop's kitchen, coating the candy in sugar and other ingredients.

"Sugarplums have been used for hundreds of years," Ward's voice explained. *"It was a way for Nikolaos of Myra to give children a gift without being caught. Even Nikolaos' powers had limits, but he knew that sometimes the best gift you could give a child with nothing was a dream. He delivered dreams in the form of sugarplums to sleeping children. But they're no longer used outside of Poppel. Just secretly between the Foundlings now."*

Ward's voice faded as the room came back into focus.

Henry was intensely staring at Maggie with both concern and intrigue. "What happened?"

"I think we found our way out of here." Maggie turned to Ward and added, "I will need a couple more of those."

CHAPTER ELEVEN

NESTLED ALL SNUG

The shimmering outlines of three sugarplums popped up from the ash pit and glided across the Great Room of Chelsea Manor. But Louis didn't see them from the sofa where he was soundly asleep. While a pair of faintly visible sugarplums disappeared into the hall and up the winding staircase to the second floor, one trace of purple dust floated along the sofa toward the napping boy.

When Louis let out a sluggish yawn, the sugarplum bits trickled into the gaping mouth. He smacked his lips a few times before letting out another yawn and then swallowing the specks completely. A few seconds later, Louis' eyes snapped open and he sat up.

Feeling dazed, Louis slipped off the sofa and moved toward the fireplace. His mind was foggy as fragments of the vision began to fuzzily return.

Maggie.

Something about Maggie.

As the images began to piece together, Louis ran out of the Great Room and up the stairs. As he turned to go to the third floor, Catharine came drifting down the steps.

"Maggie's not in her room," she said as though reading Louis' mind.

Before Louis could respond, Clemmie staggered from his bedroom at the end of the hallway. His eyes were barely open as he scratched his disheveled hair.

"I just had the strangest dream," Clemmie said with a yawn and then shook his head. "About Maggie and that Livingston fellow."

"And they disappeared down the fireplace," Louis supplied.

Clemmie froze in place as his eyes snapped open. "How did you know?"

"And now they're being held in an underground village," Louis continued.

Clemmie took a step back with his hands out in front of him. "How are you doing this?"

"Maggie's gone," Catharine explained.

"Gone?" Clemmie blurted. "What do you mean she's gone?"

"She's not in her bedroom and all three of us had a dream about her and Henry Livingston." Catharine threw up her hands. "He must have kidnapped her."

"Or they both were taken away by someone," Louis suggested, still not ready to confess what he'd witnessed in the Great Room earlier.

"Or we just… all had a dream," Clemmie simply said, fluttering his fingers in the air.

"In my dream, Henry broke into Chelsea Manor," Catharine said. "He has something to do with all of this. I just know it."

"I don't think we should make assumptions," Clemmie said, folding his arms. "Maggie could very well be in the Manor right now. Probably reading a book in the library. And by chance we just all had similar dreams about that strange Livingston man."

Ignoring her brother, Catharine turned and headed down to the main floor. Clemmie and Louis initially hesitated but then followed.

"I dreamed they escaped through the fireplace," Catharine said, crossing the hall.

"That wasn't a dream," Louis quickly said.

Catharine and Clemmie both stopped and looked at their cousin.

Louis noted the inquisitive stares and sighed. "Around midnight I came downstairs to see if there was anything left to eat from dinner. That's when I saw Maggie and Henry vanish through the fireplace in the Great Room. I fell asleep on the sofa waiting for them to come back. But then I had that dream where they were riding in a sleigh and being chased by men in black coats."

"That's what I saw!" Clemmie's voice cracked. "Now you must tell me honestly. Was I talking in my sleep?"

Catharine marched over to the fireplace. Upon closer inspection, she caught something Louis had missed. "What's this?"

Clemmie and Louis peered over Catharine's shoulder. Her finger was pointing to the back of the fireplace.

"Where did that come from?" Louis squinted at the dull gleam embedded within the brick.

Catharine cautiously pressed the emblem and the ash pit opened.

"That's where they went!" Louis exclaimed.

Catharine grabbed hold of her robe and scooted toward the edge of the hole.

"What are you doing?" Clemmie asked. "You're not actually going down there?"

"Of course, I am," snapped Catharine. "Someone has our sister. And much to their future suffering, I am going after her."

And with that, she jumped into darkness. A moment later, a faint *thump* indicated she landed somewhere below.

"Are you hurt?" Louis asked hoarsely.

There was no response.

"Catharine?"

"Yes, yes. I'm all right," Catharine's voice called back. "There's a passageway down here. I'm going to find Maggie."

"Wait for me!" Louis swung his legs over the opening and nervously dangled them, his face growing paler by the second.

"Well, are you going down?" Clemmie asked.

"Don't rush me!"

Louis then took a long gulp before dropping through the hole after Catharine. Clemmie inched closer and peered down. He couldn't see anything, but he heard Catharine and Louis' muffled voices.

After a few moments, Louis called up. "Clemmie, are you coming?"

With great reluctance, Clemmie situated his body near the hole. But before he could drop down, he noticed that the golden emblem had wiggled out of place. Clemmie poked it with a finger, loosening it even more until it finally separated from the brick.

Clemmie held the emblem in his palm and stared at the engraved letters.

"Clement Moore Ogden!" Catharine hollered.

"Yes, coming," Clemmie hissed into the hole. He slipped the emblem into his shirt's breast pocket, and then he fell through the opening.

Seconds later, Clemmie landed in a pile of ash. Catharine and Louis were standing in a tunnel entrance; the light coming from the other end of the tunnel outlined their dusty bodies.

"Ah, there you are. I was worried you became lost on your way down," Louis quipped before he and Catharine disappeared into the tunnel.

Feeling his pocket to make sure that the emblem was still intact, Clemmie stood up and chased after his sister and cousin.

Lloyd had gone out alone to release three sugarplums near the Sleigh Pit. But when he returned to Snop's backroom, he brought along a familiar face.

"Harriet," Maggie exclaimed, recognizing the Foundling.

"Did you release the sugarplums?" Ward asked Lloyd.

Lloyd nodded. "And then I ran into Harriet." He turned to Harriet. "Tell them what you just told me."

"The Sister Wheel has been found."

An audible sigh rippled through the group.

"The missing Sister Wheel appears to be just a rumor started by a couple of drunk Garrisons," Harriet said. "So Castriot knows that Alfred and Lizzie didn't take it."

"Well, that's a relief," Maggie said.

"Yes, but Castriot also knows you're hiding," Harriet stressed. "And he's placed a crew of Garrisons in the Sleigh Pit to make sure you don't escape."

"So if your family comes looking for you," Lloyd explained. "They're going to be captured."

"Catharine and Louis are both smart people. And Clemmie…" Maggie paused and then added. "Well, Clemmie fancies himself as rather brilliant. They won't come down here alone. Once they realize I'm missing, they'll wake up the rest of my family. And then Catharine, Clemmie, and Louis can lead everyone down the ash pit."

"Why didn't we send the sugarplums to the adults in the first place?" Henry asked.

Ward shook his head. "When a person is older, it's less likely they'll believe their dreams. We're even taking a chance that Catharine, Clemmie, and Louis will figure out the truth. Still, we should prepare as though they did realize what's happened and that they're coming through the Sleigh Pit. Alone."

"What can we do?" Maggie asked.

"Well," Ward said, shifting into action with the clap of his hands. "The Garrisons won't guess that Alfred and Lizzie are with me, but the longer Wendell and Lloyd are away, the more suspicious it'll be. They need to go back to the workshop and say that when the earlier incident happened, Alfred and Lizzie took off and they chased after them."

It was agreed that while Wendell and Lloyd returned to the workshop, Ward and Harriet would stay with Maggie and Henry to make sure the rest of the family arrived unharmed.

Once Wendell and Lloyd left, Ward went over to a huge wooden crate in the corner that had the word *FLOUR* stenciled diagonally across its side. He reached over the top of the lid and touched around until there was a *click*. Ward then slid its panel open, revealing stone steps within the crate.

Maggie sighed. "I think I've gone through enough hidden passages tonight."

"There's a series of tunnels that connect all of Poppel. When the Garrisons took over, they went through every inch of this place," Ward said and then nodded toward the crate's opening with a smirk. "But they didn't find these tunnels. So the Foundlings can still get around Poppel without being caught by the Garrisons."

"And we can get to the Sleigh Pit through here," Harriet added, joining Ward near the crate.

"Ward!" A crackly voice hollered from the front of the shop.

"It's Houten," Ward groaned and then turned to Harriet. "Take them down to the pit. I'll deal with the old man."

Harriet nodded and gestured to Maggie and Henry who followed her into the flour crate just as Ward grimly shut the panel behind them.

"We must be getting close," Louis whispered, peering at the upcoming tunnel.

Catharine, Clemmie, and Louis were huddled in a sleigh as it rolled along the clanking chains. From the rickety sleighs to the oil lamp lit caverns, everything looked exactly as it had in their dreams. But they still weren't confident about finding Maggie anytime soon.

"Oh, are we, Louis?" Clemmie brushed ash from his shoulder. He had been pretty sour since having his clothes dirtied. "I'd be interested to hear how you can tell. Everything down here looks the same."

"Well, this can't go on forever," stated Catharine, squinting into the darkness.

"It very well may," grumbled Clemmie. "We could be traveling in a loop. Circumnavigating the entire globe! How would we know?"

There was no chance to answer. As the sleigh entered another lit cavern, a blockade of Garrisons could be seen awaiting their arrival.

"Uh oh," Louis groaned, recognizing the black coats.

The Garrisons held rifled muskets and upon seeing the occupied sleigh, they perched the guns on their shoulders, pointing them at the intruders.

"Off!" one Garrison shouted.

Catharine, Clemmie, and Louis scurried from the moving sleigh and crouched on their knees with hands raised above their heads.

"More of them, Cockrell," a slender Garrison with a long nose said. "I'm starting to suspect that they didn't just accidently wander down here."

Cockrell, a thick man with barely any neck, stood in the middle of the pack. Gray sideburns curved along his swollen face as he lifted an arm, signaling the Garrisons to put down their firearms.

"Easy, fellas," Cockrell bellowed as he walked his tree trunk legs toward the Moore grandchildren.

"Are you here for Alfred and Lizzie?"

Catharine, Clemmie, and Louis eyed each other with uncertainty.

"We're... lost," Louis said weakly, not daring to mention Maggie's name.

Clemmie apparently wasn't thinking along the same lines.

"We're looking for Maggie," Clemmie stammered.

Catharine shot him a piercing glare. She also knew it wasn't a good idea to mention their sister's name.

"Maggie?" Cockrell grunted. "Who's Maggie?"

"Our... dog," Clemmie recovered, realizing his mistake. "Our dog, Maggie. She's a Norfolk spaniel—about yay high." Clemmie cautiously moved his wrist to his chest and waved it a couple times.

"Yes, our dog," Catharine jumped in. "She chased a mouse through a hole in our fireplace. We came down here, but have been unable to locate her. Perhaps you have seen her."

"Yes, perhaps you have seen her," Clemmie repeated mechanically. "The dog. The dog named Maggie. Maggie is her name."

"Mostly white," Louis added. "With black spots on her back. And big ears."

Placing hands next to each side of his head, Louis wiggled his fingers like floppy ears.

Cockrell looked back at the other Garrisons who seemed in no hurry to search for a dog.

"So if you could just help us find her, we can be on our way," Clemmie said, standing up from the ground.

"Enough!" The flab of Cockrell's face shook angrily. "We're not looking for any dog. You're coming with us. There'll be no more talking until Castriot sees you."

Three Garrisons grabbed Catharine and Louis and stuffed them in the arriving sleigh while Cockrell and another Garrison took Clemmie into the sleigh behind it.

"Here, Maggie," Clemmie called halfheartedly with a whistle. "Come on out, girl."

"Stop that," Cockrell growled.

As Clemmie finished another high-pitched whistle, the other Garrison smacked his shoulder with the butt of a musket.

"Oomph," Clemmie moaned, rubbing the bruised muscle.

He remained quiet for the rest of the ride.

Soon Catharine and Louis arrived at the Sleigh Pit with Clemmie's sleigh following minutes later. The Moore grandchildren were then roughly pulled off the sleighs and lined up between two tunnel entrances.

"Before you're taken to Castriot, would you like to share the truth about your whereabouts?" Cockrell asked.

There was silence until Louis stuttered, "Who's Castriot?"

Under his dense nose, Cockrell's lips curled into a sly smile.

"You will soon find out. And once you have, you will not easily forget."

Cockrell nodded and the Garrisons grasped the arms of Catharine, Clemmie, and Louis. But suddenly the oil lamps in the Sleigh Pit went out, and like a cloak being thrown over the room, it became completely black. The Garrisons let go of the intruders and instantly clutched their rifled muskets. But it was too dark to shoot.

"What is going on here?" the voice of Cockrell boomed. "Who's there? What's happening?"

Catharine, Clemmie, and Louis were clustered together, but then shadowy figures unexpectedly swept through, whisking them away one by one. The grandchildren didn't make any noise, hoping that whatever had grabbed them was better than the Garrisons.

Catharine, Clemmie, and Louis were led through a passageway and then into a round chamber that emerged out of the darkness. Although it was crowded with half a dozen people, Catharine instantly laid eyes on a brunette girl.

"Maggie!"

"Shh!"

Catharine turned and saw Henry Livingston dressed in a green coat and black hat. He was not only the person who had hushed her but also the one gripping her arms. As the two made eye contact, Henry appeared stunned at the sight of Maggie's older sister. He didn't even notice that Ward had let go of Clemmie and Louis.

Maggie's stomach dropped as she watched how Henry continued to hold Catharine. But her eyes were pulled away as Louis gently grabbed her shoulders.

"Maggie, what happened to you?" Louis asked.

Meanwhile, Catharine was glaring at Henry as he still absentmindedly held her arms. "Release me, Mr. Livingston."

Henry relaxed his grip and flushed pink. Catharine instantly marched over and wrapped her sister in a hug. "Maggie, are you hurt?"

Harriet stepped forward. "I thought you said your name was Lizzie." She looked at Henry, adding, "And it's Alfred, isn't it?"

The Moore grandchildren and Henry swapped glances.

"Who are you, really?" Ward asked.

Ward had met up with Henry, Maggie, and Harriet right before the other Moore grandchildren arrived. The plan was to sneak Catharine, Clemmie, and Louis into the tunnel located between the piles of broken sleighs in the back of the Sleigh Pit. But when they saw Cockrell and the other Garrisons, they knew they had to make quick adjustments. Maggie and Harriet put out the oil lamps while Henry and Ward snatched the Moore grandchildren.

"We don't need to say anything until I'm told where we are," Catharine said, rubbing Maggie's back protectively.

Maggie explained about following Wendell down the fireplace. She told about Henry getting punched by McNutt and then being captured by the Garrisons before finally becoming new Foundlings. She finished with the sugarplums they had sent to Chelsea Manor. Maggie was sure that of everything discussed, the sugarplums would certainly be the part needing further inquiry. But Catharine was hung up on just one detail of the story.

"What were you doing in Chelsea Manor?" Catharine twisted about to face Henry.

Henry appeared taken aback by Catharine's attack. But with a reluctant sigh, he repeated what he had told Maggie earlier in the library.

"That's impossible," Clemmie said, placing his hands stiffly on his hips. "Clement Clarke Moore not being the rightful author of *Twas the Night Before Christmas*? I don't believe it."

But before Clemmie could debate Henry on the literary merits of Major Henry Livingston and Clement Clarke Moore, Harriet chimed in.

"You're related to Major Henry and Sidney Livingston?"

Henry nodded.

"And you four are the grandchildren of Clement and Catharine Moore?"

"Yes," Clemmie replied dully. "So?"

All the Foundlings looked around at each other, making the Chelsea Manor visitors feel as though they were being kept out of an important secret.

"What is it?" Catharine asked, not hiding her frustration.

"What is it? What is it!" a voice crackled from the doorway. "You are the grandchildren of Clement Clarke Moore and Major Henry—both related to the Van Cortlandts, and the keepers of the two remaining Sister Wheels."

A stout, plump man wobbled into the room; his cane striking the stone floor with each step. Bushy white hair swirled out from underneath his blue top hat while his wrinkled eyes squinted through oval glasses, staring at the Moore grandchildren huddled together.

Ward stepped forward grudgingly. "What are you doing here, Houten?"

Houten cackled hoarsely. "You think I can't move around these tunnels, eh? Well, I'm sorry to say that while I'm slower than you Foundlings, this old body can still trudge along. And these nearly blind eyes can still spot when a panel on an empty flour crate is cracked open."

Ward groaned, realizing that in his hurry he had left the tunnel entrance ajar.

"That little light show you just pulled in the Sleigh Pit won't go over well," Houten continued. "You best head back up to Myra Lane unless you want the Garrisons to think you're aiding the Van Cortlandt descendants. And if you don't think they'll eventually figure out their true names as you all just did, you are gravely mistaken."

Houten's eyes moved to Maggie and then over to Henry. He raised his crooked finger and pointed at the pair. "It's like seeing the second coming of Catharine Moore and Sidney Livingston." Catharine, Clemmie, and Louis came into focus and Houten added, "And those three as well. No doubt from the Van Cortlandt bloodline."

"What are you saying, Houten?" Ward asked.

Houten strained his eyes in Ward's direction and smacked his gums as he spoke. "Ward, these intruders are the only hope for Nikolaos of Myra returning to Poppel."

Chapter Twelve

The Sister Wheels

The Foundlings were sent back up the tunnel to Myra Lane, leaving Henry and the Moore grandchildren with Houten who smelled like peppermint.

Facing the group, Houten planted his cane steadily between his bowed legs.

"It's been so long since I saw a Van Cortlandt descendant. Mrs. Catharine Moore and Mr. Sidney Livingston were always running around here with young Margaret. Such lively little ducks."

"You knew my father?" Henry tilted up his top hat, exposing his untidy bronze hair and intrigued expression.

"Sidney? Why, of course, I knew Sidney Livingston. I knew Major Henry, as well. And Major Henry's uncle, Pierre Van Cortlandt, the great-grandson of Oloff and Annette Van Cortlandt." Houten looked at Maggie. "And your grandmother, Catharine Taylor Moore, was a descendant of the Van Cortlandt family. Catharine's grandfather Philip was the great-great grandson of Oloff and Annette Van Cortlandt. And you know who Annette Van Cortlandt was?"

"The daughter of Grace Loockerman—the eldest of the three sisters," Louis replied as though answering a question in school. The story Maggie had told the other grandchildren was still fresh in his mind.

"Indeed," Houten nodded. "But there is a portion of the tale I am certain you do not know. After Nicolas Poppelius went to help the Martyrs of Gorkum, the three girls were left with the unlimited time. So Grace, Sarah, Lily, and the Foundlings continued living their extraordinary long lives even after Nicolas disappeared."

"Disappeared?" Henry repeated.

"It was reported that Nicolas Poppelius as well as eighteen others were mutilated and hanged outside of the town of Brielle in the western part of the Netherlands."

Maggie let out an abrupt noise at the horrific image.

"Do not distress, young duckling," Houten reassured. "That is just how the story goes. But it is not so. Nicolas Poppelius rescued those men and fake remains were sent to Belgium where they were appropriately placed in the Church of St. Nicholas. Nikolaos of Myra and those men secretly vanished, but no one knows to where. In the meantime Grace, Sarah, and Lily continued to run Poppel."

"Until Grace married Jan Loockerman," Henry said.

"Indeed. But not every sister supported Grace's decision to leave Poppel. For when one sister gave away her immortality—it was taken from them all."

"Oh, really. How so?" Catharine hastily asked, clearly disbelieving the story.

But Houten didn't catch her incredulous tone and continued to explain.

"The Sister Wheels, of course. Nikolaos of Myra gave each sister a wheel. When brought together, the wheels granted unlimited time to those in Poppel. But if one sister left—the gift was broken. When Grace married Jan Loockerman, Sarah supported her—even if that meant giving up their everlasting youth. But Lily did not. Angrily, Lily took her wheel and went in search of other means to not inevitably succumb to death. Meanwhile, Grace and Sarah welcomed old age and passed their Sister Wheels on to Annette Loockerman before she headed to

America. Annette eventually gave the two wheels to her eldest son, Stephanus, who continued the tradition of passing them down the Van Cortlandt line, along with the secret of Poppel."

Houten whacked Henry's leg with the cane. "Follow me, little ducks."

Not allowing time for questions, Houten wobbled through the doorway. And like a true gaggle, Henry and the Moore grandchildren closely followed the slow moving man, all remarking at once.

"So we're the descendants of Stephanus Van Cortlandt?" Catharine asked.

Maggie added, "Wouldn't that mean our families have the two Sister Wheels?"

Clemmie aggressively wiped the endless layer of ash from his jacket. "And I would like some clean clothes, if that is at all possible."

Henry was the last to speak. "What do you know about the poem *'Twas the Night Before Christmas*?"

Houten continued down the tunnel, encircled by the flock of people.

"You all must keep your voices low," Houten whispered. "First, we'll go see Hostrupp so everyone will receive new clothes. It has become even more imperative that the Garrisons never find any of you." Houten turned to Maggie. "Stephanus Van Cortlandt passed the Sister Wheels and Poppel information to his son Philip, who split the wheels between his two sons, Pierre and Stephen. The Livingstons married into Pierre's lineage and carry Sarah's wheel while your Van Cortlandt relatives are Stephen's direct descendants and have Grace's. Mrs. Catharine Moore and Mr. Sidney Livingston were the last in the two Van Cortlandt lines to know the history."

"What do you know about our grandmother?" Catharine asked.

"And my father," Henry added, coming up behind Catharine who didn't appreciate his encroachment and shot an annoyed glance.

Houten stopped walking and squinted up at the young faces.

"I had known Mr. Sidney Livingston since he was a boy. Major Henry and his son used to come all the way down from Poughkeepsie a couple of times a year. Eventually, it became too long of a trip for Major Henry, but Sidney would visit Poppel when he was studying at the seminary in the city."

"And that was when he met our grandmother," Louis added plainly.

"Well, yes and no," Houten said. "Sidney first met her daughter, Margaret, who had received the family secret from her grandmother, Elizabeth. Mrs. Catharine Moore had never known about Poppel until her daughter began mysteriously disappearing down fireplaces. It was then Mrs. Moore befriended Mr. Livingston and the two of them became deeply bonded."

"And Grandfather Clement knew about this?" Maggie asked.

"Mr. Moore knew of Mr. Sidney Livingston calling on Mrs. Moore and the children at Chelsea Manor. But was he aware of the Van Cortlandt family history, the Sister Wheels, and Poppel? No, I do not believe he knew any of that. Even when *Twas the Night Before Christmas* was published and later tied to his name, Mr. Moore thought it was simply a childish poem by the Poughkeepsie man he despised. And a man he eventually drove out of New York by a fallacious plagiarism claim."

The group reached the trapdoor that connected the tunnel to the backroom of Kleren. One by one, they climbed through the floor and were met by a grinning Hostrupp.

"Well, well," Hostrupp said, softly patting his palms together. "They just keep arriving."

Houten was the last person to be pulled up. It took the combined efforts of Henry, Clemmie, and Louis to hoist the plump old man into the backroom.

"So these are the newcomers causing quite a stir outside!" Hostrupp's mauve eyes danced as he examined Catharine, Clemmie, and Louis. "You're very, very lucky. The Garrisons have

115

already come through here, searching under this and that, turning the entire place inside out. Trying to track you special folks down! But some Foundling clothes will help you troublemakers blend."

Catharine was the first to get changed. While her sister disappeared into a dressing room, Maggie spied a row of trousers hanging in the corner. Grabbing a pair off a hook and a shirt lying nearby, Maggie slid into a broom closet before anyone took notice. A few minutes later, Maggie emerged wearing more comfortable clothes.

"What is all this?" Hostrupp stopped adjusting the collar of Louis' silver jacket when he caught sight of Maggie's brown trousers and white shirt. "Foundling ladies are not to be wearing male attire."

"If I'm going to be chased by Garrisons, I'm going to be wearing something I can actually run in," Maggie defended.

Taken aback by Maggie's passion, Hostrupp didn't argue and actually looked over at Catharine to see if she had similar objections.

"I'm content with my clothes," Catharine said bluntly, pinching the fabric of her skirt.

"Wonderful," Hostrupp replied, clapping his hands.

If Hostrupp's goal had been to make Catharine less stunning, he had failed. Her deep red dress with white trim caused her to be even more striking in appearance. And Maggie couldn't help but notice Henry having difficulty taking his eyes off her sister.

Clemmie walked out of the corner dressing room wearing a lavender suit and hat with a light beige vest. "I've trouble believing that I won't be easily spotted dressed as a lilac bush."

Clemmie dropped an armful of clothes on the floor. Something within the pile clinked against the ground before rolling out of a pocket. It didn't take Maggie much time to recognize the emblem from the Chelsea Manor fireplace. Even Houten's nearly blind eyes identified the golden object instantly.

Houten pointed his cane at the emblem lying in the middle of the floor. "Where did you get that?"

Clemmie bent over and scooped it up. "It came loose from the fireplace in Chelsea Manor."

"Do you know what that is?" Houten asked flabbergasted.

Clemmie stared down at his hand and shook his head. Catharine and Henry came over and peered at the small trinket.

"Why, it's a Sister Wheel!" Hostrupp observed. "How fascinating! How marvelous!"

"Sister Wheel?" Maggie echoed.

"Why didn't you tell us you were carrying it?" Houten snapped, whipping up his cane and prodding Clemmie's chest with it.

Clemmie looked flustered and responded slowly. "Because... this isn't a wheel."

Houten smacked his forehead with the palm of his hand. "A clock wheel, you silly boy! The wheels of a clock contain round centers that hold emblems like the one in your hand. And in the case of the Sister Wheels, they allow the unlimited time. At least when they all are placed inside the original Horologe brought all the way to Poppel from Belgium."

Houten hobbled over to Clemmie and snatched the wheel out of his outstretched hand. Turning it around in his crooked fingers, Houten eyed every bit of its golden surface.

"Outstanding," Houten said, bringing the wheel up to his narrow gaze. "No doubt it once belonged to Grace. Passed down through Stephen's side of the Van Cortlandts before being given to Mrs. Catharine Moore's daughter, Margaret, and then hidden in Chelsea Manor's fireplace." Houten looked at Clemmie and murmured darkly, "Castriot would kill to have it."

"But why?" Henry blurted. "I thought Castriot didn't want Van Cortlandt descendants returning to Poppel for fear of exactly this—uniting the Sister Wheels and bringing Nikolaos of Myra back."

"Yes, if all the Sister Wheels were united in the Horologe that would bring an end to the Garrisons. But in case you hadn't realized, Poppel already has one of the three wheels."

"They accused us of stealing it earlier!" Maggie exclaimed. "But whose would they have?"

"Lily's," Louis remarked thoughtfully. "It has to be Lily's. But how could that be? What became of her?"

Houten stiffened. "That is a story for another time and place. All I'll say is that the Foundlings acquired Lily's wheel centuries ago. And since that time have enjoyed long lives down here. If Grace's Sister Wheel were to be added to Lily's in the Horologe, it would further extend the time given to Poppel. Which is why we must not let the Garrisons know who you are and what you have. They would first make sure the Sister Wheel is taken and then see to it that all of you are destroyed."

Clemmie loudly gulped.

"But how did the Garrisons come to know about the Sister Wheels?" Catharine asked. "I have a hard time believing that the Foundlings were so forthcoming with all this information once the Garrisons had taken over."

Hostrupp jumped in again. "Oh, when the Garrisons invaded long ago it was terribly, terribly terrible. Foundlings have always been extensive records keepers, going back over a thousand years when Poppel was first founded in Belgium. But when the Garrisons attacked Poppel ever so suddenly, we had no time—no time at all—to hide our records away, including the mighty fine tale of the three sisters. One of the very first things they did in Poppel—the very first—was hole themselves up in the Boeken Kamer, where they quickly learned all there was to Poppel and its legends."

"Boeken Kamer?" Henry repeated.

"Poppel's library," Harriet quickly supplied.

Clemmie let out a laugh. "Of course, Poppel has a library. On top of everything else, why wouldn't it! I imagine Poppel will also be getting its own postal service and navy any day now."

Harriet glowered. "The library is where we keep all our books and records, including those that came all the way from Belgium centuries ago."

Receiving Harriet's glare, Clemmie became stoic once again.

"So if the Garrisons have Lily's wheel and we have Grace's," Louis said slowly, counting on his fingers, "there is only one left—Sarah's."

"And that means it would be somewhere in the lineage of Stephanus, which went from Pierre Van Cortlandt to Major Henry to…" Maggie trailed off.

"My father," Henry whispered, his eyes growing large.

Houten nodded. "Yes, Sidney Livingston would have been the last to know the whereabouts of Sarah's wheel."

"But you said that the wheel and story was always passed on to another family member," Catharine said. "My mother, Margaret, would have been the last one in our family to know, but she died too suddenly to pass it on. However, Sidney just died recently. Why would he not tell Henry anything?"

Before Henry could respond, Maggie interjected, "What makes you think he didn't?" Maggie turned to Henry. "You said you have letters and journals from your father. Did he ever once mention Poppel, or perhaps, the wheel?"

Henry thought carefully for a moment. "I… I don't know. He wrote so much about Catharine and Margaret. But if there were any references to Poppel, it must have been done rather cryptically, because I don't recall anything specific."

Reaching into his jacket's inner pocket, Henry pulled out a thick stack of yellowed papers that were tied together by a taut piece of twine. He went over to the corner and dropped the pile on the ground. The rest of the room watched as he rifled through the mound of letters, searching desperately for something perhaps overlooked.

"He shouldn't bother," Houten said gruffly. "Even if he could pinpoint the exact location of Sarah's wheel, there's still one element missing."

"And what is that?" Maggie sighed, exhausted by the thought of even more parts to the already convoluted story.

"Although each individual wheel can be placed into the Horologe, there is only one tool that could successfully unite all three. And it hasn't been heard of since Grace, Sarah and Lily still ran Poppel in the 1500s. It could be with either line of the Van Cortlandt families or it could have been left far away in Belgium altogether, never to be seen again."

"What kind of tool is it?" Louis asked.

"Oh, I don't even know exactly," Houten said, scratching his deeply wrinkled forehead. "Some key or crank, I suppose."

A large commotion suddenly sounded from outside of the shop.

"What is that?" asked Catharine, as the voices of a gathering crowd grew louder.

Henry looked up from the corner where he remained bent over, rummaging through the papers. Clemmie and Louis started moving toward the front of the shop to investigate, but Hostrupp pulled them back.

"No, no. You will certainly be seen. Most certainly."

Hostrupp grabbed a long rod that had been leaning in a corner of the backroom. He flicked it up at the ceiling until it hit a knot in the wood. A moment later, the ceiling opened and a ladder came sliding down.

"Up here. Very secret attic from where we can view Myra Lane. Come with me quietly. Very quietly."

Hostrupp scurried up the ladder with Clemmie and Louis following right behind. Catharine and Henry went next, but Maggie hesitated, looking at Houten. The old man clearly could not climb unassisted.

"Don't worry about me," Houten snapped, whacking the ladder with his cane. "Get up there and see what's happening. Then report back."

By the time Maggie made it into the attic, covered in old boxes of fabric and frayed ribbons, Hostrupp and the others were huddled around a dusty window facing Myra Lane. Maggie joined them, forcing herself into a gap between Henry and Clemmie. And there she was able to see what had everyone speechless.

It was Francis.

Francis had followed them to Poppel.

CHAPTER THIRTEEN

NEW HEAD GARRISON

Francis stood on the stone platform under Myra Lane's post clock. He was front and center of the growing Foundling crowd, sandwiched between Comstock and Cyrus who were slyly clutching the sleeves of his striped nightshirt.

At first Maggie thought her cousin was being paraded about as a captive, but she quickly realized he wasn't being held prisoner—he was being celebrated.

"At last," Comstock bellowed. "The Van Cortlandt heir has returned to Poppel. Here stands, Francis Casimier Moore, grandson of Clement Clarke Moore—the man we owe a great deal of thanks."

Smiling cruelly, Cyrus gripped Francis' sleeve tighter.

"Wait!" a voice roared from the crowd.

A moment later, another Garrison came bounding up to the post clock, each hand bracing the shoulder of two similarly sized bodies.

"What is that you have there, Chatham?" Cyrus hissed, peering down from the platform.

"They say their names are Gardiner and Gertrude," Chatham replied, yanking the children forward. "They arrived to the Sleigh Pit right after Francis."

Cyrus twisted his head toward Francis. "Relatives of yours?"

Francis gulped before murmuring, "My cousins."

The Garrisons promptly cheered and after some persuasion, the Foundlings reluctantly followed suit. Francis didn't seem to know how to take such a reception, while Gardiner and Gertrude were clearly frightened.

"Francis, Gardiner, and Gertrude—welcome to Poppel!" Comstock exclaimed. "Your arrival has been anticipated for many years."

Looking overwhelmed, Francis stammered, "What's Poppel?"

"Your new home," Cyrus answered foolishly, causing Gertrude to burst into tears and Francis to jump off the platform in a panic. But Comstock and Cyrus grabbed his arms and hauled him back up just as Gardiner sprung forward, attempting to shove the Garrisons away from his older cousin.

The Garrisons had almost controlled the situation when a voice boomed from the other end of Myra Lane.

"Silence!"

Castriot stood near the banquet hall stairwell where McNutt had punched Henry. The mere presence of the Head Garrison caused a sudden shift in the crowd. Everyone watched as Castriot strolled down Myra Lane. He didn't speak until he was standing between Comstock and Cyrus, blocking Maggie's view of Francis.

"How dare you scare our guests, Cyrus," Castriot said before turning to Gardiner and Gertrude. "You have no reason to be frightened. We are very pleased to have you here. Your family and our village have a long and pleasant history. Obviously, you may leave when you wish, but we hope you will stay for a little while."

Castriot then extended his right arm toward the crowd and a couple of Garrisons appeared, arms overflowing with candy and toys. With their tears now sniffled away, Maggie watched as the twins giddily flocked toward the gifts.

Castriot moved to the side and Maggie spotted Francis again. She was pleased to see that he wasn't as easily enticed by the offerings. But Castriot quickly responded to the boy's hesitation.

He swooped down to Francis' level and whispered into his ear. Castriot and Francis exchanged words quietly.

"What are they saying?" Clemmie grumbled, pressing his face against the dusty window.

Francis and Castriot continued to talk until Castriot finally straightened up. The Head Garrison peeled off his black jacket and placed it over Francis' nightshirt. Castriot then tousled Francis' hair in a fatherly manner, leaving the boy with a rather smug grin.

Wearing only an undershirt and high-waisted trousers did not take away Castriot's fearsomeness. He faced the crowd, hand on Francis' shoulder, and announced, "The descendants of Oloff and Annette Van Cortlandt have returned to bring Poppel back to its former greatness and ensure its future dominance. I hereby declare that Francis Casimier Moore will be the new Head Garrison. And all of his requests and demands must be obeyed."

Castriot stared down at the twins who had stopped munching on the slices of yellow cake in their hands. "Gardiner and Gertrude, you will join the Foundlings until you can prove yourself as useful as your cousin, Casimier."

Two muscular Garrisons came up behind the twins and lifted them away before they could even cry out.

"Margaret Ogden!"

Maggie stiffened at the sound of her name. Her stomach shifted uncomfortably.

"Henry Livingston, Louis Moore, Catharine and Clement Ogden," Castriot announced. "These other Van Cortlandt descendants have infiltrated our walls in an attempt to destroy Poppel. They must be tracked down and stopped. Any Foundling that is seen harboring these intruders will be locked in the Kelder." Castriot paused, licked his lips and added, "Forever."

A gasp trickled through the crowd, but Henry, Maggie, and the other Moore grandchildren couldn't hear it over their own audible concern. However, they did not discuss anything until they climbed down the ladder and were once again safely tucked away in the back of Kleren.

Maggie was the first one down and immediately saw that Houten was no longer there. But the room had still gained quite a few faces. Ward, Harriet, Wendell, Lloyd, Nellie, and Violet had apparently snuck into the shop during the uproar in Myra Lane. By the time Clemmie, Catharine, Louis, and Hostrupp squirmed down the ladder after Maggie, the backroom was crammed with bodies.

"Where's Houten?" Maggie asked outright.

"He had to go back to Snop," Ward explained. "He couldn't risk not being there when the Garrisons come looking."

Nellie spotted the concern on Maggie's face and added, "He said to tell you that his help was no longer needed. And that we would assist you on the next step."

"Which is what?" Catharine asked.

Lloyd stepped forward. "We have to get the third and final Sister Wheel."

"Oh, well, if that's all," Clemmie huffed.

Henry walked over to the pile of letters and journals still in the corner. Bending over, he scooped the papers into his arms. "Neither Major Henry nor my father left any clue to where the family's Sister Wheel was hidden."

"Maybe you weren't supposed to know."

All eyes in the room turned to Louis.

"What do you mean?" Henry looked up as letters spilled out of his overflowing arms.

"Well, Pierre Van Cortlandt passed the Poppel secret onto Major Henry," Louis said thoughtfully. "But that doesn't mean Major Henry's uncle gave him the Sister Wheel. Pierre probably left it to someone in his own immediate family."

"So that means it could be found…" Clemmie paused before chuckling dryly. "Absolutely anywhere! Good sleuthing, Louis. Sure glad we brought you along."

Louis glowered. "Well, if we were left with just your quick thinking, we'd still be in the sleigh tunnels searching for an imaginary dog."

Before Clemmie could retort, Henry assertively blurted, "Van Cortlandt Manor."

The group looked over at Henry as he stood up with his arms still clinging to the papers.

"I've passed the Van Cortlandt Manor estate many times. It's halfway between Poughkeepsie and New York City. As far as I know, Stephanus Van Cortlandt's descendants still reside there."

"Are you sure?" Maggie asked.

Henry nodded. "Stephanus Van Cortlandt was the former mayor of New York, so it's a well-known estate. Major Henry's aunt had married into the Van Cortlandt family, but until tonight I hadn't realized Pierre Van Cortlandt was Stephanus' grandson. And if he knew the secret of Poppel and the three sisters, Sarah's wheel is likely still at Van Cortlandt Manor."

"Even if that is true and we have narrowed its location down to Van Cortlandt Manor," Catharine said. "The idea of finding it in the entire Van Cortlandt Manor property is extremely difficult at best and impossible at worst."

"And didn't Houten say not to bother," Clemmie added glumly. "Even if we found the last Sister Wheel, we still don't have the tool needed to combine all three wheels together in the Horologe."

A light suddenly went on inside Maggie's head. "I know where it's at."

Maggie had only whispered the words, but she still received everyone's attention.

"Where what is at?" Catharine asked.

"The key for the wheels," Maggie explained. "Grandfather Clement's servant, Charles, used to work at Great Grandmother Elizabeth's childhood home and he mentioned a key that didn't work with any of the clocks. It was for the Sisters Wheels. I just know it."

"So let me understand this," Clemmie interrupted as he extended his arms with palms out. "Our good man Henry here has a general idea of the last Sister Wheel's location—a huge manor on a possibly infinite chunk of property miles north of New York. And Maggie has a hunch that a teeny weeny useless clock key is kept somewhere in a large house that probably has had many different families living in it since our great-grandmother called it home."

"What are you trying to say?" Catharine said with a sigh.

"That we have a better chance at being struck by lightning than ever finding any of these ridiculous items," Clemmie stated sharply. "What we should do is figure out how to escape and then notify the authorities about our cousins being kidnapped. Or at least report Gardiner and Gertrude missing. I am not too greatly upset at the idea of the Garrisons keeping Francis."

There was silence in the backroom as the Foundlings and Hostrupp exchanged defeated glances.

Clemmie looked around at the gloomy faces. "Well, if it upsets everyone so much, we can retrieve Francis, too, I suppose."

"Don't you see that the Garrisons are the authorities?" Harriet snapped. "There is no one from the outside who can help. The Garrisons are not only protected by the city—they are part of those who control the city."

"Well, this keeps getting better and better," Clemmie said, slumping against the wall and angrily folding his arms across his chest.

Nellie stepped forward. "Van Cortlandt Manor is near the village Furnace Brook. Poppel gets its food and supplies from that village and its surrounding farmland. I used to be assigned to the steamboat that travels back and forth from there."

"You can't go, Nellie," Harriet said, clearly upset at the possible suggestion. "If the Garrisons catch you, you'd be kept in the Kelder forever."

"If Poppel never returns to its time without the Garrisons, I'd happily take that fate," Nellie replied. "And we're one Sister Wheel and key away from making that possible."

"I'll go with you," Henry jumped in. "It's my family's wheel. I should be the one trying to find it."

"Very good, very good," Hostrupp said. "Yes, you two should take the steamboat to Furnace Brook. To Furnace Brook you must go. Just remember—you must remember—that you'll be out of Poppel and time will return back to normal. So you must be quick—very quick—if we are to do this on Christmas."

"I'll go with them to Van Cortlandt Manor," Catharine said. "The more people we have looking, the better."

Automatically, Maggie said, "I'll come, too."

Maggie tried convincing herself that she wasn't jealous at the idea of Catharine and Henry traveling together, and she simply volunteered because she didn't want to be separated from her sister.

"But we still need the key," Louis pointed out. "Maybe Maggie, Clemmie, and I should go look for that."

As Maggie peered out the corner of her eye at Henry, who was stealing quick glances of Catharine, Maggie fought the sudden urge to push Louis down the floor's trapdoor.

Ward nodded. "I can come with you. Houten will cover for me in the shop."

"Ward and Nellie," Wendell said meekly. "Do you know what you two are doing?"

"They have nothing to lose," Lloyd added, hesitantly nodding toward Henry and the Moore grandchildren. "But once you two leave, you can never come back unless the Garrisons are defeated. You do understand that, don't you?"

Ward and Nellie looked at each other and nodded.

A sudden shift occurred and all the Foundlings started bustling about. Ward began instructing Wendell, Lloyd, and Harriet on what they should do while the rest were away. There was mention of a weapon stash and implementing a secret attack against the Garrisons.

Meanwhile, Hostrupp was busy answering questions from Clemmie and Louis while Maggie watched Nellie talking with Henry and Catharine who were standing closely together. Although Maggie was worried for her sister's safety, when she saw Catharine and Henry's shoulders brush against one another, Maggie's heart stung with resentment. She wished she was going to Van Cortlandt Manor, but before she could attempt one last protest, someone tugged on her sleeve.

Maggie looked down to see Violet's big, sweet eyes.

"What can I do, Liz—uh—I mean Maggie. What can I do to help?"

Violet spoke with such sincerity that Maggie had to muster all her strength to keep from wrapping the little girl in a hug and then storing her safely away until everything was over.

Maggie bent down to Violet's level. "I have an important task for you. It seems my cousins, Gardiner and Gertrude, are becoming Foundlings. They're going to be very scared and will need someone to show them around Poppel. Keep your head down and make sure my cousins do the same until we're back. And definitely do not tell anyone where we are and what we're doing. Or that you ever spoke to any of us."

A hand touched Maggie's shoulder. It was Henry.

"It's time to go," he said solemnly.

Before Maggie could respond, Catharine swooped in and wrapped her younger sister in a tight embrace. "Be ever so safe," she whispered into Maggie's ear and then planted a light kiss on her cheek.

"We must be quick," Nellie said, pulling back her long, blonde hair into a low ponytail. "The steamboat could be leaving any minute for Furnace Brook."

Nellie headed toward the trapdoor with Catharine and Henry.

Before disappearing down the hole, Catharine gave Maggie, Clemmie, and Louis an affectionate look.

"Good luck," Henry wished to everyone, but Maggie felt it directed her way.

And then they were gone.

Before anyone even had a chance to get overcome with emotions, Ward jumped into action.

"Harriet, take them near the Sleigh Pit. I'll go to Boeken Kamer to retrieve the directions to their great-grandmother's house."

"No, I should be the one to go," Harriet said. "I know the Boeken Kamer better than anyone."

Ward sighed. "That's true."

"You take Clemmie and Louis down by the Sleigh Pit," Harriet instructed and then turned to Maggie. "I want you to come with me. You know your great-grandmother's family history, and we'll need that information in order to look up how to get there."

Maggie tensely agreed.

"What are you thinking?" Louis asked Maggie before they parted ways.

Maggie looked over at the Foundlings she had only met that night. Their expressions surprisingly held no trace of fear, but instead were full of determination.

"I'm thinking that our Christmas Eve has only just begun."

Chapter Fourteen

Stoomboot and Boeken Kamer

Catharine and Henry struggled to keep up with Nellie as they dashed along the Foundling tunnels. Nellie darted with ease through the passages while her followers stumbled behind.

Eventually, the air became colder and a strong scent of salt water hung in the air. A chilly breeze struck the group before they rounded the final corner. Through a stone archway, a canal appeared with a mighty steamboat quietly bobbing in the water.

"Stoomboot hasn't left yet," Nellie whispered, pointing to the boat.

"Stoomboot," Henry repeated. "The Dutch word for steamboat."

Nellie looked at Henry as though he had made the most obvious observation.

"The shops in Myra Lane... they are all Dutch words as well," Henry shook his head; mortified he had just realized this.

"Of course, they are," Nellie said. "Poppel was founded in Belgium after all."

Henry's cheeks flushed. His embarrassment was only heightened by Catharine's amused expression.

"Captain Noble is neither a Garrison nor a Foundling. He's just an old man who's compensated well for steering this boat to

Furnace Brook and back," Nellie quietly explained. She motioned for the other two to follow her as she shuffled onto the dock. "He's not an enemy of the Foundlings, but he certainly will not come to our defense if we're discovered hidden away on his boat."

Captain Noble was reclined in a chair on the top deck of the boat. A pipe was stuck between his crinkled lips, resting above his chin's prickly white beard. His portly chest heaved in and out as he snoozed the evening away.

Nellie carefully led them across the ramp linking the wooden dock and boat. Creeping slowly over the swaying deck, they kept their eyes on the old captain. But he didn't stir even when Nellie opened one of the hull's hatches.

Nellie gestured for Catharine and Henry to jump down the hatch. And as the three of them landed on a pile of flour sacks below, footsteps were heard stampeding toward the steamboat.

"Captain Noble," one Garrison called, but after getting no response he loudly repeated, "CAPTAIN NOBLE!"

"Wha—What?" Captain Noble jerked awake. His pipe clattered against the deck.

Catharine, Henry, and Nellie gathered around the lattice hatch to listen.

"Captain Noble, we are here to inspect the boat. We must make sure the Van Cortlandt descendants aren't trying to escape," the voice said and then added harshly. "Since you clearly haven't been awake long enough to guard the one vessel that leaves Poppel."

"Van Cortlandt descendants?" Captain Noble repeated with a yawn. "What in the blazes are you blathering about?"

Ignoring the captain, the Garrison turned to his men. "Search the lower compartments."

Nellie dragged Catharine and Henry down into the hull where paths were cleared between the mounds of crates and sacks.

"Over here." Nellie pulled aside a heavy sack at the far end of the hull.

Catharine slipped behind the sacks, but it was apparent that there was only room in the compartment for two people. Henry gestured for Nellie to take the final spot, but she rolled her eyes and shoved Henry down next to Catharine. Nellie had just enough time to cover their bodies before the Garrisons stormed down from the deck, raining into the hull like a black-coated flood.

"You there!" a Garrison shouted. "What are you doing?"

Catharine and Henry nervously listened from their hiding space.

"I am going to visit Furnace Brook," Nellie explained in a steady voice.

"Alone?"

"Yes, alone."

"Surely, you know about the missing Van Cortlandt descendants," the Garrison snidely said.

"Yes, but I have not seen anything around here," Nellie lied. "I'm going to visit Furnace Brook and its workers, as I do every Christmas. You can ask Captain Noble, if you don't believe me."

"Search around! See what you can find," the Garrison leader ordered, still eyeing Nellie suspiciously.

The Garrisons began peeking around the crates while Nellie continued to defend herself against the inquisitive Garrison.

"You can ask any worker at Poppel. They know I visit Furnace Brook when I can," Nellie stated firmly.

A pair of Garrisons inched toward the concealed Van Cortlandt descendants. As they began to take turns pulling aside sacks, Nellie knew that in only a matter of time, Catharine and Henry would be discovered.

"My presence on this steamboat is not unusual," Nellie said as she watched the Garrisons out of the corner of her eye. They reached for the sacks hiding Catharine and Henry.

"I am offended by your questioning!" Nellie shouted. As planned, the Garrisons were taken aback by her outburst and momentarily turned away from the sacks.

"I insist that you have your men leave this boat so it may continue to Furnace Brook as planned."

But the Garrisons went back to ignoring the agitated Foundling, and Nellie watched in horror as they grasped the sacks concealing Henry and Catharine.

Holding her breath, Nellie braced for the inevitable.

"No one else is down here," a Garrison declared from the other end of the hull.

And after being only a moment away from discovering the hidden Van Cortlandt descendants, the Garrisons let go of the sacks and walked back to the others.

Nellie's relief was short-lived, however.

"Very well," the leader replied. "Everyone here will carry on to Furnace Brook in case something was overlooked." He paused before adding, "In the meantime, I'll take this Foundling to the Kelder."

"But… but… I have nothing to do with the Van Cortlandt descendants," Nellie cried as the Garrisons hauled her away. "I had nothing to do with it! Don't put me in the Kelder!"

Nellie's screams echoed throughout the hull until there was only silence.

Harriet pushed a bookcase open and peered out of the gap. After confirming the Boeken Kamer was empty, Harriet stepped out and gestured for Maggie to follow.

"There is also a door hidden behind the maroon curtains in the banquet hall that leads here. But it's safer to use the tunnels," Harriet explained. "The Garrisons rarely monitor this place. It no longer holds much value to them."

The Boeken Kamer was covered ceiling-to-floor with stacks of old books. Harriet walked around tables piled high with thick, worn tomes. Running her hand across a few battered covers, she continued proudly, "Boeken Kamer houses all of Poppel's records.

They go as far back as the fifth century when Nikolas of Myra and the three sisters arrived in Belgium. Only a few Foundlings work in the Boeken Kamer. We make sure all the records of the city and its inhabitants are kept up-to-date by what is reported to us from those working the Sleigh Pit."

"So you are bookkeepers," Maggie said simply.

Harriet huffed. "It's a rather important position. Poppel could not run without the records. Not only would we not know how to navigate the Sleigh Pit, what needs to be delivered and to where, but the entire history of Poppel would be lost."

After glancing around again, Harriet pulled Maggie onto a ladder that connected to the room's second level of bookcases.

"There's something you should see before we find the Van Cortlandt address. But we must be quick," Harriet muttered under her breath as though someone could be listening.

Harriet shuffled along the second level's narrow ledge. Although the path in front of the bookcases was railed, Maggie still latched onto the bookshelves as she tried to stay close to Harriet.

"There's no need to be frightened," Harriet said, stopping in front of a corner bookcase. But her tone was anything but reassuring.

Maggie watched in shock as Harriet began to scale the shelves, fearlessly climbing toward the ceiling as though she had done it hundreds of times before. When she reached the top shelf, she pulled on a thin green book. Then the entire bookcase slowly opened, revealing a crevice just large enough for a person to slip through.

When Harriet climbed back down to Maggie, they both entered the dark chamber. Harriet grabbed a candle from the back of the bookcase and lit it with a match. The light billowed throughout the space as they approached a short table in the back of the secret chamber. Lying on top of the table was a massive book with elaborate carvings on its dusty, purple cover.

"It belonged to Nikolaos of Myra," Harriet boasted. "Not many people know of its existence."

Harriet lifted the fragile cover. Bits of dust and paper fragments swirled up from the pages in the glow of the candle, which Harriet held off to the side so wax wouldn't drip on the frail paper full of ornate calligraphy.

"The last pages in the book were added after Nikolaos of Myra disappeared."

With a permitting nod from Harriet, Maggie delicately turned one page at a time. The pages were filled with some kind of ancient script, but Maggie didn't bother studying the foreign words. Instead she focused on the mosaic illustrations.

The images of Nikolaos of Myra didn't resemble the St. Nicholas described in *'Twas the Night Before Christmas*. Nikolaos of Myra was thin with a short shadow of a beard, receding hairline, and piercing eyes. The next illustration was of the three sisters about to be sold into slavery by their oppressive father. Grace, Sarah, and Lily appeared young and beautiful but deeply unhappy. A page later showed Nikolaos of Myra giving the sisters their gold.

Maggie's favorite illustration was Nikolaos of Myra receiving the gift of unlimited time as the four of them sailed across the sea. The waves reached up toward the silver ship and its glowing passengers like a spirit guiding them to a new home.

"The Sister Wheels were given to Nikolaos of Myra on the twenty-fifth of December over a thousand years ago," Harriet said. "This was before December twenty-fifth was known across the world as Christmas Day. And the wheels can only be reunited on the day they were first bestowed onto Nikolaos of Myra. Which is why it's imperative we act now."

"If we haven't much time, then why are you bothering to show me this?" Maggie asked.

"Because I don't know you," Harriet said bluntly. "And if we're going to place all our trust in someone I don't know, I want that person to at least understand what they're trying to save."

Page after page, the story unfolded, from the early days of Poppel to Nicolas Poppelius coming to the Martyrs of Gorkum's aid. Then there was the blissful union between Grace and Jan Lookerman, where Sarah joined them in the village of Turnhout, and then a haunting illustration of Lily embarking on her own. But when Maggie turned the page to see what became of the youngest sister, a horrifying illustration was sketched into the brittle paper.

Harriet quickly shut the book, nearly slamming Maggie's finger within the pages.

"What was that?" Maggie asked as the frightening outline of the horned figure pulsed through her mind.

Harriet grabbed Maggie's hand and led her out of the chamber. "We should find the Van Cortlandt address and return to the others."

Maggie wanted to ask Harriet about the terrifying image in the book, but Harriet was now too focused on their task to reply. Or at least that's how she tried to appear when brushing off Maggie's questions.

They headed back to the first level where Harriet dashed between rows of bookcases. She began climbing another ladder, but this time Maggie did not follow. Moments later, Harriet jumped back down; a crimson book filled with jagged beige paper was stuffed under her arm. She dropped the heavy book onto the wooden floor and swiftly flipped it open, her eyes scanning and fingers turning each page before Maggie could even make out a single word in the thinly scribbled columns.

"Oloff and Annette Van Cortlandt's grandson, Philip, had five sons of his own, but only two married and had children: Stephen and Pierre. Pierre married Henry's great great-aunt Joanna and inherited Van Cortlandt Manor where Henry and your sister, Catharine, are headed now," Harriet read quickly, her finger slithering down the columns of names and dates. "The older son, Stephen, meanwhile, inherited his father's house in the city and lived there with his two sons, Philip and William. Philip inherited the house for his large family, most of which either died young or childless. But his daughter, Elizabeth, and her husband, William Taylor, were eventually given the house."

"Elizabeth Van Cortlandt Taylor? That's Grandmother Catharine's mother. Well, Grandmother Catharine clearly didn't inherit the house, so who did?"

"Your grandmother's brother, Sir Pringle Taylor," Harriet read. "But he currently resides in England, so the Van Cortlandt house stands empty."

"Where is it?" Maggie asked.

After closely studying the text, Harriet's eyes popped open.

"Ten Sylvan Terrace."

And with that, Maggie and Harriet slipped out of the Boeken Kamer just as quietly as they'd arrived.

Maggie and Harriet met up with Ward, Clemmie, and Louis near the Sleigh Pit. The plan was to go as far as they could within the Foundling tunnels and then sneak upon a sleigh running toward Sylvan Terrace, which was located near the northern end of Manhattan.

"When you get to the caverns with the passages leading to the ash pits, look for the inscriptions above the doorway," Harriet explained. "You want to exit at 188D. Ward will know what to do."

"Aren't you coming with us?" Louis asked.

"The fewer Foundlings to get involved, the better," Harriet said.

"And we need as many Foundlings as we can in Poppel right now. We've been planning an uprising against the Garrisons since they took over," Ward explained. "Because we're monitored closely, it's been difficult to build weapons of our own. Over the years, we've had to sneak into the workshop during the night and between Garrison shifts."

"And have you actually built anything?" Louis asked. "Or are you just going to fight them with sugarplums?"

Ward's eyes widened. "We've made many weapons. The problem is even if we did overthrow the Garrisons, more officials from the outside could be sent down and we'd be right back where we started." Ward's voice dropped and he added, "Or they may just wipe out Poppel and the Foundlings completely."

"But," Harriet interrupted. "We won't need to worry about that once Henry and Catharine return with the final Sister Wheel and all of you retrieve the key."

"And what if we aren't successful?" Maggie asked hesitantly.

"Then the Garrisons will still know the Foundlings helped the Van Cortlandt descendants," Ward said. "And we'll have to protect ourselves either way."

"Then maybe we shouldn't go," Clemmie suggested a bit too eagerly.

Ward shook his head. "It's too late to turn back now. And even if it wasn't, we need to take this chance. So we shall either bravely save or tragically lose Poppel. But whatever happens, it will happen tonight."

CHAPTER FIFTEEN

FURNACE BROOK MEN

The steamboat treaded up the Hudson River as Catharine and Henry remained below in the hull, huddled behind sacks of cargo. The water was relatively calm that night, but every bump tossed about the stowaways.

Exhaustion eventually caught up with Catharine and Henry, and they were soon drifting in and out of sleep. Henry would occasionally stir awake, fearing that the Garrisons were about to discover them. Also, Catharine had gravitated to the nook of his arm after falling asleep, and Henry found it difficult to focus on anything but how her body situated perfectly within his own. But sleep did finally overtake him.

However, Henry wasn't asleep for long. Loud screams erupted in the air outside and feet pounded on the deck above.

Henry's eyes shot open.

"What's happening?" Catharine whispered, but she was barely heard over the sound of gunshots.

"Someone's attacking the boat." Henry pushed aside a sack with his shoulder before leaping out of the hiding space. "Stay here," he instructed Catharine.

But Catharine ignored Henry and toppled out from the gap, chasing after him. Henry was climbing the mound of sacks when she caught up.

"I told you to stay hidden," Henry said, pulling Catharine up beside him.

Catharine shot him a glare as she crouched near the hatch. "And for your own wellbeing, we're going to pretend that you hadn't."

Henry quickly joined her at the top of the mound and they both anxiously peered out of the hatch.

The deck of the steamboat resembled a battlefield—and the Garrisons had lost the fight.

Garrisons were slumped on the bloodstained deck as well as one man wearing a gray jacket. Being the closest body to the hatch, the gray-jacket man's motionless eyes were quite visible. A single bullet had pierced his heart, and dark blood pooled around his body. The man's outstretched hand rested inches from a pitchfork that he must have held in his last moments. But his death seemed relatively peaceful when compared to the murdered Garrisons who had been sliced and stabbed by less conventional weapons.

Henry stood on the deck next to the hatch, bent over with hands bracing his knees. He tried to steady his breath as the smell of death filled the cold air. But he couldn't contain his dry heaving. Out of the corner of his eyes, he saw a group of men approaching. Bloodied scythes, sickles, and hammers gleamed in their hands.

"Henry!" Catharine cried, leaping from the hatch.

Grabbing the pitchfork from the dead man, Catharine jumped in front of Henry, aggressively waving the weapon at the strangers.

One man tentatively stepped forward. Thick sideburns ran down his stubbly cheeks.

"We mean you no harm, Catharine."

"How do you know my name?"

"I'm Albers from Furnace Brook. Ward sent sugarplums preparing us for your arrival. We were told you must be taken to Van Cortlandt Manor, and also that the Garrisons could be on your trail." Albers looked down at the dead bodies and sighed. "But we didn't know they were on the steamboat with you. I'm afraid we surprised them as much as they surprised us. Terrible tragedy."

Another man with curly blond hair tilted up the straw hat on his head before spitting over the side of the boat. The ball of saliva splashed into the river.

"Any dead Garrison is a good one."

"Not if it costs us the life of our own, Wesseling," Albers said, nodding down at the body in front of Catharine and Henry.

"Ah, Schaddelee," Wesseling murmured, respectfully touching his hat's brim with two fingers. "Ain't much of a thinker, but had a good heart."

An older man next to Albers sniffled through his bulbous red nose that hung over a gray handlebar moustache. Bringing his forearm up, the old man blew his fat nose into his sleeve.

Albers rubbed the man's shoulder. "There, there. It will be all right, Boe."

A few other men tried to hide tears as they looked at their dead friend.

"Where is Captain Noble?" Catharine asked.

Albers pointed toward the wheelhouse. "Captain Noble is unharmed. My men are keeping watch over him, and will do so until you have successfully returned from the Van Cortlandt Manor. Then we can head back to Poppel."

Henry finally regained his composure and approached the armed men, carefully stepping around the bodies. Catharine continued to keep a safe distance, pitchfork firmly grasped in her hands.

"You know how to get to Van Cortlandt Manor?"

"Henry Livingston, is it?" Albers passed the bloody scythe he was holding to his left hand and then dropped it to his side. "A Poughkeepsie lad, I hear."

Henry couldn't take his eyes off the glistening weapon even when Albers reached out and offered his empty right hand. Henry slowly shook it, but his eyes remained on the scythe.

"We know the history of the Van Cortlandts quite well," Albers said, looking around at the other men.

"How are we getting to Van Cortlandt Manor?" Henry asked.

"Don't worry none," Wesseling spat, nodding toward the shore. "We'll get you there."

Bordering the river, there was a visible stretch of rocky land in front of a wintry forest where a dozen horses pawed at the ground, exposing snowless patches of brown flattened grass. Shaking their long manes, the horses let out a cadence of snorts and whinnies.

While Boe and the rest of the Furnace Brook men carried the dead bodies off the steamboat and lined them along the dock, Albers and Wesseling took Catharine and Henry over to the horses.

"Van Cortlandt Manor is a few miles south of here," Albers explained, grabbing the reins of a white horse. "Wesseling and I will ride with you, offering whatever assistance we can."

Catharine looked over at the dock just as Schaddelee's body was delicately placed beside the row of dead Garrisons.

"I think your men have done enough," she said coldly. Seeing Albers and Wesseling stiffen at her comment, Catharine added, "We do appreciate all of your help."

"Our job isn't complete until you've successfully reached Van Cortlandt Manor," Albers said. "But we shouldn't experience any trouble. This area is fairly peaceful. I'd be surprised if we came upon so much as a squirrel."

"I'm not too concerned about getting there," Henry admitted. "It's finding what we're searching for that may pose the greatest issue."

Albers locked eyes with Henry and whispered, "The Sister Wheel."

"You know of it?"

Albers smiled for the first time—not out of happiness but rather understanding. "We in Furnace Brook do not experience the same, shall I say, *life* as those in Poppel."

143

"You mean extended time," Catharine said bluntly.

Albers nodded. "Some in Furnace Brook resent this. Others are happy for a life of more freedom, since we're not always under the watchful eyes of the Garrisons."

"We're allowed to live our lives," Boe said, approaching the group with an armful of coats. Henry and Catharine each took one to put over their colorful Poppel attire. "Our village is east of here, and we farm, raise our families, and occasionally the Garrisons will come by to check on our work. But so long as we deliver what is asked, there's no trouble. It's a simple existence, but I wouldn't trade places with a Foundling for any extra day of life."

Albers frowned. "Not everyone from Furnace Brook has felt that way." And without saying an additional word, he stomped away to gather the other horses.

Catharine and Henry looked to Boe for an explanation.

"Ah, poor Albers," Boe whispered, shaking his head. He took off his hat and slipped it underneath an arm. "Once was in love with a young Furnace Brook girl. But Albers crossed a Garrison, and as revenge, the Garrison offered the girl a position in Poppel."

"And she went?" Henry asked.

Boe nodded. "Crushed Albers' heart. Not just that she had left, but knowing that she's still the youthful girl he had loved, while he fights to hide the gray hairs that sprout up, more frequently nowadays."

Albers returned guiding a horse on each side of him. He handed a set of reins to Wesseling. The blond man effortlessly hopped on the horse and looked down at Catharine.

"You can ride with me, lovely," Wesseling said, reaching down to her.

Catharine hesitantly grabbed his hand.

"I should've worn trousers," Catharine muttered as she climbed behind Wesseling with the assistance of Henry.

As Catharine uncomfortably situated sideways in her dress,

Henry glowered at Wesseling, not appreciating the man's wandering eyes.

"Don't worry, girl," Wesseling said to Catharine, even though his wink was directed at Henry's brutal glares. "I'll take it nice and easy."

There was a pause before Catharine harshly replied, "Sir, you better be addressing the horse with that tone."

Embarrassed, Wesseling was only able to mutter, "Yes, ma'am."

Albers rubbed the neck of the unoccupied horse next to Wesseling and looked over at Henry. "Although we're not going far, I think we're too heavy to double up. Would you be comfortable riding her alone?"

"Yes, I am quite capable," said Henry defensively as Wesseling beamed down at him.

"Very good," Albers replied, bringing over the horse.

Catharine's gaze was focused on the forest up ahead. "We haven't much time."

Waving goodbye to Boe and the others, the riders dashed through the great mass of trees.

Henry looked back only once before the forest completely vanished the sight of the river.

As the Furnace Brook men returned to the dock, no one spotted the face that was peeking between the blades of the steamboat's paddlewheel. Although Catharine had never encountered the face before, Henry would have recognized it, for the bruise on his chin offered a chilling reminder.

McNutt.

The redheaded Garrison had crouched behind the paddlewheel when the Furnace Brook men raided the steamboat. And after listening to their conversation, McNutt realized that the new Foundlings were indeed the feared Van Cortlandt descendants and they were trying to unite the Sister Wheels.

Not wanting to end up like the dead Garrisons, McNutt patiently planned his next move. Unlike many of the Garrisons, McNutt was unarmed. But even if he had a weapon, he wouldn't have tried fighting the Furnace Brook men after seeing what had occurred earlier. McNutt knew that his best chance was to flee as fast as he could.

As the Van Cortlandt descendants disappeared on the horses, McNutt knew he only had a small window of time before he would lose them. He lowered his body into the freezing river, making sure not to make even a pinprick of a splash. After taking a deep gulp of air, he dipped down until he was completely underwater. If the Furnace Brook men happened to see his submerged form, McNutt knew he would be met with a quick, fatal blow.

So when his knees made contact with the shallow riverbed, he splashed up with a gasp and blindly bolted toward the unguarded horses. He immediately felt the sting of water upon opening his eyes. Everything was eerily quiet, but once McNutt's ears popped, the frightening curses of the Furnace Brook men could be heard closing in on him.

McNutt safely reached the forest's edge, but as he mounted a horse, a scythe came slicing through the air, missing his arm by only inches. However, the furious men startled the horse as much as they'd scared McNutt, and soon the animal was charging away.

McNutt steered the horse down the rift in the trees the others had gone through. With angry shouts filling the air, McNutt rode on, knowing he would soon be chased as aggressively as he pursued the Van Cortlandt descendants.

But McNutt had to keep Catharine and Henry from obtaining the Sister Wheel. No amount of Furnace Brook men would stop him.

CHAPTER SIXTEEN

SIR PRINGLE TAYLOR

Ten Sylvan Terrace was a three-story yellow row house with green shutters located on a narrow cobblestone road that once functioned as a carriageway to an old mansion. Coach lights illuminated the other identical row houses crammed along Sylvan Terrace. But Maggie didn't see any of that when her underground sleigh came upon the tunnel marked 188D.

"Here we are," Ward announced, hopping off the sleigh and sprinting toward the tunnel entrance. Maggie, Clemmie, and Louis quickly followed.

The passage was different than the one under Chelsea Manor. Instead of being led directly to the ash pit, the tunnel was full of doors. Ward hurried past the entrances, muttering directions under his breath. Upon reaching the end of the passage, Ward turned left and disappeared through a doorway.

"This way," his hushed voice called.

The pit was smaller than the one under Chelsea Manor. But there was still a mound of ash just below the ceiling, and Maggie wondered how they would get inside the house.

Apparently thinking the same thing, Louis stretched out an arm and lunged upward, trying to touch the ceiling in hopes of triggering an opening. But his efforts fell short and he landed clumsily on top of the ash pile.

Clemmie let out a hearty chuckle while Ward stared blankly at Louis before walking over to a darkened corner. He returned a moment later with a ladder.

Wet ash flew from Louis' mouth as he blew a raspberry. He looked at Ward in annoyance as he steadied himself up on his knees. "And how did you find that?"

"Every ash pit has one," Ward said simply, placing the ladder against a barely visible square frame in the ceiling. Maggie spotted a smirk twitching at the edge of Ward's lips as he added, "We're Foundlings, Louis. Not birds." Ward scrambled up the ladder and slapped his palm on the frame's center, causing the square to vanish. "It's about knowing where to strike."

Ward looked down at the Moore grandchildren and raised his eyebrows. "Is everyone ready? We are breaking into someone's home, so no one will come to our defense if we're caught. Surprisingly, not even the Garrisons." Ward's tone was light, but the underlying seriousness did not go unnoticed by Maggie. "So if you have any sneezes, coughs or other unnecessary noises, please kindly make them now."

As Louis climbed the ladder after Ward, Clemmie gave Maggie a supportive shove, insisting she go next. The wobbly ladder creaked under her feet, but Maggie quickly reached Ward and Louis' extended hands. They pulled her into the dirty cellar of Ten Sylvan Terrace with Clemmie arriving shortly after.

A window on the front end of the cellar let in a cool glow from the street outside. Old furniture and wooden barrels were packed against the walls with the exception of a round table with mismatching chairs. On top of the table, situated in the center of the room, was a single candle imprisoned within its own melted wax.

The back area was made extra dark by boarded up windows. In the corner there appeared to be a kitchen covered in tilting stacks of plates. A squeaking mouse weaved through the dishes, apparently indifferent to the intruders.

"Do you think we should search down here?" Ward asked.

Like Maggie, he seemed to notice there wasn't a grandfather clock in sight.

"Only if we don't find a clock upstairs." Maggie tried to sound confident, but the truth was, if they didn't find a grandfather clock, she didn't know where else to look. The key could have been easily discarded years ago.

But Maggie tried not to worry about that possibility yet.

After emerging from the cellar and into the foyer on the main floor, Maggie could see the street through the window on the front door. The doorway to the left led to a parlor packed with furniture, including a regal grandfather clock ticking softly next to the fireplace. Silently, the group crept closer, and Clemmie, easily the tallest of the four, reached on top of the clock. But after churning up a cloud of dust, Clemmie's hand returned with nothing.

Maggie, Louis, and Ward opened the glass panel and went about looking for the key inside the clock, clunking the weights and chains aside and feeling around the bottom. Ward even peeked under the clock, in case the key had fallen.

"Are you sure it's not up there?" Maggie pleaded with Clemmie.

Rolling up his sleeves with a sigh, Clemmie made a second attempt at the top of the clock. Once again, his dusty hand returned empty.

"Anywhere else it could be?" Ward whispered, scanning the dark room.

Although the key could very well be hidden amongst the parlor's numerous bookcases, searching through the endless shelves was a bit improbable. Instead Maggie nodded toward the desk in the corner.

Clemmie and Ward began rummaging around the desk, opening screeching drawers and shuffling through stacks of papers. But after a few minutes of unsuccessfully searching, Clemmie and Ward gave up.

A knot twisted in Maggie's stomach as Ward patted her shoulder, trying to ease the disappointment. "We still haven't looked upstairs."

Ward led them back to the foyer and then crept up the staircase to the second floor. When reaching the top, he held out his hand to signal the others to wait while he checked if the coast was clear. Ward disappeared for a few moments, but when he returned, he waved them up.

The group stayed close together at first, just four shadows moving along the hallway. Then Maggie and Louis went down the hall to the farthest door while Clemmie and Ward started with the nearest.

Maggie and Louis opened the door and found a bedroom with white sheets eerily draped over the furniture. None of the ghostly figures looked to be clock shaped. But Maggie and Louis still picked up the ends of the sheets and peered underneath. They were just peeking below one that turned out to be a dresser when a door slammed in the hallway and then another violently swung open.

"Who the hell are you?" a deep voice shouted.

Maggie's insides dropped.

The house wasn't as empty as they thought.

Maggie and Louis scrambled to the bedroom door. Glancing out into the hall, the cousins not only spotted the silhouettes of Clemmie and Ward, but also a thick shadow of a man whose width was greater than the other two combined. A long shiny object was angled in front of Clemmie and Ward, and it took Maggie a moment to recognize that it was a sword.

The man had to be Sir Pringle Taylor.

"What are you doing in my house?" Sir Pringle wiggled the antiquated sword under Clemmie and Ward's chins.

A few seconds of silence ticked by as Ward's arm rose above his head. Maggie thought she spied something in his hand. And then with one sudden motion, Ward threw the object to the ground, releasing a storm of powder. The wide figure of Sir Pringle collapsed into a coughing fit while Clemmie and Ward stumbled toward the stairs.

"Run!" Ward shouted.

Maggie and Louis covered their faces as they struggled through the hazy hallway. But a familiar spice permeated the inside of her mouth.

Cinnamon.

Ward had dropped some kind of cinnamon explosion.

The spice-tinged air stung Maggie's eyes, but it was the only opportunity to get by Sir Pringle who was against the wall, wheezing and wailing. His sword continued to fiercely wave as though dueling with the pungent scent. And Louis had to quickly dodge a blow while lunging toward the staircase.

Maggie had reached the main floor when Sir Pringle bounded after them.

"Hurry!" Ward cried, holding open the cellar door and waving to the others frantically.

They rushed down the cellar steps as Ward slammed the door behind them.

Maggie, Clemmie, and Louis charged toward the fireplace while Ward desperately held the door shut at the top of the stairs. Sir Pringle was trying to heave open the door from the other side.

"Go down!" Ward called. "Now!"

Heeding Ward's instructions, Clemmie and Louis dropped down the fireplace opening. But Maggie hesitated.

"Come on, Maggie!" Clemmie yelled.

Maggie watched as Ward made one last effort at holding Sir Pringle at bay. Knowing he couldn't keep the door closed much longer, Ward forcefully threw it open, knocking Sir Pringle back. Ward then ran toward Maggie whose legs were dangling in the fireplace hole.

"Drop!" Ward shouted.

Maggie plunged straight down, landing between Clemmie and Louis on the mound of ash just as Ward and Sir Pringle neared the fireplace. Ward leapt toward the opening and the Moore grandchildren watched in horror as the Foundling's ankle was grabbed by a beefy hand in the middle of his desperate dive. His body was quickly pulled back up into the cellar.

The ladder rattled in Maggie's hands as Ward and Sir Pringle scuffled on the floor above.

"Get... off... me," Ward grunted, frantically trying to break free from Sir Pringle's grasp.

"Where are your little friends? Why don't you get them to help you?"

Maggie started back up the ladder, but was stopped by Louis.

"Don't go!"

But Maggie brushed away Louis' hand and continued climbing. When she peeked through the fireplace hole, Sir Pringle held Ward in a headlock, the sword poised under the Foundling's throat.

"Now tell me, what are you doing in my house?" Sir Pringle growled, his heavy jowls quaking around his shaggy white moustache.

Sir Pringle was a hefty man; dressed head to toe in vertically striped long johns with white buttons that were straining to keep his large gut from bursting out the front. A blue nightcap sat high on his hairless head, leaving his thick, unkempt eyebrows to rest alone on the top of his wrinkled face.

Ward wiggled in Sir Pringle's locked arm.

"Stop it," Sir Pringle grumbled. "Stop moving."

Sir Pringle brought the sword closer to Ward's neck and nicked the skin like a razor that slipped while shaving.

"Release him," Maggie declared, kicking her feet to avoid Clemmie and Louis who were trying to pull her back into the ash pit.

Maggie hopped out of the fireplace and stood in front of Sir Pringle and Ward. She had hoped Sir Pringle would be caught off guard by her reappearance, but she didn't quite anticipate him to react as he did.

After seeing Maggie, Sir Pringle dropped his sword and backed into the wax-covered table, looking as though he had just seen something not of the living world.

A fat finger quivered Maggie's direction. "You... you... you."

The words were repeated over and over until Maggie finally asked, "What about me?"

Sir Pringle began pacing around the table, frantically muttering, "This is not real. A dream. All a vision of the mind."

Maggie and Ward shared an uncertain look while Clemmie and Louis' heads popped out of the fireplace hole.

"What's happening?" Clemmie hissed.

Ward picked up the sword Sir Pringle had dropped. "I am unsure."

"A ghost. A spirit," Sir Pringle continued muttering.

"Who?" Ward asked.

Sir Pringle waved his hand at Maggie as he fell into one of the chairs behind the table. "You—you look... Catharine. It can't be."

"Catharine?" Ward repeated and glanced over at Maggie.

Maggie stepped forward and Sir Pringle jerked back in his seat.

"Grandmother Catharine?"

"Grandmother?"

"Your sister, Catharine. She is my grandmother," Maggie explained slowly. "She married Clement Clarke Moore and had my mother, Mary."

Sir Pringle continued to stare at Maggie with a gaping mouth.

"These are my cousins, Clemmie and Louis. They also are Clement and Catharine's grandchildren."

Sir Pringle glanced from Maggie to the two boys. "I wouldn't believe it, but you look so much like Catharine. But I don't understand. Why are you here?"

Maggie hadn't expected to be explaining the Nikolaos of Myra, Poppel, and Van Cortlandt history again that night. But starting with Grandmother Catharine and Sidney Livingston, Maggie condensed the epic family tale into a short narrative while Sir Pringle quietly listened.

"I always knew that Clement Clarke Moore was a bad sort," Sir Pringle spat.

"I beg your pardon?" Maggie asked, not expecting that to be his first comment.

"I never met the man. I lived in England when he married my sister and didn't return to America until after she had died. But I knew about him. And when Moore was named the author of that Christmas poem, I sensed something was awry."

"The poem is hardly the issue here," Ward said, placing his hands on his hips "If we don't find the key for the Sister Wheels, the Garrisons will see to it that the Moores and Livingstons are destroyed."

"Is that so? And why is that my problem?" Sir Pringle said, straightening up in his chair. "Why should I help you?"

"Because you are a Van Cortlandt descendant," Ward continued. "They will come for you as well. I assure you that they don't want to take any chances."

"Well, there's no reason for them to seek me out," Sir Pringle sniffled. "I know nothing about these Sister Wheels. But I can say with absolute certainty that the key is not here."

"How can you be so sure?" Clemmie asked.

Sir Pringle stared confidently at Clemmie. "Because when I inherited the place, I went through the entire house, and I can tell you, there was no key."

Maggie sighed. "Then where else could it be?"

Sir Pringle rested his fat hands on top of his belly. "You said that one of the Sister Wheels was found in the fireplace at Chelsea Manor?"

Maggie nodded.

"So it was obviously put there by Catharine and her daughter,

Margaret, since they were the only ones who knew of this Pebble or Poople place."

"Poppel," Ward corrected firmly.

"Right, Poppel," Sir Pringle snorted. "So if Catharine had gone through all the trouble of bringing the Sister Wheel from Sylvan Terrace to Chelsea Manor in order to carry on the family secret, wouldn't you think she would have also taken the key and hid it somewhere in the Manor as well?"

Maggie looked over to Ward, Clemmie, and Louis. They stood silent, processing Sir Pringle's valid point.

"But where in Chelsea Manor?" Maggie turned back to Sir Pringle. "It would be nearly impossible to find and we haven't got much time."

Sir Pringle stuck up his finger. "Not nearly as impossible as you think."

"What do you mean?"

"Whatever we may think of your grandfather, I know my sister and I doubt she would have kept all of this from Clement Clarke Moore."

"You think Grandfather Clement knows where the key is?" Maggie asked.

She hadn't even considered that possibility.

"Again, I never met Moore. And I do not doubt what you say about the Christmas poem," Sir Pringle said. "But Catharine never would have married a man she didn't trust. She may not have told him everything, but it's unlikely that she didn't confide any of this to him. I know that Catharine died rather suddenly. But if this key were as important as you say it is, Catharine would have told Moore. I'm sure of it."

"So what do you suggest?" Maggie asked.

Sir Pringle cocked one of his bushy eyebrows and curled his lip. "You have to return to Chelsea Manor."

Ward threw up his arms in frustration. "It will take forever to get there from here. It's a long way south and on a completely different track in the sleigh tunnel. We would have to go all the way back to Poppel to switch to the correct one."

Sir Pringle shot up to his feet, knocking over his chair in the process.

"I have a horse and carriage," he announced. "I can take you."

But before the Moore grandchildren and Ward could accept the proposal, a familiar purple ball floated up from the fireplace hole that had been left open.

Ward spotted the sugarplum first and quickly dove toward the gleaming sphere. He knew its arrival likely meant bad news. So popping the sugarplum into his mouth, he gently began to chew.

Sir Pringle and the Moore grandchildren watched as Ward's eyes filled with dread.

"What has happened?" Maggie asked nervously.

Ward took a big gulp, swallowing the rest of the sugarplum.

"War has begun in Poppel."

CHAPTER SEVENTEEN

KRAMPUS

Three horses came to a halt in front of the entrance to Van Cortlandt Manor. Jumping down from his horse, Albers ran over to the wooden gate and swung it open.

"Wesseling and I will keep watch here," Albers said, grabbing the reins of his horse and steering it over to the stone wall that surrounded the estate. "I'm afraid we wouldn't offer much assistance searching for the Sister Wheel. But we will be on the lookout and ready to ride back to the steamboat on a moment's notice."

"I wouldn't say you couldn't be of use searching for the wheel," Henry said gruffly, sliding off his horse. "You have as good of a chance as we do at finding the blasted thing."

Albers and Wesseling exchanged looks while Catharine shot Henry a scowl. No one appreciated Henry's cynical attitude.

"But thank you for getting us this far," Henry quickly recoiled. "We can handle it from here." He then added softly, "I hope."

Henry went over and helped Catharine down from Wesseling's horse. With a crooked grin, Wesseling's eyes seemed to trace the outline of Catharine's frame as she dropped to the ground. Watching the man's lingering gaze, Henry firmly held Catharine's arm. But she shrugged out of his grip with an annoyed frown, unaware of what was causing Henry's sudden intensity.

"Is there something the matter?" Wesseling asked as Henry continued to glare. But before Henry could reply, Catharine had latched onto his hand and tugged him away.

"I'm not fond of how Wesseling leers at you," Henry whispered as the pair passed through the gated entrance.

"Oh, Henry, really," Catharine scoffed as she trudged through the snowy path, her hand still intertwined in Henry's. "Of all the things to get flustered about now. Don't you think we have greater things to focus on than Wesseling's unbecoming stares?"

"I'm just trying to protect you," Henry said haughtily, releasing Catharine's hand with an exaggerated yank of his wrist.

Catharine rolled her eyes. "Your assignment tonight is not to be my protector."

Her prickly tone caught Henry off guard just as he stepped onto snowy tracks left by carriage wheels. Unable to soundly plant his feet, Henry clumsily stumbled to the ground, nearly taking Catharine down with him.

Catharine spun around and looked at Henry, her mouth curling into a smile. "Some protector," she said in a low voice.

But before Henry could stand back up, a familiar purple sphere came floating through the trees and hovered near his spread legs.

A sugarplum.

Henry plucked it out of the air and hesitantly placed it between his lips while Catharine eyed him closely. After a few chews, Henry's face lit up. "It's Maggie."

"What about Maggie?" Catharine exclaimed. "Has something happened to her?"

Henry shook his head. "She's returning to Chelsea Manor in search of the key. And we're to retrieve her there when the steamboat heads back to Poppel."

Catharine let out a relieved sigh, but her face was still heavy with concern.

"Maggie will be okay," Henry said. But Catharine's eyes narrowed at his reassuring tone.

"How do you know?" Catharine snapped. "I don't think any of us really understood how grave the situation had become. We just saw men slaughtered like animals. You could barely keep from heaving at the sight of the dead bodies."

Henry looked away, embarrassed. "I had never seen death like that before," he mumbled, his face flushing in the chilly winter air. "I had never seen death until my father passed away. And those dead men reminded me of that. He's really all I ever think about. I don't think seeing him die will ever leave me."

Catharine's features softened. "No, it doesn't ever leave you. I witnessed my mother's death. And I was only a year old."

Henry turned back to Catharine. "And you still remember?"

Catharine nodded. "I never talk about those memories. But I have them. My family believes I recall nothing of that time. My mother became ill rather suddenly. And I was forbidden from her bedroom on her final day of life. That has stayed with me for the past seventeen years."

Unexpectedly, the clouds that had been covering the moon parted. And the moon's fresh light illuminated a path containing deeply carved carriage tracks that branched off from the main road.

"It must lead to the Manor," Catharine whispered, helping Henry to his feet and guiding him toward the path.

The tree-lined trail curved up a hill and soon Catharine and Henry spotted Van Cortlandt Manor. The two-story rectangle building was made of red and yellow bricks that varied in size and shape, adding quaintness to the rather charming home. Its low snow-covered rooftop drooped over the white picket porch that wrapped around the second story. A wide staircase on the front of the house came down from the porch and then split into two separate stairways going opposite directions. Their rails were draped in sagging garland.

Catharine and Henry carefully approached the Manor as the hard snow crunched beneath their feet. Although the outside of the house had a warm and welcoming quality, the paned windows were dark and foreboding.

But then a galloping horse sounded in the distance.

Henry's back stiffened as he glanced around. "What's that?"

"It's probably Albers or Wesseling, going to guard a different entrance," Catharine whispered and then pointed to the porch. "We need to see if anyone's inside. You check the second floor and I'll look below."

Henry watched Catharine disappear into the shadows under the porch before he turned toward the front stairs. His feet froze at their base, but then an ominous breeze, funneling through the nearby trees, propelled him up the porch steps. Also, the muffled sounds of Catharine moving below strangely gave Henry a great deal of comfort.

Henry pressed his forehead against a window and squinted through the cold glass. An empty dining room appeared on the other side of the wall. Any dishes from a possible Christmas Eve dinner had been cleared from the table. Nothing inside stirred.

Not even a mouse.

Henry crossed to the other end of the porch and looked through the windows of what appeared to be the parlor. But seeing nothing of interest, Henry turned the corner and moved to the side of the house. The last window belonged to a small bedroom. Henry was surprised its two beds were empty, since the sheets and blankets were strewn about as though they'd been recently slept in.

Stepping back from the window, Henry listened for Catharine's footsteps under the porch. But his ears were met with silence. Bending down, Henry tried to see if there was any sign of Catharine between the wooden planks. But a glow in the window he had just been looking through caught his eye and he glanced up to find a face staring directly back at him.

Henry stifled a scream and fell backward onto the porch.

The glow was actually the pale skin of a dark haired boy peering out the window. The boy seemed unaffected by Henry's presence as he continued to blankly stare. Henry watched closely, expecting the young boy to go running to his parents at any moment. But the boy didn't flinch.

Gently getting up from the ground, Henry slowly walked to the window. The boy's eyes were fixed on him the entire time. Reaching out to the window, Henry placed his hand carefully on the glass above the boy's head.

"Hello," Henry whispered. But by the time his breath had faintly fogged the window, the boy had already disappeared into the shadows of Van Cortlandt Manor.

Catharine crept along the bottom of the Manor, peering into the windows of the main floor. There was a kitchen, back chambers, and a couple of windows with their curtains drawn. But when Catharine finally came out from below the porch, she noticed that the Van Cortlandt Manor front door was now ajar.

Thinking that Henry had gone into the house, Catharine began to whisper his name, but then stopped. She didn't know who could be listening. Instead she cautiously climbed the porch stairs and peeked through the entrance. There was an empty hall with a door on its right wall, leading to a parlor, and a door to the dining room on the left.

Catharine hesitantly tiptoed inside.

"Who are you?"

The chilling voice came from a young boy standing at the end of the hallway. Rather than being frightened, the boy's voice was forceful with an air of authority.

Catharine glanced at the boy who returned a somber stare, not breaking eye contact for even a moment. His hair was dark and curly, and he looked harmless enough; dressed head to toe in an oversized, baggy cotton shirt that stretched down to his ankles.

"Don't be afraid," Catharine whispered soothingly.

"I'm not afraid," the boy replied with his hands innocently clasped across his belly.

His tone caused Catharine to shift between feet with unease.

"I'm a distant relative. And I'm looking for something that belongs to our family," Catharine gently explained.

The boy didn't reply, but a smirk formed on his mouth.

There was a sound of footsteps running along the porch outside. Catharine spun around just as Henry burst through the front door.

"Catharine," he said, exhaling rather loudly. "A boy…"

Henry trailed off when he saw the child standing behind Catharine.

"What about him?" Catharine whispered.

"No, not this boy," Henry said. "I saw another boy who looks very similar. But he vanished."

Catharine glanced back at the peculiar boy, realizing that there was more than one child awake in Van Cortlandt Manor.

Henry cautiously approached the child. "Who are you?"

The boy's smile disappeared. "Romeyn." He then added simply, "You're here for the wheel."

Henry and Catharine exchanged surprised looks.

"How do you know that?" Henry straightened his back.

Romeyn was silent, but two other young voices chimed in.

"Bels told us."

Henry and Catharine turned around to see two more boys who looked similar to Romeyn. One stood in the parlor's doorway and the other in the dining room.

"Who's Bels?" Catharine asked. "And who are you two?"

"My brothers." Romeyn nodded to the boy who was a little shorter than him. "James." Then walking over and gripping the shoulder of the shortest boy, Romeyn added, "And Theodoric."

"Uh, would you boys be able to help us?" Henry stammered. "We don't want to wake the rest of the household."

Romeyn, James, and Theodoric's nearly identical faces lit up for the first time. But it wasn't a comforting sight. Catharine sensed that something was quite off with the children.

"Who is Bels?" Catharine asked again.

"Bels is our friend," Theodoric squealed.

"Well, how does this friend know about the Sister Wheel?" Henry asked, bending down to Theodoric's level. "And where does Bels say the wheel is?"

All three boys jerked a finger up to their lips and sharply hissed, "Shh." Then they whispered together like a chorus, "We know where to find the wheel."

"Henry," Catharine said, touching his arm with her hand. "I don't like this." She spoke as though the three boys weren't there.

But Henry pressed on. "Where's the wheel?"

The boys laughed and then scampered around in a circle.

"In the orchard."

"With Bels."

"In the orchard with Bels."

Then dropping to their knees, the boys scampered down the hallway and finally out the front door of Van Cortlandt Manor.

Henry started after them, but Catharine held him back. She didn't say anything, but she wore a troubled expression.

"What other choice do we have, Catharine?" Henry said, breaking away from her and running out of the Manor after the boys.

Catharine tentatively followed, trying to prepare for whatever awaited them in the orchard.

When the Furnace Brook men finally reached Van Cortlandt Manor, Albers and Wesseling were still waiting near its entrance gate.

"What is it?" Albers immediately asked, riding over to meet them.

"There was another Garrison hiding on the steamboat," Boe exclaimed. "He rode after you. But we lost sight of him halfway here."

"We haven't seen anything," Wesseling said. "Was he armed?"

"He didn't appear to be," Boe replied, pulling the brim of his hat down.

"Send some of your men back to the steamboat. Have them bring it this way," Albers directed. "We'll patrol the perimeter of the estate. He shouldn't be too hard to find."

"Garrisons are cowards and rarely act alone," Wesseling added. "He was probably just fleeing the area, not wanting to risk the same fate as the others."

But McNutt was closer than anyone knew.

Less than a mile away on the other end of the Van Cortlandt property, McNutt had finally come to a halt. He had ridden to the Croton River, running along the east side of the estate. It was there McNutt found an abandoned ferry house.

Shivering, McNutt tied up the horse on a fence post and hurried into the desolate building. His wet clothes were frozen to his body and he trembled violently. But McNutt was able to scrounge up a pair of well-worn trousers and a dry shirt in a neglected storeroom.

Catharine and Henry were no doubt in Van Cortlandt Manor by this time. But McNutt planned to cut them off before they met up with the Furnace Brook men again. Now he just had to watch and wait.

After warming his body and dumping the frozen Garrison clothes in a sack, McNutt returned to his horse. He almost hoped that the two descendants had been able to recover the Sister Wheel. It would make their inevitable capture by McNutt an even greater accomplishment to the other Garrisons at Poppel.

"Romeyn," Henry called. "James! Theodoric!"

The boys had run far ahead of Henry, and as he stood on the

edge of the orchard that was packed with rows of bare trees, he could no longer spot them.

Then someone rushed up behind him. Henry jumped, but let out a relieved sigh when it turned out to be Catharine.

"Where did they go?" she huffed, out of breath.

A chorus of giggling voices floated throughout the trees before Henry could reply. Never had children's laughter sounded so menacing.

Henry gripped Catharine's hand tightly, more to calm his own nerves than to offer her any comfort. Together they walked through the orchard, looking around for the brothers.

"Romeyn," Henry tried again.

But just as swiftly as the giggling began, it stopped. Instead a chilly silence swept through the trees.

"Boys, come out right now," Catharine ordered.

Before Catharine could call again, a figure appeared a few rows away. Henry turned his head and immediately locked eyes with one of the boys. Henry and Catharine ran toward him, but as they neared, the boy shot through the trees and disappeared again.

"Stop!" Catharine shouted. "Come back."

"Where's the Sister Wheel?" Henry called.

Then the young voices returned.

"Jingle bells, jingle bells. Jingle all the way."

The boys sang the familiar verse over and over again until their voices seemed to completely surround Henry and Catharine. Finally, the children popped up in the distance between the orchard trees.

Henry and Catharine watched carefully, but the boys didn't move. They stood barefoot on the snow wearing only their wispy nightshirts, looking at their visitors through the gray trees.

"We have the Sister Wheel," James announced.

Henry and Catharine slowly approached the children, expecting them to take off any moment. But they remained in place until Henry and Catharine were standing right in front of them.

The youngest, Theodoric, stuck out a small fist.

Henry reached his hand out and Theodoric dropped a familiar golden wheel into his palm. Then the boys scattered, leaving Henry and Catharine feeling more unnerved than relieved that they were finally in possession of the Sister Wheel.

And then they heard it.

Bells.

It wasn't like the mighty church bells that boomed through the city on Sunday mornings, or the crisp tinkling of tiny silver bells that accompanied carolers. The clinking of chains and rattling of rusty bells sounded through the air as though a deathly procession marched right toward them.

A strong wind whipped through the orchard, kicking snow from the tree branches down at Henry and Catharine. After a moment of no visibility, Henry realized there was more than wind in the trees. They watched as a dark shadow bounded from branch to branch. The figure's face was hidden, except for a pair of yellow eyes and two horn-like structures that stuck out of its head. The rest of its body appeared thick and hairy like a wild animal. But its movement resembled a human—an incredibly strong human.

As the creature moved through the trees, the bells and chains wrapped around its body sang out mercilessly.

Catharine clutched Henry's shoulder. "What is it?"

"I don't know," Henry mumbled, slipping the Sister Wheel into his jacket's breast pocket.

But Henry's shaking hand missed the pocket and the wheel tumbled to the ground. As soon as it landed on the snowy earth, the creature in the trees stopped moving. The Sister Wheel's shiny appearance against the white backdrop had caught its attention. With a deep growl, the creature launched itself from the tree, pouncing down on Henry in lightning speed. Catharine let out a scream as the creature slashed and gnashed its sharp claws and fangs at Henry's clothes and skin.

Catharine looked around for something to fight the beast away, but all she saw was a broken branch barely hanging onto a tree. Catharine gripped the rough bark and pulled on the branch, trying to break it free. After a couple swift kicks, the branch loosened enough for her to pull it off.

Hoisting the large branch in her arms, Catharine turned toward the creature that was still mauling Henry. She thrust the branch at its hairy body. Although no damage was done, it was enough to distract the creature and allow Henry the chance to roll away.

Henry's clothes were torn, revealing scratches on his arms and chest that oozed blood, dotting the snow like wilting rose petals. But he had managed to protect his head and face.

Catharine and Henry could fully see the creature now. It was human in shape, but taller than the average man. Its hairy body was grayish white except for the head, which was as bald and bony as a skull. A pointy nose jutted out of the face while two brown horns twisted up from the head. Between the creature's sharp teeth, a long tongue stretched far from the mouth, whipping about like a black leathery rope.

The tree branch could only distract the creature so long before it looked ready to pounce again; its chains and bells drummed off its body, signaling the next attack. But the sound of galloping hooves stopped the creature in its tracks.

A horse carrying McNutt appeared in the distance, charging down the orchard. The Garrison was no longer dressed in his black garments, and a square spade was raised in his hand, ready to swipe. The creature ducked away from the impending rider while Catharine and Henry dashed to the side. McNutt made an attempt at the creature's head, but just narrowly missed. He quickly halted the horse and steered it around for a second try.

Henry then remembered the Sister Wheel still lying on the snow. He knew with McNutt distracting the creature, it was the best chance to get the wheel back without the creature seeing. Henry dived toward the Sister Wheel. He snatched it up and dropped it into his pocket. Stumbling back to Catharine, he grabbed her hand and tugged her away from the fighting.

McNutt returned to the creature and tried again to strike it with the spade. But the creature seized the handle of the spade in midair, pulling McNutt off the horse and tossing him onto the cold ground.

The horse continued galloping toward Catharine and Henry. After grabbing the reins and pulling herself up on its back, Catharine reached down for Henry's less battered arm and helped him hop on. With much struggle, Henry was finally situated on the horse behind Catharine.

"Go quickly," Henry's voice shivered into Catharine's ear.

Every movement of the horse caused Henry to wince in pain.

"We have to go back to the Manor," Catharine said. "Your injuries must be attended to as quickly as possible."

"No, Catharine," Henry snapped. "We can't risk going back. We have the wheel. Let's just go."

But before they could flee the orchard, painful cries sounded from nearby. McNutt was cornered against a tree trying to fight the creature back with the spade. But the creature was relentless.

"We must go," Henry said, sensing Catharine's hesitation.

"We can't just leave him," Catharine said. "He came to our aid."

"He's a Garrison," Henry harshly replied. "He's after the Sister Wheel."

An idea struck Catharine. "Give me the Sister Wheel."

"What?" Henry stammered.

"Now!"

Henry fumbled in his jacket, and then placed it in Catharine's hand. She aimed the horse at the creature and, with her arm extended, she charged. If the Sister Wheel was sought so desperately, she believed it must also be a rather powerful object.

Catharine's theory proved to be correct, for as they drew nearer, the creature lunged away when spotting the Sister Wheel in her hand. Not satisfied with its small retreat, Catharine jumped from the horse and chased after the creature, feeling propelled by whatever strange powers the Sister Wheel contained.

The creature let out a final growl before disappearing between the trees and into complete darkness.

"Bels! Bels!"

The children's voices returned to the orchard.

Catharine couldn't see Romeyn, James or Theodoric, but she certainly didn't want to stay and witness them summoning the frightening creature back. Catharine looked over at McNutt leaning against a tree, trying to catch his breath. Catharine then turned to Henry still slumped on the horse.

"We need to dress your injuries," she said to Henry who was coddling his right arm.

"There's a ferry house next to the river," McNutt spoke for the first time; a slight accent slipped through his words.

Henry stared at McNutt. The sight of the Garrison seemed to cause the bruise on his chin to sting stronger than all the fresh wounds scattered over his body.

"How can we trust you?" Henry spat.

"Castriot wants the Van Cortlandt descendants captured alive and returned to Poppel with the Sister Wheel. And I will see to it that you two are brought back safely." McNutt frowned. "At the very least, I owe you that."

Catharine reached up and rubbed Henry's knee. He shivered in response.

"What do you think we should do?" she asked softly.

Henry's eyes reluctantly looked up from where her hand touched his leg.

With a sigh, he whispered, "We do still have to retrieve Maggie. And I don't think she'll be too pleased if we're late."

Chapter Eighteen

Down the Chimney

A horse-drawn carriage flew down the darkened streets of New York carrying a rather jovial Sir Pringle and an anxious Maggie who was gripping the rattling carriage door with all her strength.

Clemmie, Louis, and Ward had said their goodbyes back at Sylvan Terrace before slipping down the ash pit.

"By the time you find the key at Chelsea Manor, it won't be safe for you to travel by way of the sleigh tunnel," Ward advised Maggie. He reached into his pocket and pulled out a sugarplum. "Use this to contact Catharine and Henry. It will find them. And then they can find you."

Maggie kept a hand on her pocket that held the sugarplum, guarding it from the turbulence of the bouncy carriage. But she worried that if the sugarplum wasn't sent soon, the steamboat wouldn't stop near Chelsea Manor. And then Maggie would have no way of returning to Poppel.

Before the pointed rooftops of Sylvan Terrace were even in the distance, Maggie brought the sugarplum to her face and thought deeply about how she wanted Catharine to retrieve her at the river pier near Chelsea Manor. Then the sugarplum shot out her hand and into the night, searching for its recipient.

As they arrived at the Chelsea estate, Sir Pringle stopped the carriage in front of the Manor. Maggie looked up at the mansion looming above the area, a huge shadow sitting upon a pearly white hill. It dawned on her for the first time that all of Chelsea Manor was locked for the night. There was no way of getting inside without waking the family.

"Well," Sir Pringle said, leaning back in his seat and sliding a pipe between his lips. He lit the bowl with a match and then quickly flapped his massive hand, putting the tiny flame out. "You better be on your way."

"I can't get inside," Maggie mumbled, feeling rather foolish. "The doors are locked for the night."

"What?" A cloud of smoke puffed out of Sir Pringle's mouth as he twisted his thick neck in the young girl's direction. "We came all this way and you're telling me this now?"

Maggie nodded sheepishly. She wanted to disappear in the heavy fur coat Sir Pringle had given her to wear.

Sir Pringle looked over at Chelsea Manor and gestured at it with his pipe. "Surely you will be let inside if you ring the doorbell."

Maggie shook her head. "That will wake the entire house. And there's no time to explain to everyone what has happened."

"Well, you better think of something," Sir Pringle huffed. "I didn't come all this way to sit in this carriage, smoking my pipe."

Maggie studied Chelsea Manor, her eyes drifting from the bottom front steps to the top of the roof. An idea suddenly struck her, and at the same time, frightened her to the core.

"Do you—do you have rope?" Maggie stammered.

Before leaving Sylvan Terrace, Sir Pringle had scrambled around, pulling tools off shelves and shoving them into a box that was placed in the back of the carriage. Although Maggie wasn't certain, she thought he had grabbed a coil of rope hanging from a rafter in the cellar.

Sir Pringle's face lit up. "Why, yes, I do."

Maggie examined the west porch and its neighboring sycamore tree before settling upon the Manor's chimney. It didn't take long for Sir Pringle to guess her plan. And a minute later, he was demonstrating to Maggie proper rope techniques.

"So this is the knot to make if you don't want to die," Sir Pringle instructed bluntly.

Maggie watched nervously. With the task of climbing a tree ahead of her, she thought a knot would be the least of her worries.

Maggie shook the dense coat off her body before wrapping the bulky rope around her arm. The weight of the rope threw off her balance and she worried about climbing with the additional barrier. But with a supportive shove from Sir Pringle, Maggie scampered across the road.

After walking up the snowy hill, Maggie climbed the railing of the Manor's west porch, and tossed the rope onto its rooftop. Stretching her arms as high as possible, Maggie grabbed the rooftop's edge and pulled herself up. Situating the rope back upon her shoulder, Maggie slowly stepped toward the lowest branch hanging over the corner of the porch. She carefully threw her legs around the branch, and after feeling confident enough to stand, she reached toward a higher branch.

Using this method of pulling, straddling, and standing, Maggie made it halfway up the tree with relative ease. But then Maggie mistakenly looked down for the first time. Seeing the ground far below, her breath halted in her throat.

Maggie glanced at the third floor windows still needing to be passed before reaching the rooftop. The nearest branch was some distance away, and she would have to fully jump off her branch to grab hold. Even in the cold of winter, Maggie's feet began to sweat, pleading to remain firmly planted. But she had to make the leap. It'd now be just as difficult to go back down the tree, as it would be to continue upward.

With her legs shaking, Maggie leapt into the air. But she slipped and fell just short of the above branch. With the tips of her fingers, she grabbed hold of a branch a few feet below, preventing her body from falling all the way to the ground. Using her strained muscles, she pulled her body up and slid onto her stomach. The fall had returned her fear of heights with an even stronger pulse. And she hugged the branch with her remaining strength.

"Get up, Maggie," Sir Pringle's voice hissed from below. "You can make it."

Sir Pringle stood at the base of the sycamore. His waist appeared thicker than the width of the tree trunk.

"I'll catch you if you slip," Sir Pringle reassured. "You're not dying on my watch."

Somehow the sight of portly Great Uncle Pringle restored some of Maggie's energy. She didn't doubt that Sir Pringle's massive body would save her if she were to fall again. Also, Maggie had grown so tired of being in the tree that she would rather die trying to get to the rooftop than stay lying on a branch for another minute.

Maggie readjusted the rope still wrapped around her shoulder and stood up, using the tree trunk to brace her body. She followed the same path as before, but this time she successfully reached the previously missed branch. And from there she pushed her way to a top branch that connected to the rooftop. Sliding along on her stomach, she finally made it onto Chelsea Manor.

After getting her footing on the uneven shingles, Maggie tied the rope around a branch just like Sir Pringle showed her. And then she took the rope's other end and tossed it down one of the rooftop's chimneys.

Now came the part Maggie was dreading the most. As terrifying as the climb up the tree had been, it seemed like a pleasant memory compared with the prospect of plunging down the Manor's chimney by rope. And as Maggie reflected on the events of this fateful night and contemplated the task she was about to undertake, an explosion of red, green, and gold tinsel appeared in her mind.

The dream.

Realizing that her annual Christmas dream was a harbinger for her current predicament, Maggie lunged at the chimney, gripping its top tightly. And as she looked out into the wintry night, the air became cloudy, as though an old man was smoking a pipe nearby. But through the haze, she saw an illusion of New York with lofty towers and brilliant lights. It was not a city she knew, but rather a place that would one day come to be.

The cold and heights were starting to affect her mind, Maggie realized. And she shook her head, forcing the hallucination away.

Maggie refused to recreate her dream.

She refused to fall like St. Nicholas.

Maggie crawled up the brick chimney and swung one leg into its dark opening. Not feeling any smoke or heat, Maggie took a deep breath and began scaling the chimney. In the dark, her feet searched for oddly shaped bricks and gaps in the mortar. Step by step, Maggie carefully made her way down, all the while getting covered in a layer of soot.

The rope roughly rubbed her palms, chafing the skin. But Maggie pressed onward—or rather downward. After a few minutes of steady climbing, a dim light shone beneath her feet. She was almost to the hearth.

Unfortunately, the rope didn't reach all the way to the bottom, and Maggie was left dangling a few feet over the charred logs. With hesitation, her raw hands released their grip on the coarse rope and Maggie tumbled down. Landing on top of the logs with a *thump*, she managed to fall in between the andirons.

Maggie crawled out of the hearth and into the empty bedroom she shared with Gertrude. The portrait of late Aunt Margaret seemed to stare at Maggie with concern, as if aware of the burden her niece carried that night. But having little time to waste, Maggie hurried out of the room and down the shadowy stairs until she reached the circular hall where the grandfather clock struck five o'clock in the morning.

Maggie went to the front door and pulled it open. Sir Pringle swept inside the doorway, as though emerging from the night like an apparition.

"Well done," Sir Pringle whispered, stepping into the foyer and tucking his right hand into his brown and black plaid jacket. "Now where is Moore?"

Maggie pointed up the stairs. The pair then quietly snuck up to the second floor and slipped into Grandfather Clement's master bedroom. A four-poster bed sat on the far end of the room. Its curtains were drawn, separating them from the sleeping old man. But they still could make out Grandfather Clement's gruff snores.

Sir Pringle wasted no time. He stomped over to the bed and threw open the curtains. Maggie worried his abrasiveness would harm Grandfather Clement's old heart and she quickly leapt to Sir Pringle's side only to see her grandfather was still soundly asleep.

"Moore," Sir Pringle bellowed. "Clement! Wake up, you."

Sir Pringle prodded Grandfather Clement's stomach with his thick thumb.

Grandfather Clement finally opened his eyes to see his granddaughter and a massive man peering over the bed. Startled, Grandfather Clement gripped the duvet to his chin.

"What is all of this?" Grandfather Clement tried to shout, but his voice had been weakened by slumber.

"Grandfather…" Maggie started, but Sir Pringle cut her off.

"We've never met, Moore, but I am Pringle Taylor."

Grandfather Clement was silent.

"Catharine's brother," Sir Pringle continued.

"I know who you are," Grandfather Clement muttered harshly. "What are you doing at Chelsea Manor? And in my bedroom? I will have you kicked out at once."

175

"No, Grandfather," Maggie interrupted. "Listen, please. Something has happened. Something terrible."

Grandfather Clement's stony eyes turned to Maggie.

"I discovered Poppel. Accidentally," Maggie quickly explained. "But now the Garrisons are after all of us—Catharine, Clemmie, Francis, Louis, and the twins. They know we have the Sister Wheels. But we can't bring them together in Nikolaos of Myra's horologe without Grandmother Catharine's key."

Maggie expected Grandfather Clement to have at least some reaction to what she was saying. But if he knew what she was talking about, he didn't show it.

"You knew about Grandmother Catharine visiting Poppel, didn't you?"

Grandfather Clement shook his head slowly. "I haven't slightest idea what you are rambling on about."

Something about his tone, however, suggested the opposite. And Sir Pringle found Grandfather Clement's response particularly unsettling.

"You don't, huh?" Sir Pringle pulled his hand from his jacket, brandishing a shiny bowie knife.

"Sir Pringle, please," Maggie gasped. "Don't threaten my grandfather."

But Sir Pringle ignored the girl.

"We may have never met before. But I don't like you, Moore. Catharine was one of the brightest, liveliest people I knew. And her marriage to you killed all of that. She became nothing more than your housewife, wasting her brilliant mind and soul. No wonder she died so young. No doubt being married to you aged her heart considerably."

Maggie had never cared a great deal for Grandfather Clement, and the recent revelations of the night surrounding the Livingstons and the Christmas poem didn't help the matter. But her back stiffened at Sir Pringle's harsh words.

"Stop it," Maggie snapped. "You don't know what you're talking about, Sir Pringle."

But the damage had been done. Grandfather Clement's face was now a mix of rage and brokenness—an expression Maggie had never witnessed on any person, and especially not her grandfather.

Indifferent to Sir Pringle's knife, Grandfather Clement thrashed out of bed. Able to move only as fast as his body could allow, the old man plodded across the room and out the door, leaving Maggie and Sir Pringle frozen in surprise.

Initially, Maggie feared Grandfather Clement was going to wake up the sleeping family members, which would only complicate matters. But instead the old scholar could be heard creaking down the east stairway. And Maggie and Sir Pringle quickly followed.

"Grandfather," Maggie said as they came upon the hall on the main floor.

Grandfather Clement's posture became rigid at the sound of his granddaughter's voice, but he continued toward the Great Room. It was dark except for the moonlight shining through the tall windows.

"Grandfather, I know about Sidney Livingston and the Christmas poem. I know that is why Henry came here tonight."

Grandfather Clement still didn't respond as he entered the Great Room and collapsed into his armchair, eyes fixated on the fireplace. The opening to the ash pit was closed once again.

Maggie hesitantly approached him.

"I don't blame you for taking credit for the poem," Maggie said, trying to be diplomatic. "It was to save the family from speculation and scandal. And I don't believe what Sir Pringle said was true."

Sir Pringle's heavy feet shifted in the Great Room doorway.

"You loved Grandmother Catharine," Maggie continued. "And she deeply loved you. I never will believe differently. But I also will not believe that you didn't know about Poppel. She trusted you too much to keep that from you."

Grandfather Clement's eyes blinked a couple times and then squinted at the fireplace. "It's gone," he muttered.

Maggie was unsure what he meant, but then she realized Grandfather Clement had spotted the small gap in the brick where the Sister Wheel had broken loose.

Maggie nodded. "It's in Poppel. And if we don't bring Grandmother Catharine's key there, the Garrisons will come after us. The entire Moore family will be put in danger."

Grandfather Clement's eyes widened as though finally realizing the severity of the situation. Getting up from the chair, Grandfather Clement shuffled to the west end of the Great Room and entered the gentlemen's parlor.

"Where's he going?" Sir Pringle asked nervously. "He doesn't keep any weapons in there, does he?"

A minute later, Grandfather Clement returned with his hand balled into a fist.

"I never understood Poppel. Not in the way Catharine and…" Grandfather Clement paused. Maggie knew that he was about to say Sidney's name. "Not in the way Catharine understood it," Grandfather Clement continued. "And I never quite knew what the wheel and key meant. Maybe I was never supposed to."

Grandfather Clement opened his hand, exposing a tiny golden key. He brought it up to his face and studied it closely.

"She only trusted me with the information years later—after Poppel was revealed by the poem. She knew something bad was starting to happen. But it couldn't be stopped."

"Well, if you hadn't stolen the poem, none of this would have happened," Sir Pringle grumbled from the other side of the room.

But Grandfather Clement didn't respond.

Maggie looked past her grandfather and into the open door of the gentlemen's parlor. Through the parlor window, a speck of light floated in the distance, along the Hudson River.

It was a steamboat.

"I must leave," Maggie whispered.

Grandfather Clement looked down at his granddaughter. His expression seemed almost loving. But then it quickly turned firm again as he dropped the key into Maggie's hand.

"If you must, you must."

Maggie slipped the key into her pocket. She glanced at Sir Pringle standing in the doorway and said, "Whether you like it or not, you both are family. Take care of him."

Then Maggie hurried into the kitchen and through its backdoor, returning to the wintry landscape. After wiggling the blue sled out of a snow pile, Maggie grabbed it with both hands and trudged across the yard.

The Hudson River glistened as a steamboat slowly docked in the distance. Maggie dropped the sled down. Although it had only been yesterday morning when she had last made the same ride, it now felt so long ago.

Positioning herself on top of the sled, she thought about aiming farther than the stone wall on this attempt. And how Henry wouldn't be coming to her side if she crashed.

It was now Maggie's turn to save Henry, and so much more.

CHAPTER NINETEEN

RETURN TO POPPEL

K rampus."

The terrifying word crawled out of Albers' mouth.

"That's what you saw—Krampus."

Maggie had never been on a steamboat, so she wasn't sure if it was the motion of the water or hearing what had occurred at Van Cortlandt Manor that caused the uneasiness in her stomach.

From the murdered Garrisons to the possessed children and the frightening creature in the orchard, Maggie was starting to believe that she had been dealt the lucky hand. The sword-wielding Sir Pringle and the descent down the Chelsea Manor chimney seemed quite relaxing when compared to Catharine and Henry's night.

Maggie sat crossed legged on the steamboat deck, wrapped in blankets. Mounds of flour sacks surrounded the group, creating a barricade to block out the wind. Catharine had not left Maggie's side since her younger sister had breathlessly leapt onto the steamboat.

Maggie had yet to see Henry and McNutt who were in the hull having their injuries treated. But she was surprised to hear McNutt's name, especially after finding out the fate of the other Garrisons. But Catharine explained how McNutt had saved them from the creature in the orchard.

"What is... Krampus?" Maggie asked.

"Whatever spirit or goodness Nikolaos of Myra embodied, Krampus is the opposite," Albers explained. "While Nikolaos of Myra gave, Krampus took. And punished. And frightened."

"What was it doing at Van Cortlandt Manor?"

"The Sister Wheel," Wesseling replied, who was sitting particularly close to Catharine.

Albers and Wesseling were the only Furnace Brook men on the deck. Boe was in the wheelhouse with Captain Noble and the others were below with Henry and McNutt.

"Krampus seeks power," Albers continued. "While Grace and Sarah vanquished their immortality, Lily held onto her Sister Wheel. Somewhere along the way she crossed paths with this creature, and her wheel was taken."

Maggie recalled the ancient book in the Boeken Kamer. The image Maggie saw before Harriet had shut the book had been Krampus. She just knew it.

"How can that be?" Catharine asked. "Lily's Sister Wheel is now guarded at Poppel."

"Krampus followed Annette Loockerman to America," Albers replied. "His plan was to gain control of all three Sister Wheels. But in the process, Lily's was taken from him by the Van Cortlandts and left to be protected in Poppel."

"Looks like he's been keeping watch over Sarah's wheel now," Wesseling added. "Probably has a hold over those children. Krampus is too strong to fight off."

It grew silent before Maggie finally asked, "What happened to Lily?"

Wesseling shrugged. "Nobody knows for sure."

"She likely came under Krampus' control like those Van Cortlandt boys," Albers added.

The hatch snapped open and Henry climbed out of the hull with the assistance of McNutt.

"Henry!" Maggie stood up so quickly she almost stumbled into the wall of flour sacks.

She wanted to run over and wrap Henry in a hug, but then she noticed his bandaged body.

Henry gave a weak smile. "I heard you were successful, Maggie."

Maggie nodded. "I recovered the key." She then distrustfully glared at McNutt.

Henry looked over at McNutt and then to Maggie. "It's all right, Maggie. McNutt helped us. And he will be an even greater assistance when we reach Poppel."

But Henry's features turned dark as he looked past Maggie. She turned to see what had caused the sudden change in him, but she only spotted Catharine and Wesseling chatting quietly with one another.

Wesseling had now inched as close as possible to Catharine; his eyes fixated on her face. When Maggie looked back at Henry, he was still captivated by the situation. And even McNutt snuck a few glances in Catharine's direction.

Maggie's mother and aunts used to talk about Catharine's beauty and how she always had the focus of any room she entered. But tonight was one of the few times Maggie witnessed firsthand the extent of Catharine's allure. Even in the midst of their precarious situation, onlookers were pausing to take note of Catharine. And watching Henry stare at her sister only elevated Maggie's seasickness.

But quickly a new concern pushed away Maggie's nausea as a group of black-coated men filed out of the hull. Maggie was so overtly startled at the sight of the Garrisons that Catharine rushed over to place a comforting hand on her shoulder.

"It's just the Furnace Brook men," Catharine said gently.

The Furnace Brook men were dressed in the tattered suits of the dead Garrisons. It was like seeing the living dead. Although the bloodstains were not too visible on the black fabric, still knowing where the uniforms came from sent waves of sickness to Maggie's already troubled stomach.

Unable to contain her illness any longer, Maggie raced to the side of the steamboat. Both Catharine and Henry voiced concern. But after a few moments of being slouched over the railing, Maggie's lone visitor was McNutt.

"Seasickness?"

Maggie tried to respond, but she ended up dry heaving underneath her knotted hair that the wind was wildly whipping into her face.

"Try looking at the horizon," McNutt supplied, helpfully.

Maggie lifted her head and looked out into the distance, trying to find the point in the darkness where sky met Manhattan. But even as McNutt continued sharing old sailing lore, Maggie knew her sickness couldn't simply be blamed on the steamboat.

"Are you going to betray us?" Maggie interrupted.

McNutt didn't respond. His back stiffened as he stared at the black silhouette of New York City.

"Don't you see why we must return Poppel back to the Foundlings? And why the Garrisons must be removed?"

"Our society is faced with an uncertain future," McNutt shot back. "Now is not the time to challenge those who protect it."

"What do you mean?"

"The Garrisons have not always done right. But an attack against them is an attack against our city's stability. And we cannot risk any part of the city not being unified."

"You really believe the situation in Poppel will damage New York City?" Maggie snapped.

McNutt's expression turned defensive. "I'm saying that what may be best for the Foundlings is not best for everyone else. Those who live above Poppel will be affected by what occurs below."

Maggie studied McNutt, thinking that if her stomach was going to become sick again, she knew whom it would be directed toward. She reached in her pocket and touched the key. Its presence helped settle her emotions.

"So you are going to betray us," Maggie stated.

"I have always stood for what is right. Whether that lies with the Garrisons or the Foundlings has yet to be seen," McNutt replied.

Maggie couldn't help but scoff at McNutt's self-righteousness.

"Well, if you fight as well as you can convincingly recite that rehearsed bit, I don't think you'll be much help to us either way."

The impact of Maggie's words was lost as a scuffle started behind her. Maggie turned to see Henry and Wesseling roughly rolling about on the deck. She was startled that Wesseling would wrestle Henry in his injured condition. But she soon realized Henry had been the one to provoke the brawl.

Before Maggie could even take one step toward the fight, McNutt aggressively gripped her arms as though trying to prevent her from intervening.

"Don't get involved," he directed.

Maggie briefly struggled against McNutt before she shrugged out of his hold and sprinted away. Albers had already separated Henry and Wesseling by the time Maggie reached the pair.

"Enough!" Albers placed a protective hand on Henry's chest while shoving Wesseling away with the other.

"I don't have to take that from a stupid Dutchman," Wesseling spat. "Wooden shoes and wooden heads."

Henry tried to take another swing at Wesseling, but Albers had a firm grip on the red-faced Poughkeepsie man.

"What is the issue?" Albers glared from Henry to Wesseling before his eyes fell on Catharine standing a few feet away. The context of their brutish slugs and grunts was suddenly clear.

"You two best deal with it before we reach Poppel," Albers said, letting go of Henry's shirt. "The Garrisons aren't going to care about some jealous squabble."

While both Henry and Wesseling shamefully looked away, Boe stuck his head out of the wheelhouse.

"Almost there," he hollered.

"Right," Albers turned to the group. "Henry, Wesseling, and I still need to get into our Garrison garb. Catharine and Maggie, go hide in the hull until we know it's safe to dock at Poppel."

"If I go down in the hull, I'm going to be sick," Maggie said, clutching her stomach and imagining the stuffy-aired space.

Albers shook his head. "You're too exposed up here."

"We'll hide over there." Catharine nodded toward the flour sack barricade they had been resting behind earlier.

Albers silently agreed and then directed Henry and Wesseling back to the hatch. McNutt followed even though he wasn't asked.

The next few minutes ticked by so slowly that Maggie thought perhaps they were once again under Poppel's extraordinary time rules. Maggie and Catharine couldn't see anything from where they crouched within the flour sacks. But as the steamboat entered the enclosed canal that led to Poppel, Maggie could see a vaulted stone ceiling push away the starry December sky.

Albers, Henry, Wesseling and the rest of the Furnace Brook men popped out of the hatch and took their place on deck.

"Stay low for now," Albers instructed Maggie and Catharine.

Maggie peeked through a crack in the stacks and watched as the steamboat pulled up to the dock. At first there was no one in sight, but then three Garrisons emerged from under the archway. It took Maggie a moment to recognize that the Garrison in the middle was Francis. He was wearing a full uniform with a black cap placed delicately on top of his dense auburn hair.

"Hello there," McNutt greeted as the fake Garrisons tried to blend into the background, not wanting to be recognized as outsiders. "We're returning from Furnace Brook. We haven't seen any sign of the missing Foundlings. What is the situation in Poppel?"

"The Foundlings staged an uprising," said the tall, lanky Garrison on the right. "But it didn't last long. We fought them back and then they all disappeared."

Francis stepped forward; clearly annoyed he wasn't given room to speak first.

"And who might you be?" he asked McNutt.

"I beg your pardon?"

"You are speaking with the Head Garrison, Sir Francis Casimier Moore," Francis snapped, projecting a leg out and placing his hands on his waist. "So when you address me it must be done with formal respect. And if not, you can take the matter up with Castriot."

Maggie could almost feel McNutt's muscles tighten at the tone in her cousin's voice.

There was a long pause before McNutt responded, quite dryly, "Yes, Sir Francis Casimier Moore."

Francis relaxed his stance a bit. "Now then, who might you be?"

"Augustus McNutt. One of the Garrisons assigned to the steamboat."

Francis became silent as he looked up at the various Garrisons on the deck. His eyes widened and his mouth drew pointy in a repressed smirk. Maggie recognized Francis' face from when the cousins would play card games. Francis would get the same expression when he knew he had the better hand but wasn't ready to admit it.

Francis turned to the other Garrisons and roughly pulled them to the side. After whispering in their ears, the two Garrisons took off, leaving Francis alone on the dock. He waited a moment before charging toward the steamboat.

"Maggie!" Francis called.

Reflexively, Maggie shot up from behind the sacks.

"No!" Albers shouted while McNutt gestured for her to stay hidden.

But it was too late. Maggie had already marched to the steamboat's railing.

"How did you know I was here?" Maggie asked, looking down at her cousin.

"You think dressing that Livingston fool up as a Garrison would hide his identity?" Francis pointed to Henry. "I knew who he was just after a glance. You're lucky I sent the others away before they realized that he wasn't a Garrison."

Henry swiftly appeared at Maggie's side.

"And where did you find this bunch?" Francis nodded to Albers, Wesseling, and the others. "Again, you're lucky the others aren't as perceptive as I am."

"You better not tell anyone we're here," Henry ordered. "It would put your cousins in great danger."

Francis glared at Henry. "I am quite aware of their predicament. I saw that Clemmie and Louis were with the Foundlings during their little rebellion. And no doubt are hiding away with them now. Gardiner and Gertrude as well." Francis looked back at Maggie and smirked. "So did you successfully retrieve the final wheel?"

"Why does that concern you?" Henry snapped.

"I'm tired of this place and want to return to Chelsea Manor," Francis whined.

Maggie found her cousin's familiar tantrum especially absurd now that he was dressed in such authoritative garments.

"Yes, we found it," Maggie admitted.

Henry sent her a sharp look.

"Well, come on. Out with it," Francis said. "I'm ready to be done with this whole ordeal."

Albers, Wesseling, and the others quickly jumped down from the steamboat and surrounded Francis on the dock. Henry, Catharine, McNutt, and Maggie were still on the deck with Boe and Captain Noble who had quietly slipped out of the wheelhouse to see what the commotion was about.

"How can we trust you?" Albers asked.

"I have more power here in Poppel than you could even imagine," Francis said, crossing his arms and raising his shoulders proudly. "I know you're seeking the Horologe and I am one of the few who know its location. What other choice do you have but to trust me?"

"Well, we could always just toss you below in the hull like a bag of potatoes," Wesseling said, aggressively bumping his chest against Francis' body. "As it so happens, we have our own Garrison here to take us to the Horologe."

Wesseling looked toward McNutt, expectantly. But McNutt's face flushed.

"I don't know its location," he murmured, shaking his head. "It's classified. Only a few Garrisons know."

The confidence Francis already contained was only magnified by this confession.

"Ah, interesting," Francis said, smiling boldly. He lightly pushed Wesseling with the tip of his finger, causing the blond man to take a step back. "Now we should be on our way."

Albers and Wesseling decided to come with Francis, Maggie, Catharine, and Henry as they searched for the Horologe. Albers wasn't eager to put his trust in Francis while Henry certainly didn't care for the boy. And even Catharine seemed to have her doubts. But Maggie knew that Francis was their best chance at finding the Horologe.

The other Furnace Brook men were ordered to stay out of sight in the meantime.

As the group walked through the underground passages, it dawned on Maggie that they still didn't have the other two Sister Wheels in their possession. One was already in the Horologe and the other had been left with the Foundlings that had stayed behind.

"We have to find everyone else," Maggie whispered to Catharine and Henry.

"What was that?" asked Francis, who was walking a few steps ahead of them.

"We'll search for the others later," Henry whispered back. "It will be much easier for them to find us than it will be to locate the Horologe."

"What's with all the whispering?" Francis spun around. His

voice rose in annoyance. "And what about the Horologe?"

Maggie was unsure of where they currently were within Poppel. They were passing through slender halls and stairways with no sign of Myra Lane, Boeken Kamer, Foundling Row or the banquet hall. It seemed Francis was leading them deeper into the ground, lower than even the Sleigh Pit and workshop. Maggie thought of the Kelder and wondered if they were close to it.

"Where are we?" Maggie asked.

Francis smirked. "Don't worry. We're almost there."

"Yes, but to *where*, Francie?" Maggie said, using his hated childhood nickname.

Francis narrowed his eyes and swiftly turned back around. Not saying another word, he marched further down the hall.

"Probably not best to antagonize him," Catharine whispered to Maggie.

Finally, Francis and the group came to a dead end. Or at least that's what they thought. The oil lamp hanging on the wall gave off a soft glow, so they didn't immediately notice a door in the corner, blending perfectly into the wall.

"Here we are," Francis announced. He opened the door with one hand and gestured to Maggie with the other.

"After you," Francis said, directing her through the ominous doorway with a sly grin.

CHAPTER TWENTY

HOROLOGE

The inscription *Horologe Hall* was carved into one of the many large columns of the underground hall. The size and splendor of the space caught Maggie by surprise, but she didn't dare speak. It would have been impossible to even whisper without the words being echoed throughout the two rows of columns dividing the three vaulted aisles of the hall.

Francis led Maggie and the group down the center aisle. Albers and Wesseling carefully trailed behind. Francis strutted along with his head held high while a clock mightily ticked away in the distance. But just as they were halfway down the aisle, Francis stopped and motioned for the others to do so as well.

As Maggie watched to see what Francis would do next, a pack of Garrisons exploded into the hall from where they had just entered. Maggie recognized Comstock, Cyrus, Cabell, Crowther, Calhoun, and Crofoot as well a dozen others. A few held rifled muskets while the others had swords drawn. The Garrisons staggered into position, stationing themselves throughout the hall.

There was no escaping.

Finally, Castriot stormed into the hall, carrying nothing but an overly stretched smile. Maggie almost shook with anger when she spotted McNutt walking behind the Head Garrison.

190

"Most impressive, Francis Casimier," Castriot boomed. "You have done what was once believed to be unthinkable, you have gathered the Sister Wheels. Or at least, those who carry them."

Maggie looked over to Francis. He stoically avoided his cousin's stare. His expression was hard to read, so Maggie couldn't tell if he had intentionally led them into a trap.

"McNutt was kind enough to alert us of your recent arrival on the steamboat and reported that Francis was leading you to the Horologe Hall," Castriot continued.

Maggie now understood. Francis had been honest, even though Castriot thought he had been acting on behalf of the Garrisons. As predicted, McNutt was the one who betrayed them.

"Now," Castriot said, stepping forward. "Hand over the Sister Wheel."

The Garrisons inched toward the group, their muskets remaining steadily positioned.

"We don't have it," Henry lied.

Castriot looked back at McNutt.

"I checked his clothes on the steamboat. He doesn't have it," McNutt stated. He then nodded to Catharine. "Search her."

One Garrison with a musket and another holding a sword advanced on Catharine. She resisted at first, gripping tightly the side pocket of her dress that held the Sister Wheel.

Castriot had yet to mention anything about the Horologe key, and Maggie was starting to think he didn't know about it.

"Give it to them," Maggie instructed just as one Garrison raised his sword in the air near Catharine. Maggie made eye contact with her sister. With a reassuring look, Maggie repeated, "Give them the wheel."

Catharine hesitantly pulled the Sister Wheel out of her pocket. With one final act of defiance, she tossed it on the floor a few feet from Castriot. Cyrus quickly scooped the wheel up and handed it over to the Head Garrison.

Holding the wheel up and slowly rotating it between his thumb and pointer finger, Castriot examined its round edges.

"Perfect," he muttered. "Now we only have one left to find. Francis told me he saw Clemmie pick it up back at Chelsea Manor before coming here. Clemmie no doubt is hiding away with the Foundlings. But I'm sure if he thought his sisters and cousins were in danger, he would happily surrender it. What a gallant and final gesture on his part."

The group fell silent, realizing the Garrisons were not going to let them go peacefully once all three Sister Wheels were collected. But Maggie still noticed the Garrisons seemed unaware a key was needed to fully unite the wheels.

Maggie slowly placed her arms down at her sides. Her right hand brushed against the outside of the pocket, searching for the hard key.

Nothing.

Her left hand felt around on her other side for the key.

Again nothing.

Somewhere between the steamboat and the Horologe Hall, the key had disappeared.

A wave of anxiety rushed through Maggie's body, but she tried not to let it show. Castriot was no longer interested in the Moore grandchildren as he approached the Horologe with the Sister Wheel in hand. The other armed Garrisons directed the intruders to follow until they reached the end where an extravagant bronze clock was mounted on the high stone wall.

Cyrus scurried up a metal ladder leaning against the wall and opened the clock's large face, revealing an intricate display of gears and wheels, rotating and clicking away. Comstock took the Sister Wheel from Castriot and passed it up to Cyrus who attempted to place it in one of the spaces within the turning gears. But he soon saw that it didn't fit. Cyrus studied the Sister Wheel and then the clock, realizing the wheel was too small.

A second later, the golden wheel came soaring between the heads of Catharine and Henry before slamming into Francis' black-coated chest. The wheel rattled noisily as it finally hit the ground.

"It's a fake!" Cyrus shouted. "It doesn't match the other Sister Wheel."

Castriot tore around, glaring at the Van Cortlandt descendants. He glided toward them like a snake pursuing its prey. Before Castriot could strike, however, the entrance door at the other end of the hall burst open once again. Maggie's heart jumped thinking it was more Garrisons, but it turned out to be the Furnace Brook men, led by an ever jubilant Boe who was swinging a spade wildly around. The Garrisons didn't even have time to mount their muskets before the Furnace Brook men collided violently with them.

Maggie's body was jerked sideways as Henry pulled her toward the door. Catharine and Francis were already far ahead, escorted by Ward and Harriet. The Foundlings had snuck in behind the Furnace Brook men who were staying behind in the Horologe Hall, making sure the Garrisons didn't follow the Van Cortlandt descendants.

Clemmie and Louis were waiting in the doorway. Maggie was so happy to see that they were unharmed that she ran up and wrapped her arms around Louis. But the embrace was short-lived.

"We have to get back to the tunnels," Clemmie directed, starting down the hallway.

"What happened since we left?" Maggie asked.

"Castriot knew we had been hiding all of you," Harriet said. "He started locking Foundlings up in the Kelder and even tortured some for information."

"Gardiner and Gertrude…" Catharine trailed off.

Harriet shook her head. "The twins are unharmed. They were the first to be hidden away. Although the Foundlings fought back, we were no match against the Garrisons."

"By the time Clemmie, Louis, and I returned from Sylvan Terrace, all the Foundlings had retreated to the tunnels," Ward added. "It's the only place the Garrisons didn't know how to reach us."

Ward stopped in the middle of the corridor. After quickly glancing around, he reached up to one of the oil lamps and pulled it down. An opening in the wall appeared and the group slipped inside the tunnel where they were met with a floating light.

It was Lloyd.

"Follow me," he whispered, holding a candle up to his face where the light reflected in his glasses. He turned and clambered up a flight of steps.

No one spoke as they maneuvered through the winding passage. When Lloyd finally stopped walking, Maggie recognized they were under the Kleren shop. One by one they climbed into the backroom where Hostrupp and Madame Welles were waiting.

"Where is the Sister Wheel and key?" Madame Welles immediately asked.

Henry explained how the Garrisons deemed it to be a fake since it hadn't fit in the Horologe.

"Where is it now?" Madame Welles' eyes scanned the Van Cortlandt descendants.

No one responded. The last time anyone saw the wheel had been when Cyrus angrily threw it. It was probably still lying on the floor in the Horologe Hall.

But then Francis extended his arm out to the group. The Sister Wheel was resting in his palm.

"I picked it up," he mumbled.

Madame Welles' face brightened. "Wonderful!"

"But if it's a fake, what good is it?" Clemmie asked.

She sneered. "It's certainly not a fake. Do you really think that monstrous clock in the Horologe Hall traveled all the way from Belgium? That decoy was built here in New York. Even the Foundlings never knew where the original Horologe was kept."

"Which is where?" Maggie asked.

Hostrupp emitted a giggle. "In plain sight. Oh, so very plain sight."

He motioned for everyone to follow him to the front of the shop where all the windows had been boarded up, and the door was now barricaded by chairs, racks of clothes, and piles upon piles of useless, yet colorful, ribbons.

Maggie noticed the pendulum wall clock with pear-shaped weights hanging on the wall. Its blue and white porcelain dial indicated that it was almost seven o'clock in the morning.

"This is it," Hostrupp said shrilly. "Beautiful mahogany wood, silver features. Made in Holland." He turned to Maggie. "Do you have the key?"

Maggie was silent. She didn't know how to tell everyone that the key—the vital instrument in freeing Poppel—had gone missing between the steamboat and the Horologe Hall.

"It's… gone…"

'What?" Madame Welles snapped. "What do you mean it's gone?"

"I had it on the steamboat, but it wasn't in my pocket when we reached the Horologe Hall," Maggie admitted. "It's lost."

"It's not lost," Henry interrupted. "McNutt took it. I bet you anything. You heard him tell Castriot that he searched my clothes to see if I had the Sister Wheel. He probably did it when I was changing into the Garrison uniform."

"Was there ever an opportunity where McNutt could have taken the key from you?" Catharine asked.

Maggie thought for a moment. The only contact she had with McNutt was when he tried to hold her back during Henry and Wesseling's fight. Although the gesture had seemed unnecessary, she hadn't given it too much thought at the time. But now the reason behind his actions seemed rather clear.

"Yes," Maggie finally answered. "Yes, I think McNutt took it."

"I'm going after him," Henry spat, heading toward the back.

"Wait," Madame Welles called. "Where is Nellie?"

Henry spun around. "Nellie?"

"Yes, the girl who took you and Catharine to Furnace Brook. Where is she now?"

Henry and Catharine exchanged glances, realizing that no one else knew about her capture.

"She was taken to the Kelder," Catharine said.

"No," Madame Welles gasped, cupping her mouth with her hand.

"We'll get her out," Louis stepped forward. "Once everything is said and done, we'll free all the Foundlings in the Kelder."

"No, you fool," Madame Welles barked. "Nellie was given the wheel that came from Chelsea Manor—Grace's Sister Wheel."

Ward sighed. "So now we're missing the key and one of the wheels."

"Two of the wheels," Lloyd added. "Francis is gone."

Everyone quickly looked around and saw that Lloyd was right; Francis had managed to slip away. But to where exactly no one knew.

"Seems as though we have another double-crosser on our hands," Ward said, sprinting toward the backroom. Before anyone could say anything, Ward disappeared through the trapdoor.

"So now both Sister Wheels and the key are gone," Henry forced a laugh of despair. "Looks like we're starting all over again from the beginning."

"It's more terrible than that," Madame Welles said grimly. "Francis has escaped with valuable pieces of information—the truth about the Horologe and the location of the Foundling tunnels."

Hostrupp let out a squeal. "My, my. Perhaps this is the rare occasion—the rare occasion indeed—where Poppel doesn't have much time. No, no. Not much time at all."

Francis had been told to head to the Krog if trouble arose. So the moment the others were distracted by the clock in Kleren, he snuck back down to the tunnels, and soon he was stumbling out into the hallway near the Sleigh Pit.

With the Sister Wheel clutched in his palm, Francis ran through Myra Lane. It wasn't until he neared the stairs that led up to the banquet hall that he heard someone running behind him. A sharp sting accompanied the sound of footsteps as something pelted the nape of his neck.

Francis glanced back and spotted Ward aggressively chasing him, a thin pipe between his lips. Ward reloaded his mouth with a handful of jellybeans and soon another round was shot in Francis' direction. The beans smashed against the stones under Francis' feet as he ascended to the top of the stairs. Francis made it halfway through the banquet hall before something struck his legs, tripping him right underneath the chandelier. Ward had hit Francis with a whip made out of taffy, allowing him the opportunity to tackle Francis from behind.

"Get off me," Francis grumbled while Ward tried pinning him to the ground. But the Foundling struggled to keep Francis' flailing arms and legs still.

"Hand over the wheel," Ward shouted. "Hand it over!"

Francis tried to push Ward off, but the Foundling continued to grapple with Francis' chest, attempting to retrieve the Sister Wheel hidden away in the boy's pocket. Freeing his arms, Francis punched Ward solidly in the face. Stunned, Ward fell backward, giving Francis the chance to wiggle out from the Foundling's grasp and roll away.

Francis hurried to his feet and reached for the revolver Castriot had given him. He pointed it down at Ward who was kneeling on the ground. Ward's eyes looked up at the gun in both fear and surprise.

Francis had never shot a gun before. Even when the Foundlings were uprising, Francis had been kept away from most of the action, for a Garrison of his importance couldn't be in harm's way.

"What are you waiting for?" Ward halfheartedly provoked with a gulp.

Francis considered shooting the air to further frighten the Foundling, but as he was still pondering his options, a shot rang through the banquet hall. A second later, Ward hurled forward, blood dripping out of his mouth.

Stumbling back into a table, Francis let out a horrified scream, thinking his gun had accidently gone off. But then Francis saw Cyrus standing on the mezzanine in front of the Krog doorway. His bony face held a satisfied smirk.

"I knew you couldn't do it yourself," Cyrus snarled. His tone made it sound like Francis should be thankful he had shot the Foundling. Cyrus then motioned with his gun for Francis to join him. "Get up here, boy."

Francis stared at Ward's motionless body and then up at Cyrus. Although Cyrus repeated his request for Francis to join him up on the mezzanine, somehow Francis couldn't muster the strength to unlatch his trembling fingers from the table behind him.

Chapter Twenty-One

The Wheels and Key

The Horologe Hall was empty when Maggie returned with Louis and Clemmie. The three of them came searching for McNutt, but he was nowhere to be seen.

"Over there," Louis said, pointing to the far end of the hall where black-coated bodies were lying near the fake horologe.

"Are they Garrisons or..." Clemmie trailed off as the group neared the unmoving bodies.

While some Garrisons had been killed, the greatest number dead were the Furnace Brook men, as Maggie had feared.

"Boe and Wesseling," Maggie muttered sadly, recognizing the older man with the bulbous nose as well as the blond-haired young man who had shown great interest in Catharine.

Maggie, Louis, and Clemmie respectfully bowed their heads, but the moment of mourning was interrupted by a cough. The Moore grandchildren jumped, expecting Castriot to be lurking in a corner.

But no one appeared.

It wasn't until the hollow cough sounded again that they finally tracked the noise to one of the columns. They cautiously tiptoed behind it and were shocked to see Albers slouched against the column, gripping his bleeding right arm.

Clemmie dropped next to him. "What happened?"

Albers breathed heavily. "They got my men. And then the Garrisons escaped with Castriot."

"Was McNutt with them?" Maggie asked. Albers gave a puzzled look, so she added, "The redheaded Garrison."

"I... I don't know." Albers paused for a moment and then shook his head. "No, I don't think he was with the others. He may have slipped out earlier."

Clemmie unbuttoned the top of his shirt, exposing a copper ascot. Maggie arched an eyebrow as her brother untied the ascot from around his neck.

Maggie and Louis gave Clemmie questioning gazes, and he looked back at them sheepishly.

"Is that silk?" Louis asked in disbelief.

"Hostrupp said I could have it."

Maggie suppressed a tired eye roll, imagining Clemmie exploring Kleren for an accessory to complete his outfit. Only Clemmie would be concerned about looking dapper in the midst of battle. But Maggie soon regretted judging Clemmie, for he quickly used the ascot to bandage Alber's wounded arm.

Albers admired Clemmie's work, but then asked solemnly, "Where are the Sister Wheels?"

"There was a setback," Clemmie reluctantly admitted. "Two are now missing."

Louis sighed. "My brother Francis took off with one."

Alber's pale face turned even whiter. "Could he be working with Castriot?"

Maggie bit her lip. She didn't want to believe it. It was easier to think that only McNutt had betrayed them, and not Francis, too.

"Catharine and Henry went after him," Louis said. "So they'll soon find out."

"And the second wheel?" Albers asked.

Maggie explained that it had been given to the Foundling named Nellie, and that she was now being held in the Kelder.

Albers' eyes shot open as he struggled to get to his feet.

"I must go," Albers stammered.

Louis and Clemmie tried to keep him sitting.

"You've done enough to help," Maggie said. "You should rest."

"We sent Foundlings to retrieve Nellie and the wheel," Clemmie added.

Albers fiercely shook his head. "No, no, no. You don't understand. I must go to her. I must go."

Even with Louis and Clemmie's best efforts, Albers could not be restrained. Soon he managed to get to his feet and bolt toward the doorway.

"But... but do you even know where you're going?" Louis called after him.

However, it was too late. Albers had already disappeared.

"I'll go after him," Clemmie said. "Ward showed me how to get to the Kelder. He probably will get lost trying to find it." Clemmie then took off after Albers, leaving Maggie and Louis alone.

"Now we're not any closer to finding McNutt or the Horologe key," Maggie observed glumly.

"Well, if any good comes out of this, it's the realization that Clemmie isn't completely useless," Louis joked with a forced chuckle. "Where did Clemmie learn to bandage an arm? I didn't even know he could read."

Maggie's eyes lit up and she grabbed Louis' hand, tugging him toward the doorway.

"I know where to find McNutt."

The Kelder was farther than the workshop, deeper than the Sleigh Pit and colder than the steamboat. But since Albers didn't know how to get there, Clemmie had no trouble catching up to the injured man.

"Albers, the Foundlings have already gone down to find Nellie,"

Clemmie explained again. "They probably have reached her by now." But Albers brushed aside Clemmie's comments and kept insisting he must go to her.

Giving into Albers' persistent pleas, Clemmie led him toward the Kelder through the Foundling tunnels. Clemmie had a candle, but its glow only extended so far, and he didn't see the other Foundlings walking his direction until Lloyd nearly smacked into Clemmie's elbow.

"Is that you, Clemmie?" Harriet asked and then let out a gasp when she saw Albers, thinking he was a Garrison.

"It's all right," Clemmie said quickly. "He's from Furnace—"

"Were you able to get Nellie?" Albers interrupted.

"No," Lloyd said. "The Kelder is too well guarded."

"We were coming back to get more Foundlings," Harriet added, and then eyeing Albers' uniform said, "But maybe now we won't need them."

Minutes later, Albers walked down the Kelder passageway alone while Clemmie and the Foundlings waited in the tunnels. They had directed Albers to Nellie's cell and briefly orchestrated a plan that depended entirely on deception.

Two Garrisons confronted Albers as he entered the Kelder, which was a grisly, dirt-covered burrow full of windowless, wooden doors.

"I'm here to retrieve a Foundling," Albers stated in a steady voice.

The Garrisons looked at Albers with uncertain expressions. He still had his bloodstained tourniquet around his arm.

"There was an accident in the Sleigh Pit," Albers explained, nodding to his injury. "We need the Foundling to help clean up the mess."

"Which?" grunted one of the Garrisons.

"Cell number four," Albers replied, trying not to appear too anxious. "The blonde girl."

The two Garrisons exchanged hesitant looks, causing Albers to lose his composure.

"Do I need to get..." Albers paused, trying to remember the name the Foundlings had given him. "Cockrell? Do I need to bring Cockrell down here? Or are you going to follow orders and take me to cell number four?"

One Garrison pointed down the hall. "On the right," he directed.

Albers nodded and marched on, trying to hide his apprehension.

Reaching the cell marked number four; Albers unlocked the iron bolted door and pushed it open. He stepped into the darkness, unable to see his own hands in front of him.

But then a set of blue eyes appeared. They were frightened at first, but a look of recognition soon swept into them as a voice muttered, "Albers?"

Albers shivered, but he didn't know if it was the temperature of the cell or the reunion he had anticipated for over the past decade.

"Albers?" the voice repeated.

"Nellie," Albers replied softly. There was so much he wanted to say, but all he managed to choke out was, "Do... do you have the wheel?"

A pair of familiar arms quickly wrapped around his chest as a head of blonde hair settled under his nose. It smelled like a past he had nearly forgotten. But instead of giving him back the comfort he thought he had once lost, he became very aware of his age and the years he would never get back.

Although he wanted to stay in the embrace longer, the sound of footsteps approaching pulled them a part. The Garrisons were coming.

"Do you have the wheel?" Albers repeated, looking down at Nellie.

Albers stared at the girl's glowing skin. He couldn't remember her ever looking so youthful. Although he had imagined this reunion from the moment Nellie left Furnace Brook, convinced that the passing of time was insignificant when it came to love, he now realized that time may be the only thing that mattered.

"How do you know McNutt is here?" Louis whispered as Maggie led him through the tunnel Harriet had shown her earlier.

Maggie didn't respond. The truth was she really only had a slight hunch.

The Boeken Kamer was eerily quiet as they slipped out of the bookshelf. Maggie and Louis tiptoed through the rows of books. With Henry and Catharine probably closing in on Francis and Ward, and Clemmie retrieving Nellie and the Sister Wheel, Maggie needed to find the redheaded Garrison.

"McNutt!" Maggie called, knowing she was taking the risk of someone other than McNutt hearing her.

But nothing stirred.

"McNutt!" she called again.

Maggie began to worry she had led them astray. But then out of the last row of bookshelves, McNutt finally emerged.

"You!" Without hesitation, Maggie charged toward him. "You betrayed us! You led Castriot to the Horologe Hall! People died because of you!"

Wide-eyed with his mouth slightly open, McNutt looked stunned. "Maggie, I did not betray you. I know you don't believe me, but you must."

Maggie folded her arms and looked at McNutt doubtfully.

"When we arrived in the steamboat and Francis sent the other Garrisons away, he must have told them to alert Castriot of your arrival. After I left the Furnace Brook men behind, I ran into the Garrisons just as they were coming to find you. I know it may be hard to believe, but it was Francis who betrayed you, not I."

"Considering that Francis just fled with one of the Sister Wheels," Louis said, "It's not too hard to believe, actually."

Maggie didn't speak, but she knew that Francis' actions did give McNutt's version of the events some credibility.

"How did you know I was here?" McNutt asked.

"Your reputation precedes you," Maggie said, but seeing McNutt's confusion, she added, "I remembered that you had a book when Henry and I first ran into you."

Maggie also wanted to say that McNutt probably needed an isolated space where he could get away from the other Garrisons who hated him. But she didn't.

"Did you take the key from me?" Maggie asked instead.

McNutt was quiet for a moment, but then nodded. "I suppose you'd like it back."

Maggie looked at him with uncertainty. "You didn't give it to Castriot?"

McNutt shook his head. "He doesn't even know about its existence."

"Then how do you know about it? And why did you bother to even steal it?"

McNutt scratched his prickly red hair. "Henry and Catharine had mentioned the key on the way back from Van Cortlandt Manor. I wasn't sure what I would do with it. I just knew I didn't want you to have it until I was sure of what should be done. But now I don't know what's right anymore." McNutt reached in his jacket's pocket and pulled out the key.

"I hope you know what you're doing," he said, handing it over to Maggie.

Maggie sighed. "Oh, how I wish that I did."

Catharine and Henry didn't see Ward's body when they rushed into the banquet hall, searching for any sign of Francis or the Garrisons. It wasn't until Henry's foot smeared along a puddle of blood that they finally noticed the dead Foundling.

Henry gasped while Catharine bent down to examine the body.

"They shot him," she observed, touching Ward's neck.

The ominous sound of guns being cocked filled the banquet hall. A moment later, Garrisons stepped out from behind the columns under the mezzanine, pointing their rifled muskets toward Catharine and Henry.

"Yes, another unfortunate casualty that your interference in Poppel has caused." Castriot appeared on the mezzanine with Francis at his side. Comstock and Cyrus lingered in the background.

Unknown to everyone else in the banquet hall, Maggie, Louis, and McNutt were just sneaking out from the Boeken Kamer through the door hidden behind the maroon curtain.

Seeing the armed Garrisons through the slit in the fabric, Maggie leaned over to Louis and whispered, "We may have to bring the Horologe to the remaining Sister Wheel. Go back to Kleren. Find the others."

Louis understood and dashed back into the Boeken Kamer while Maggie and McNutt watched Castriot stroll down from the mezzanine.

"You should have learned a thing or two from Clement Clarke Moore," Castriot continued. "He was wise enough to stay away from Poppel. But do not be confused, for he was not any less noble. I actually did not realize the extent of your grandfather's gallantry until tonight."

McNutt led Maggie over to a ladder that was against the wall. She slowly followed him onto the mezzanine where they hid in the shadows. Even Francis, Comstock, and Cyrus didn't see them as they walked down the creaky steps to the banquet hall.

Meanwhile, Castriot circled Catharine and Henry, looking ready to strike.

"I wasn't aware that the Livingston family also knew of Poppel's existence until Francis told us about Henry's visit to Chelsea Manor tonight. If I had known, Sidney would have been killed alongside Catharine and Margaret Moore all those years ago."

"What do you mean by that?" Catharine cried while Henry placed a hand around her shoulder to keep her from charging at Castriot.

"Didn't you know?" Castriot feigned an innocent, wide-eyed expression. "After that delightful little Christmas poem was published in 1823, exposing Poppel once and for all, we soon learned about Catharine and Margaret's connection to the village. But we weren't aware of Sidney Livingston until tonight."

"You killed Clement Clarke Moore's wife and daughter," Henry said bitterly.

Cyrus nodded from behind Castriot. "Quite right."

"Years apart, of course," Comstock cut in. "So as to not make it too suspicious."

"Both poisoned. Rather sudden deaths," Cyrus added. "Easy when one has such access to their home."

"Arsenic dusted sugarplums," Comstock said without emotion. "Delivered right to their pillows in the early morning hours. Catharine and Margaret both easily mistook the candy as messages from Poppel. An unfortunate, but understandable error."

Henry continued to restrain the thrashing Catharine, who was using all her strength to claw her way toward the Garrisons.

"That was my mother!" she cried. "You killed my mother!"

"What's done is done," Castriot said calmly. "We couldn't risk Poppel being brought to the public's attention after our takeover. And unfortunately, the knowledge they held posed a threat that had to be eliminated. However, after Margaret's death, it seems that Clement Clarke Moore must have become suspicious, conducting his own little investigation over the years. Eventually, he traced their deaths back to us, which is why it seems he finally laid claim to authoring *Twas the Night Before Christmas*."

"What does that have to do with anything?" Henry snapped. He grimaced in pain as his arms, including his injured one, were now completely wrapped around Catharine's waist as she continued to scream at the Garrisons.

"My dear, Mr. Livingston, it's the sole reason your father was able to live," Castriot sneered. "Once Clement Clarke Moore realized what had happened to Catharine and Margaret, he knew we would come after Sidney and the Livingstons if it were discovered that they knew of Poppel's existence. But as it were, Clement Clarke Moore took credit for the poem, making it highly unlikely that we would come to know the truth. At least until all of you arrived tonight."

Maggie slid down the mezzanine wall as her legs suddenly became weak. It had never even crossed her mind that Grandfather Clement's actions had been to protect the Livingstons.

"But then why didn't you kill Clement Clarke Moore, too?" Henry asked.

"Mr. Moore's death would have been too heavily profiled. We didn't want to risk the attention. And we had no interest in harming any other family members who were unaware of Poppel," Castriot explained, and then added slyly. "But now since all of you know about it, this changes matters."

Catharine stopped moving about in Henry's arms; once again becoming aware of the muskets pointed their direction.

"Francis has told me of some other important secrets," Castriot said, gesturing to Francis who no longer looked as confident as he had earlier. "He shared in great detail the existence of some hidden tunnels belonging to the Foundlings that the Garrisons are now infiltrating. And more importantly, he informed us about the location of the true Horologe."

Francis' face was white and he looked down at the floor. He didn't resemble the same arrogant boy Maggie could imagine running to the closest authority figure, eager to share his important news. Instead he appeared trapped and afraid. She watched as Francis stepped back into the shadows behind the columns.

Castriot didn't notice Francis slink away as a crowd emerged through the doors. Armed Garrisons roughly escorted Clemmie, Albers, Nellie, Lloyd, Harriet, Wendell, and a dozen other Foundlings into the banquet hall. Madame Welles, Hostrupp, and Houten were also in the group.

Maggie was relieved that Louis hadn't been caught. But her stomach sunk when a Garrison walked in carrying the Horologe, stripped right off the wall in Kleren.

"Ward!" Wendell sobbed, spotting the dead Foundling.

But as Wendell and the other Foundlings sniffled back their tears at the sight of Ward's body, Cockrell presented the Horologe to Castriot.

"A Foundling was also carrying the Sister Wheel," Cockrell gruffly said. He bowed his heavy body as low as it would go and held out his chubby hand with the final Sister Wheel gleaming under the chandelier's light.

Castriot's eyes lit up. "At last!"

The Horologe was placed down on the table in front of Castriot who didn't hesitate to open the clock's face, exposing its rotating gears. Castriot reached in his pocket and pulled out the Sister Wheel given to him by Francis, so he was now holding a wheel in each hand. He set one wheel down in the Horologe, not aware that he still needed the key to truly unite all three.

Maggie gripped the key tucked away in her pocket. It was still there this time.

"Finally, the Garrisons have control of the Sister Wheels," Castriot announced and then tossed the third wheel to Cyrus. "Dispose of that one. Melt it down and destroy it. Then the possibility of St. Nicholas returning is gone forever."

Cyrus gleefully took the wheel and started toward the mezzanine steps.

"With just the two wheels, we will be able to further extend our time in Poppel," Castriot explained. "Unfortunately, none of you will be here to take advantage of it."

Castriot nodded to the Garrisons who tightened their grips on the muskets and aimed for the captives crammed in the middle of the hall. But before they could shoot, the chandelier came shrieking down from the ceiling before crashing against the floor, striking near Castriot and sending shattered glass soaring across the room.

Amidst the chaos, Maggie spotted Francis in the darkened corner standing next to a dangling rope. It was clear he had been the one to loosen the line, causing the chandelier to drop. But she lost sight of her cousin as Cyrus came bounding up the stairs right in front of her hiding place.

McNutt jumped out from the darkness and tackled Cyrus, slamming his body to the ground. But nobody in the banquet hall noticed McNutt as they dealt with the shift caused by the chandelier. The Foundlings wasted no time in turning their aggression onto the Garrisons. This took the Garrisons by surprise, making their guns useless as the Foundlings attacked.

While McNutt and Cyrus struggled up on the mezzanine, Louis, Violet, Gardiner and Gertrude snuck out from behind the maroon curtain.

Louis and the twins immediately went to help Catharine and Clemmie who were trying to strip Garrisons of their weapons. But as Clemmie pushed around the plump Cockrell and Catharine tangled with Cabell, Violet crept across the banquet hall, dodging between people and tables until she reached the unguarded Horologe. Under the nose of Castriot, who was distracted by those protecting him from the ambush, Violet grabbed the Horologe with both of her arms, clutched it to her chest and scurried away. Violet was almost up the mezzanine before Castriot noticed what had happened.

"The Horologe!" he shouted, trying to get his men's attention. "After it!"

Violet ran toward the Krog's stairs with Maggie following just as McNutt was able to pry the Sister Wheel out of the hand of the badly beaten Cyrus. McNutt quickly got up and bolted after Maggie and Violet.

"Where are you going?" Maggie called to Violet as they entered the Krog, which smelled strongly of liquor and smoke.

But as Violet dashed up one last set of stairs behind the bar in the Krog, Maggie realized the answer.

Violet was leaving Poppel.

CHAPTER TWENTY-TWO

SENECA VILLAGE

The morning's pale light poured into the Krog as Violet burst through its door that led to the outside. The sun had yet to rise, but Maggie's eyes still struggled to adjust to the bright air as she stepped through the doorway. Squinting around at the surroundings, it soon became clear she was in a rural part of Manhattan. Small wooden houses were scattered along dirt roads while a cemetery stood in the distance. There also was an old stone church that happened to contain the secret Poppel entrance from which Maggie and Violet emerged.

An older black man had been walking up the road, but froze when he saw Violet running out of the church's back door, clutching a clock half her size. He watched as Maggie came chasing after her with a young redheaded man bounding behind.

"I have it!" McNutt choked out. "I have it."

"Toss it!" Maggie shouted to McNutt as Violet set the Horologe onto the dirt road.

McNutt flung the small wheel through the air and Maggie effortlessly caught it. But just as she was about to open the Horologe, a pack of Garrisons stormed through Poppel's door. The last ones slammed the door shut before barricading it with their bodies, preventing the Foundlings and Van Cortlandt descendants from escaping.

When the old man saw the army of black-coated men explode from the church, he turned on his heels and hobbled down the empty road.

Maggie inserted the last Sister Wheel into the Horologe and tightened the three wheels with the key. Apprehensively, Castriot and the Garrisons watched, waiting to see what would happen.

But nothing changed.

Castriot let out a hoarse laugh. "Where is your great Nikolaos of Myra?"

The rest of the Garrisons cackled with relief as they began closing in on McNutt, Maggie, and Violet. Meanwhile, the other Garrisons were holding back those still in Poppel. The pounding of hands vibrated on the inside of the church door.

"Now then," Castriot said, marching forward. "Hand over the Horologe."

Violet picked up the Horologe and pressed it to her body while Maggie defensively stepped in front of the young girl.

"You have no business attacking these children," McNutt shouted to the Garrisons. "If anything, you should be pleased they were able to collect the Sister Wheels."

"Why, yes, very pleased indeed." Castriot took out his revolver and without hesitation shot McNutt in the left leg.

Violet muffled a scream. Maggie was also horrified to see McNutt collapse to the ground, gripping his lower leg as he groaned in agony.

"You've been helping these intruders," Castriot emotionlessly said, walking slowly toward McNutt. "That kind of disloyalty will not be tolerated."

Castriot raised his revolver again, but before he could take another shot, a bullet whizzed through the air, striking his fingers and embedding itself in the church wall. Castriot dropped his gun and grabbed his bloodied hand with a painful yell. Falling to his knees, Castriot looked toward the dirt road that the old man had retreated down just moments earlier. The road was no longer empty as twenty black men and women, a few armed with rifled muskets, stood ready to fight.

"You shot the church, Nat!" one of them called out to the man holding the sizzling musket.

Nat lowered the barrel of the gun and glared at the Garrisons. "I don't know who you all are, but there's to be no harming of these here children in Seneca Village. You understand?"

Seneca Village.

Maggie had heard Thomas and the other Chelsea Manor servants mention it before. It was an entirely black village in the northern part of the city where former slaves had purchased their own land.

Castriot's face burned red as he gripped his wounded hand. And seeing that his assailants were landowning blacks seemed to only escalate his fury. Cyrus and Comstock immediately came to their leader's side, but he brushed them off and shouted, "Attack them!"

The Garrisons, who were armed with revolvers, started toward the villagers just as the Foundlings finally broke through the church door.

Cyrus and Comstock, however, were more interested in the Horologe and locked their eyes on Violet. As they began approaching the young girl, Maggie seized the Horologe from Violet and shoved the young girl to the side. Maggie wrapped the Horologe tightly in her arms and ran down the deserted road. Cyrus and Comstock aggressively followed. With the weight of the Horologe slowing her down, Maggie worried that the Garrisons would catch her in no time.

But in the mist up ahead, Maggie spotted peculiar shadows. As she kept running, these shadows transformed into solid images within the cloudy distance. Dozens of these figures were quickly approaching as yellow lights bounced above the ground. Maggie soon realized the lights belonged to the eyes of a stampede of deer.

But something more startling than the charging deer caused Maggie to freeze, even as Cyrus and Comstock drew nearer. Among the deer were nearly twenty men on horses; foggy silver figures that Maggie at first thought were illusions. Most of the men were bald and wore old robes with thick collars. They did not carry any weapons, but rode their horses with such confidence and force that they might as well have been covered in the heaviest armor.

The Horologe ticked away in Maggie's arms, as she stayed planted in the middle of the road. Cyrus and Comstock stopped a few feet behind her. After noticing the stampede of deer and horses headed in their direction, the Garrisons spun around and dashed back to the church. But it wasn't long before the storm of deer and silver horsemen caught up.

The momentum from the stampede knocked Maggie to the ground. Still cradling the Horologe in her arms, a blur of stomping hooves and dusty air whirled around her body. Maggie squeezed her eyes shut. It wasn't until the sound of galloping had moved into the distance was she able sit up and peer back down the road.

The silver and brown whirlwind reached the church, breaking up the battle that had been in progress. The Seneca Villagers and the Foundlings had managed to dive out of the way in time, but Castriot urged the Garrisons to stand and fight. However, the overwhelmed Garrisons instead took off running as the cloud of deer and horsemen reached them. The Garrisons delivered one last fighting cry before collapsing under the force of the mysterious storm that carried them down the road. And then with one final *swoosh*, the silver phantoms disappeared, taking the Garrisons away with them.

Maggie remained on the ground, an arm protectively draped over the unharmed Horologe. But then a shadow emerged out of the corner of her eye. She turned away from the church and back down the road where the stampede had started.

There was still one hazy figure standing in the mist. Its gray form was featureless, but appeared to be the silhouette of a man.

"Nikolaos," Maggie whispered.

The apparition didn't respond. And a moment later, the figure turned and soundlessly disappeared into the fog.

Maggie didn't hear the rush of feet behind her and jumped when Catharine and Louis appeared at her side.

"Are your hurt, Maggie?" Catharine asked, studying her sister with concern.

"I... I..." Maggie still gazed down the road.

"Come along," Louis said, helping her up. "We must get back to the others."

Hostrupp was first to greet Maggie as she approached the church.

"The Horologe!" he squealed. "Oh, goodness, goodness, thank goodness it is not damaged!"

Hostrupp took it out of Maggie's arms and embraced it affectionately.

Houten wobbled forward. "You fool," he snarled. "Have you nothing to say to the one that saved Poppel?"

Hostrupp looked up at Maggie, embarrassed. "Oh, yes. Sorry. So sorry. You were tremendous. Those trousers ended up working quite marvelously for you. Just marvelous, marvelous."

Houten tapped Maggie's knee with his cane. "You all right, little duck?"

Maggie looked past the church where the apparitions and Garrisons had vanished.

"The Martyrs of Gorkum..."

Houten nodded. "You brought them back."

"But what about Nikolaos of Myra?" Louis asked. "Wasn't he supposed to return?"

Before Maggie could mention she had seen Nikolaos, or at least some ghostly man she believed to be him, a loud eruption came from the side of the road. Maggie looked over where Clemmie had

Francis by the arm. Her brother was giving Francis the biggest scolding she had ever heard.

"Really, Francis, of all the stupid, most selfish and senseless acts you have ever done! What did you think would happen? You would be King of Poppel? Wear a crown? Honestly, that you would even consider putting your family in danger. Oh, if I had a birchen rod right here I would spank the skin off your behind! You must be the worst boy that ever lived!"

Gardiner and Gertrude were huddled nearby, watching the scolding with wide eyes.

"Seriously, someone fetch me a rod," Clemmie continued, flailing his arms. "I need to whack some sense into my cousin."

Catharine tried to calm her brother down. "Clemmie, that is not going to help the situation..."

Lloyd, Wendell, and Harriet were clustered together in the background. It wasn't until Maggie neared did she see that they were looking over the wounded. Albers was among those on the ground having his arm rebandaged while Nellie sat next to him, lovingly stroking his graying hair.

Maggie suddenly realized she had yet to see Violet, and she frantically looked around.

"Violet," she called. "Violet!"

Eventually, a familiar caramel-toned face appeared through the crowd of villagers.

Violet ran up to Maggie. "You pushed me down."

"I am sorry for doing that. I just didn't want the Garrisons to hurt you."

Violet smiled. "We won, didn't we?"

"Yes, we did. And all thanks to you," Maggie said. "You were very brave."

"You both were." Madame Welles marched over to the two girls. "The Sister Wheels have been reunited at last. And thanks to the Martyrs of Gorkum, the Garrisons are no more. I just wish

Nikolaos of Myra would have returned as well."

Maggie's eyes widened. "But I saw him. At least, I believe it was Nikolaos. He appeared just briefly. And then he left."

"He left?" Madame Welles' voice sounded troubled.

"Yes," Maggie replied, waiting for Madame Welles to elaborate. "Is something wrong?"

"It's just... he was supposed to return. And if he's not then..." Madame Welles trailed off before forcing a tense smile. "Well, Castriot is gone. That is what matters for now."

"But what will happen to Poppel?" Maggie asked.

"What do you mean?"

"Well, won't the city eventually realize that the Garrisons are gone?"

Madame Welles looked past Maggie where some villagers were tending to McNutt's leg.

"We have one Garrison." The old woman smiled. "And that is all we need. The city officials will still have a contact."

"What about us?"

Maggie turned around to see an exhausted Henry staggering over. Her pulse quickened and she fought the urge to embrace him.

"What becomes of the Van Cortlandt descendants?" Henry asked. "Are we not to return to Poppel?"

Madame Welles stiffened. "You have done a great service to your family and city, and especially to Poppel. But yes, you are not to return." Madame Welles then added a bit more quietly, "I hope, in the most sincere and grateful manner, that we will never meet again, for if our paths were not to cross in our remaining time on this earth, I know that all is well."

Before returning to Chelsea Manor, the Van Cortlandt descendants paid a final visit to Poppel. After all, the Horologe still needed to be returned.

Everyone crowded into Kleren until it was at capacity, forcing the remaining Foundlings to spill out onto Myra Lane. Maggie stood between Henry and Catharine as they watched Hostrupp place the Horologe back onto its rightful wall.

An unsettling realization struck Maggie. She leaned over to Henry and whispered, "So now that the wheels are reunited, does that mean that those in Poppel... can live forever?"

Henry looked at her with growing eyes, containing both fear and amazement. He scanned the Foundlings in the room as though their appearances might reveal the answer.

A soft cough sounded above Maggie's head. She turned to find Laszlo standing nearby. She had nearly forgotten about the workshop leader. He stared vacantly at the recently hung Horologe with his arms placed behind his back.

"All right," Hostrupp chirped, clapping his hands together. "Everyone must exit Kleren. Out out out! That is... everyone except for the Van Cortlandt descendants."

Slowly, the Foundlings filed out the shop. As the room emptied, the Moore grandchildren looked about with uncertainty, wondering what else could possibly be asked of them.

Hostrupp closed the door after the last Foundling left and then spun around. He clapped once more. "Now then! There are some final pieces of business that must be settled. Yes, yes. Just a few last things."

"Please don't tell me there was a fourth sister and we must head to Canada to retrieve her wheel," Clemmie muttered with an exhausted sigh.

Madame Welles cackled at Clemmie. Her laughter not only surprised the others in the shop, but also herself. It sounded as though she hadn't laughed in many years.

"Do not fear, Clemmie. All of you have done more than we could have ever hoped." Madame Welles nodded to Houten who waddled over to the group carrying a worn, leather pouch.

"You two!" Houten shook his cane at Maggie and Henry. "Come here and reach inside."

Maggie and Henry hesitantly stepped forward as Houten jiggled the pouch in front of them. "Don't be shy."

Henry reached in first, followed by Maggie. Their hands briefly touched, but before Maggie's cheeks could turn fully pink, her fingers grazed a tiny, hard surface.

Maggie and Henry locked eyes before pulling out their hands that grasped objects they knew too well.

The Sister Wheels.

Maggie glanced down at the wheel in her hand. A large *G* gleamed up at her while Henry studied Sarah's wheel. Maggie looked closer at Henry's hand. He also had grabbed the Horologe key.

"We decided long ago that if all the Sister Wheels ever had to be reunited in the Horologe to protect Poppel that we would never keep them there," Madame Welles explained. "We would like you to take Grace's and Sarah's when you leave."

"You mean you're forsaking immortality?" Catharine asked.

"No good would come from that," Madame Welles declared. "And besides, the wheels were meant to stay with the Van Cortlandt descendants."

Although Maggie and Henry agreed, a gloomy silence fell over the room. There was now nothing left to say but goodbye.

As Hostrupp opened the front door of the shop, an unexpected rumbling of celebration filled the room. The Foundlings were cheering for the descendants.

Clemmie and Louis were the first ones to walk back onto Myra Lane. As a roaring applause overtook the crowd, the pair looked back at their cousins in astonishment. Neither Henry nor any of the Moore grandchildren had ever been the recipients of such appreciation.

Francis and the twins were next to leave Kleren, followed by Maggie, Catharine and Henry. Maggie searched the crowd for familiar faces. She eventually spotted Lloyd, Wendell, and Harriet near the front window of Snop, but her heart sunk when she remembered she would never see Ward again.

As they made their way through the crowd, a pair of small arms found Maggie's waist.

"I don't want you to leave," Violet murmured, hugging Maggie.

"It's all right," Maggie said, stroking Violet's curly hair. "I'm sure we will see each other again."

When Maggie managed to separate Violet from her body, Laszlo slipped out in front of her.

"You must place the wheels somewhere safe, you understand." Laszlo's voice was no longer emotionless. Instead it was heavy with concern. "You never know when they may have to be reunited again." Laszlo's piercing eyes gazed past Maggie. She turned around to see that Laszlo had also been addressing Henry who was standing behind her. "It would be unwise not to take advantage of this opportunity."

Laszlo then disappeared into the crowd, leaving Maggie feeling quite puzzled. She stared up at Henry who seemed equally confused. But then he placed his hand tenderly upon Maggie's shoulder and said with a smile, "Well, we couldn't very well leave Poppel without one final strange encounter, now could we?"

CHAPTER TWENTY-THREE

LUSTRE OF MIDDAY

As the noon sun dangled over New York City, flicking its Christmas daylight onto the white hill of Chelsea Manor, Maggie and the other grandchildren strolled down the gravel avenue in a dreamy stupor. Clemmie carried Gertrude on his back while Gardiner clung to Catharine's hand and sleepily rubbed his eyes with a small fist. Francis lagged behind his cousins, head down with hands stuffed into his pockets and feet dragging over the uneven road.

Louis and Maggie, walking a few yards ahead of the group, were the first to see Aunt Lucretia come tumbling out of Chelsea Manor, her short arms waving wildly.

"They're here! They're out here," she shrieked back into the front door.

As they reached the bottom of the hill where a pathway curved up toward the mansion, Louis softly tugged Maggie's arm. "What are we going to tell everyone?"

Maggie looked at Chelsea Manor, remembering how she had scaled down its chimney only hours before. Noticing that Sir Pringle's carriage was nowhere to be seen, Maggie hoped he and Grandfather Clement had parted on relatively good terms.

"Well," Maggie said, peering out toward the Hudson River. Its serene waters struck her as an absurd sight. "I think it would be best if we tell them anything but the truth."

Aunt Lucretia swept the twins up the moment they stepped through the front door and took them upstairs to be cleaned. The remaining grandchildren were corralled into the Great Room by the rest the family. Maggie, Catharine, and Louis packed onto the sofa as the family circled around.

Grandfather Clement was the only person missing.

There were many times that night Maggie had wondered if she would see her parents again. So when Dr. John and Mary Ogden entered the Great Room, she was so overcome with happiness that their pressing stares didn't even register.

Surprisingly, the first question from the family was not where the grandchildren had disappeared to in the early hours of Christmas Day, but rather why they had returned wearing such unusual clothing.

Uncle Benjamin and Uncle CF stared with great uncertainty at Francis' black uniform as the boy slouched in Grandfather Clement's armchair, being the least responsive of the grandchildren.

Clemmie took the lead, situating himself confidently in front of the fireplace. He explained that the grandchildren had given the special clothes to each other as gifts and then had gone on an early morning walk, which went longer than expected.

"But why do all of you look so filthy?" Aunt Maria arched an eyebrow.

Louis and Maggie exchanged desperate glances while Catharine adjusted her red skirt, impossibly trying to hide all the blemishes from the night. None of the grandchildren—not even Clemmie—knew how to respond.

"It was my fault," a voice declared from the doorway.

Aunt Emily let out a gasp as the room turned to see Henry standing in the hall. The young man appeared significantly more beaten since they last saw him the night before. His injured face glowed with bruises while his tattered white shirt hung unevenly out of his black trousers.

Henry cautiously stepped into the Great Room.

"Come to ruin Christmas Day, too, have you?" growled Uncle William. "Out! Out I say!"

Uncle William charged at Henry, but Catharine quickly leapt from the sofa and positioned herself between Henry and her uncle.

"Let him speak, Uncle William," Catharine defended.

With her legs tucked beneath her body, Maggie twisted on the sofa to get a better view of Henry. More than anything, Maggie wanted to hear how he planned to explain their Christmas morning whereabouts.

After giving Catharine an appreciative smile, Henry gestured to the open front door, so everyone could see his horse and carriage out on the road. A cold breeze fanned the Great Room.

"Earlier this morning I came back to Chelsea Manor to apologize for the way I behaved last night—coming here unexpectedly and disrupting your Christmas Eve. Upon my arrival, the horse became startled and turned a corner too quickly, causing the carriage to tip over. The children were already awake and, seeing that I was in distress, came to my aid. They helped get my carriage upright, but I'm afraid that it caused them to dirty their new Christmas clothes. They then saw me off to an acquaintance's where my carriage was repaired. That is what delayed their return home. However, I am so very grateful for their assistance."

The room was quiet. The family stared at Henry before turning toward the grandchildren, searching their faces for confirmation that his story was true.

"Yup." Clemmie finally nodded, sucking in his lips and then popping them out again. "That's... what happened."

Dr. Ogden approached Henry. "Well, then. We appreciate you clearing up this matter. And we expect that you'll be on your way now." But Henry didn't move. "Was there something else?"

"I was hoping to speak with Clement Clarke Moore," Henry said firmly. "I want to apologize privately for what occurred."

The rest of the family assumed he meant the confrontation on Christmas Eve, but Maggie knew his apology went beyond that.

"Absolutely not," Uncle William snapped. "You have no business seeing him again. You have troubled us all long enough."

"We can pass your sentiments along to our father," Uncle CF added, but he was soon drowned out by an old, raspy voice.

"The young man can speak to me alone if he wishes."

Grandfather Clement stepped out from the gentlemen's parlor. Although he was dressed in his typical dreary attire, Maggie thought her grandfather appeared significantly more depleted. Even from across the room, Maggie could see darkness sagging under his eyes.

"Father," Aunt Emily exclaimed. "We didn't know you were there."

With his gaze focused solely on Henry, Grandfather Clement didn't respond to his daughter's comments or the confused stares from the rest of the family.

"Come along, Mr. Livingston," Grandfather Clement said simply. He then turned back into the parlor without another word.

The family watched as Henry crossed the room and entered the parlor like a remorseful child bracing for a scolding.

"Well," Aunt Maria huffed. "This has certainly been the strangest Christmas."

Louis let out a deep, guttural cough that prompted a glare from Clemmie. But he was too busy shaking his head to spot his cousin's disapproval.

"You have no idea, Mother," Louis murmured, rubbing his eyes with the palms of his hands. "You truly have no idea."

Realizing that Grandfather Clement and Henry were in no hurry to return from the parlor, the family went about their normal

Christmas activities and gathered in the dining room for brunch. However, Maggie quickly excused herself from the table, explaining that she wasn't hungry, even as her rumbling stomach gave away her lie.

Maggie grabbed her coat before walking outside and plopping down on the front porch. Bent forward with her arms around her knees, Maggie was determined to fight through her exhaustion while waiting for Henry to emerge from Chelsea Manor. But she was nearly asleep when footsteps sounded behind her. Startled, she straightened her back and looked up. Henry was standing over her. He silently glanced back at Chelsea Manor and then started down the front path. Maggie followed him halfway down the hill where they were out of earshot from the curious family members eager to know more about the Christmas Eve intruder.

"What did Grandfather Clement say?"

Henry put his hands on his waist and studied Chelsea Manor for a moment before turning to Maggie. "I told him that I knew what he had done for my family, particularly my father. And that I was very grateful he took credit for *Twas the Night Before Christmas*. I also apologized for accusing him of less than noble motives." A small smile appeared on Henry's face. "He wouldn't accept it. He said my apology wasn't necessary."

"So what are you going to do now?" Maggie asked softly, finding it difficult to speak.

In her heart, she already knew the answer, so Maggie wasn't surprised when Henry responded, "I'm going back home. To Poughkeepsie."

Saddened, Maggie looked away without saying anything. But Henry placed a reassuring hand on her shoulder. He then stuck his other hand in his pocket and pulled out a familiar key.

"This should go to you."

"The Horologe key!" Maggie exclaimed before glancing around nervously, as though the Garrisons could be lurking nearby.

"It should remain with your family," Henry said. "And with someone who is trustworthy. And as it so happens, you meet both of those requirements."

Maggie discreetly took the key from Henry and clenched it in her fist. "I'll watch over it."

Henry smiled, giving Maggie's shoulder a final rub. But before he turned to go down to the road, he looked back at Chelsea Manor. Although the entire Moore family was trying to get a glimpse of him from the dining room, he seemed more interested in the pair of green eyes peering through the front door.

"Give my regards to your family," Henry said somberly.

His glance lingered an additional second and then with a slight wave to Maggie, he wandered down the hill to where Dunder and the carriage waited on the road.

Feeling a flood of emptiness, Maggie strolled back inside Chelsea Manor. Voices drifted from the dining room, but she wasn't in a hurry to rejoin the crowd.

Maggie slowly walked into the stair hall just as Grandfather Clement came out from the Great Room. Upon seeing his granddaughter, he paused in the wide doorway.

"Henry..." Maggie started to say.

But she found herself unable to find the words as Grandfather Clement walked past her and into the dining room.

Maggie pressed the key she was holding deeply into her palm. Its hardness dug into her skin and when she unclenched her fist, a red imprint was left on her hand.

"Miss Margaret," Charles said, coming out of the kitchen with a platter of steaming sausages. "You best be getting yourself something to eat before Clemmie devours every last crumb."

Charles continued into the dining room where his sausage platter was immediately swarmed like a hive of bees. Clemmie scooped a spoonful of sausages onto his already overflowing plate while Gardiner and Gertrude didn't even wait for utensils, plucking out portions with their fingers. Catching Maggie's eye, Louis gave her a subtle nod before dishing up his own share.

Francis slouched in his chair at the corner of the dining room table. He mindlessly pushed about a slice of potato on his plate with a fork. Catharine was seated next to him, but she didn't seem to be paying any attention to the meal. With her back twisted in her chair, she dazedly stared out the window.

Charles walked back out into the stair hall empty-handed. He gave Maggie a smile, but before he could disappear back into the kitchen, Maggie called to him.

Charles turned around. "Yes, Miss Margaret."

Slowly, Maggie approached Charles, her hand still clenching the key.

"Do you remember what you told me about the clock key in Great-Grandmother Elizabeth's house?" Maggie whispered.

"Yes, Miss Margaret." Charles' eyes narrowed on the young girl's fist.

"I was going through drawers in Aunt Margaret's old room," Maggie lied. "And I found this." She opened her hand and showed Charles the key.

Charles stared at the familiar object. "Well, I'll be..." He pointed down at her hand. "May I?"

Maggie nodded as Charles picked up the key and held it above his head. Squinting into the light, he smiled. "Yes sir, this is the one. How about that!" He handed the key back to Maggie.

"I need a favor, Charles."

"Yes, Miss Margaret."

"Would you help me hide the key somewhere in Chelsea Manor? Since it used to be at Elizabeth's home, it has great sentimental value. I would like to find a place where it will be safe."

Charles nodded. And then after looking around the hall, his eyes settled on the library door. "Follow me, Miss Margaret," he whispered as he led Maggie into the library.

The library was unsettling to Maggie, recalling how she had been in the room with Henry that night. And what was even stranger was the burning in her chest just thinking about him. Maggie already greatly missed Henry, and she had to look away from Charles in order to hide the tears forming in her eyes. But when she remembered she hadn't slept in over a day, she concluded the emotions were brought on by tiredness and she quickly dabbed her eyes with the back of her hand.

When Maggie turned back to Charles, he was hauling a large book down from a high shelf. The old book was so thick he had to brace it against his chest with both arms before slamming it down on the desk nearby.

"What is that, Charles?"

"It was your grandmother's, Miss Margaret," Charles explained as he undid the leather strap wrapped across its center, securing the cover and keeping its loose pages from slipping out. "This family Bible is one of the oldest books in all of Chelsea Manor."

"I am not sure if that would be the most ideal place to keep the key. I'm worried it will be a snug fit in between the pages…" Maggie trailed off as Charles opened the book, exposing a hollow center cut within the paper.

"Someone removed pieces of the Bible?" Maggie asked, trying to imagine Grandfather Clement's reaction to such a sight. He surely would have never allowed such a thing to happen. "Who would do that?"

Charles shook his head. "I don't know, Miss Margaret. Your grandmother said it had always been this way. For as long as her family has lived in this country."

Maggie approached the book and gently gripped its edges. The defacement began in the Book of Ezekiel and reached all the way to the Gospels.

"Yes sir, it seems whoever brought this family Bible to America had something important to hide in it." Charles chuckled to himself.

Maggie flipped to the beginning of the book where there were pages for recording family names and dates. She had only scanned the pages for a few moments before one scribbled line caught her attention under the column marked *Getrouwd.*

Jan and Grace Loockerman, Oktober 15, 1608

"Getrouwd must mean married," Maggie whispered, but she wasn't heard over Anne's booming voice coming from the stair hall.

"Charles!"

"Oh, dear," Charles said, scrambling over to the door. "I must be going, Miss Margaret. You can place the key in the book. If you need help getting it back on the shelf, come find me. It is awfully heavy and I wouldn't want you to struggle." Charles then disappeared out of the room.

Maggie stared down at the family Bible. She reached into her pocket and pulled out both the key and Grace's wheel. With some hesitation, Maggie rested the two objects inside the pages. She carefully closed the cover and buckled the belt across its front. Then with immense difficulty, Maggie hoisted the Bible back onto its rightful shelf.

As she finished the rather trying task, Maggie caught a glimpse out the library window and spotted Henry on the road feeding Dunder from a bucket. After an additional minute, Henry climbed into the carriage and looked back at Chelsea Manor. Although he didn't see Maggie staring out the window, the sight of his face offered Maggie some comfort.

She knew it wouldn't be the last time she would see Henry. And as Maggie glanced at the hollow book that had traveled all the way from Belgium—no doubt secretly carrying the Sister Wheels—for some reason, Maggie sensed that she and Henry were actually destined to meet again.

After all, the descendants of the Van Cortlandts always had a curious way of reuniting.

EPILOGUE

As Maggie safely tucked the book back onto the shelf, she didn't notice the large figure perched on the sycamore tree just outside the windows near the west porch. If she had, not only would she have recognized the illustration from the ancient book in the Boeken Kamer and the creature Catharine and Henry encountered at Van Cortlandt Manor, but Maggie also would have finally identified the mysterious beast from her dreams.

For unbeknownst to Maggie, the creature who had pushed St. Nicholas off the rooftop was in fact the monstrous Krampus. But Krampus was not simply a dream. He was real.

And he had found Chelsea Manor.

Krampus knew that Maggie and Henry had the wheels. But he couldn't go after the girl.

Not yet.

There were too many people around. She was too protected.

Krampus looked at the boy from the orchard as he stood on the road feeding his horse.

Poughkeepsie.

That's where Krampus would have to go.

He watched as Henry climbed into his carriage and rode down the street.

Poughkeepsie.

Krampus darted up the sycamore and then leapt to a branch on a separate tree. And then another. And another.

Wherever Henry Livingston planned to go, Krampus would follow until the Sister Wheels were his once more.

ABOUT THE AUTHOR

Born in Minnesota, raised in North Dakota, and attended college in South Dakota; **Sonia Halbach** is fairly acquainted with the Upper Midwest. So naturally, a week after graduating from Augustana College, she hightailed it east to try New York City on for size. And it turned out to be pretty big. But with a passion for history, Halbach soon became infatuated with New York City's rich collection of stories.

So when Halbach's not trying new flavors of bubble tea, civilizing her cats, or conjuring up schemes to get locked inside The Morgan Library & Museum for a Night, she can be found researching forgotten stories on the island of many hills, which inspired her to write The Krampus Chronicles.

More information can be found at www.soniahalbach.com

Photo Credit: Joseph McShea https://instagram.com/josephmcs

THANK YOU
FOR READING

Please visit http://curiosityquills.com/reader-survey
to share your reading experience with the author of
this book!

The Deathsniffer's Assistant, by Kate McIntyre

Set in a world very similar to 1900s London, The Deathsniffer's Assistant combines the investigative murder mystery with a tale of personal and societal redemption. It is about the relationships between broken people who clash more often than not, but manage to shape and learn from one another in spite of this. The story is told from the perspective of Christopher Buckley, young and impressionable and influenced by the prejudices of his time, as he finds himself surrounded by a cast of exceptional women whose differing characters will slowly reconstruct his understanding of strength in others—and in himself.

Broken Forest, by Eliza Tilton

A seventeen-year-old boy goes on a desperate quest to rescue his kidnapped sister who's been taken to a mystical place thought only to exist in fables, but the closer he comes to finding her, the harder she falls for her enigmatic captor--and he has plans to doom them all.

The Gathering Darkness, by Lisa Collicutt

They say: "the third time's the charm" and for sixteen-year-old Brooke Day, they had better be right. She doesn't know it yet but she's been here before—twice in fact. Though, she's never lived past the age of sixteen. Now in her third lifetime, Brooke must stay alive until the equinox, when she will be gifted with a limited-time use of ancient power. Only then will she be able to defeat the evil that has plagued her for centuries.

Escape from Witchwood Hollow, by Jordan Elizabeth

Everyone in Arnn—a small farming town with more legends than residents—knows the story of Witchwood Hollow: if you venture into the whispering forest, the witch will trap your soul among the trees. After losing her parents in a horrific terrorist attack on the Twin Towers, fifteen-year-old Honoria and her younger brother escape New York City to Arnn. In the lure of that perpetual darkness, Honoria finds hope, when she should be afraid. Perhaps the witch can reunite her with her lost parents. Awakening the witch, however, brings more than salvation from mourning...

CPSIA information can be obtained at www.ICGtesting.com
Printed in the USA
LVOW10s1242261015

459775LV00005B/418/P

9 781620 079638